LOVE IN FIRE AND BLOOD

LOVE IN FIRE AND BLOOD

S.B URQUIDI

For Victor who never read mysteries
but who believed in fighting the good fight.

ISBN-13: 9781546447825
ISBN-10: 1546447822
Library of Congress Control Number: 2017907641
CreateSpace Independent Publishing Platform
North Charleston, South Carolina

This is a work of fiction. While, as in all fiction, the literary perceptions and insights are based on experience, all names, characters, places and incidents either are products of the author's imagination or are used fictitiously.

Sonnet LXVI from Pablo Neruda's 100 Love Sonnets, translated by Gustavo Escobedo, published by Exile Editions © 2016.

"There must have been a moment at the
beginning where we could have said no.
But somehow we missed it."

TOM STOPPARD
ROSENCRANTZ AND GUILDENSTERN ARE DEAD

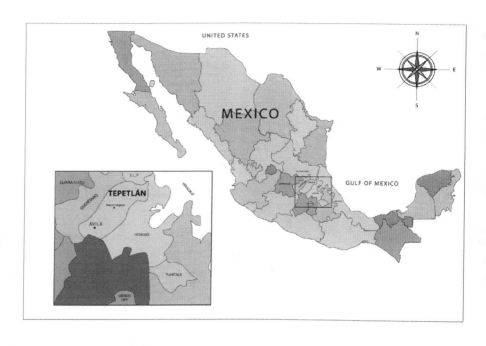

ÁVILA

SIERRA MADRE

to Mexico City

10. UNIVERSITY

1. COLONIA ALFONSO GARCÍA ROBLES

6. COLONIA INDEPENDENCIA

3. HISTORIC CENTER

5. COMMERCIAL CENTER

8. EL MILAGRO

11. SHOPPING MALL

7. AIRPORT

4. SANTA TERESA

9. EL ROSARIO

2. CHATEAU VILLE

1. Colonia Alfonso García Robles
2. Chateau Ville
3. Historic Center
4. Santa Teresa
5. Commercial Center
6. Colonia Independencia
7. Airport
8. El Milagro
9. El Rosario
11. Autonomous University of Ávila
11. Shopping Mall   M

PROLOGUE

In the few foggy seconds, while dreamland was fading and consciousness slowing seizing her mind, she felt the terror returning. Her head began to pound, the rancid taste in her mouth came back. The muscles in her back ached; the thin mat on which she had slept did nothing to protect her from the cold tile floor. Instinctively, she wrapped the coarse blanket more tightly around herself.

She had lost all sense of the time in the dark room. Near the top of the fiberboard which had been imperfectly tacked over the windows, she saw tiny chinks of light escaping into the room. It must be daytime. Perhaps still early because she couldn't remember the woman appearing with food for some hours now. Had she been in this room for a day, two days, longer? She remembered seeing a film in which a prisoner scratched on a wall the passing of each day, but she had nothing to scratch with. Her purse, her jewelry, her shoes, her belt had all been taken away.

She stank. Each terrifying part of her capture had added new layers of sticky sweat to her neck, under her breasts and armpits, down her back. Her clothes smelled worst. Dirt from the trunk of the car, sweat, and urine had penetrated and now dried on her jeans and tee shirt. She had asked the woman who kept watch over her if she could take a sponge bath, have some clean clothes. The woman had thrown her a towel but only let her splash water on her face. No new clothing ever appeared. She sensed that the woman who never spoke was also frightened. A black balaclava hid her face; a shapeless long dress, her body. It was only her faded blue eyes which betrayed fear or, occasionally, pity.

The woman wasn't young. She could tell by the tiny lines etched into her lips and the way powder caked in the deeper wrinkles around her eyes. She smelled old too, medicinal. She wasn't cruel as were the men outside the door. She looked away while her captive peed. She tried with the food which appeared regularly, not that her prisoner could eat anything. Even the thought of food made her nauseous.

Fully awake now, she threw the blanket off. She needed to move. She couldn't let her body grow stiff or her brain lazy. It wasn't the first time in her life she had felt despair lurking, like a lion hidden in the tall grass just waiting for its prey to stumble, to lose hope. As she began to pace the small space, she heard heavier footsteps coming down the corridor. A key turned in the lock. Digging her nails into the palms of her hands, she took a deep breath and waited.

Chapter 1

MONDAY, JANUARY 4TH, MORNING

When the phone rang at seven fifteen, Alma was standing at the stove stirring oatmeal for Kurt's breakfast. Kurt, sitting at the kitchen table slowly eating a dish of *papaya* heaped with honey, had been telling her yet again about the jokes during second-grade roll call. As she grabbed the phone off the hook before the shrill sound woke up her parents, she raised an index finger to her lips silencing her son.

"Alma Jaramillo?" asked the man on the other end of the line, his pronunciation automatically turning on the Spanish language button in her head.

"Sí."

"This is Humberto García Borresen, Jessica María's husband. I need to see you as soon as possible."

Startled to receive more a command than a request from someone she hardly knew, she blurted out, "Why?"

"My other phone is ringing; just come whenever you can," he answered.

"Okay, I'll drop my son off at school and head over to your house."

There was mumbled, "*Gracias*," then the line went dead.

As she hung up the phone, Kurt picked up the conversation at the exact spot where they'd left off. His name and the laughter it produced were never far from his mind. Did she know how many words began with K in the Spanish dictionary? Only about thirty and they were mostly foreign like ketchup and Kleenex. Did she know how the gym teacher pronounced Kurt? Like coot as in cooties and his middle name Sixto! What kind of a weird name was that for a kid? Where were his five sisters and brothers? his schoolmates joked. Finally, his last name, Dwyer: was his sister called Washing Machine? Ha, Ha, Ha.

Alma sighed remembering the pride with which she and Kurt's father had registered his name eight years ago. "When I was in school in L.A., they pronounced my last name as Jar AH Mill Oh," she said not really expecting that her childhood experience would be any consolation for the teasing he hated.

The bowl of oatmeal now placed in front of Kurt reminded him of what Alma called his morning "if only" list. If only Coco Puffs were on the breakfast menu instead of oatmeal. If only she would speak to him in Spanish instead of English. If only his school lunch consisted of the warm *quesadillas* sold on the street outside of the British Academy instead of the boring sandwich she put in his book bag each morning.

Alma answered by repeating her usual morning mantra. "English is your ticket to a good university abroad, street food and Coco Puffs aren't healthy." As Kurt raised his eyes to the ceiling, she wondered if he suspected what a hypocrite she was. She secretly snacked on Coco Puffs after he was asleep and wolfed down *quesadillas* fresh off the charcoal grill in front of El Diario de Ávila whenever she had a chance. Closing their conversation with a kiss on the top of his head, she silently vowed to practice what she preached. Then, she slipped off to shower and to see what was wearable in her limited wardrobe.

Last Saturday when she had been to Jessica's house to give an English class, she had worn black tights, a new long red sweater, and her black Red Wing boots. You're such an idiot she scolded herself. Who's going to be looking at you when a soap opera star is in the room? Still, she chose her best jeans, a Zara top, her red leather jacket and a fake Burberry scarf. "Hey," she called out to her son while still patting styling gel through her wavy dark hair. "First day of the new term, we can't be late."

The car ride from her house to Jessica's was only about twenty minutes if traffic was light. Then again, it was like crossing the border from Tijuana to San Diego she thought: brown earth to green grass, rags to riches. Well, not exactly. Built over a dozen years with the drips and drabs of dollars her parents had sent back to Mexico, the Jaramillo house was a crazy quilt of six rooms. What had started perhaps as a dining room or a bedroom had over the years morphed into an office, a kitchen or a bathroom. The garage was now a small general store patronized by their neighbors. The furniture and appliances for the house had been bought over time on layaway plans or picked up from relatives moving on.

Their neighborhood, officially named Colonia Alfonso García Robles, after Mexico's 1982 Noble Peace Prize winner, had once been on the edge of the city. Now no longer on the periphery of Ávila, the *barrio* hardly lived up to the ideals its name suggested. It lacked a constant water supply, shade trees, street lights, side-walks and good Internet. Still, small shrines dedicated to La Virgen de Guadalupe with fresh flowers and candles dotted every corner. There was a professional-sized soccer field for the local teams. Car thefts and house break-ins were at a minimum, drugs were perhaps available but not sold openly, and the neighbors kept a close watch on any strangers seen driving around after eight P.M. Without a doubt, she was luckier than many in this booming small city.

The García's gated community, on the other hand, had side-walks where servants could walk three abreast; street lights copied from the 1880's, retrofitted with energy saving bulbs; tree-shaded boulevards and instant Internet. Chateau Ville had a golf club with greens that never wanted for watering, smaller homes that started at twelve rooms, live-in maids, heated swimming pools and body-guards and chauffeurs who merited their own small club house.

The first thing which entered Alma's head after Kurt kissed her good-bye was why did Humberto García want to see her so urgently? It was most likely a rush translation. Just like the rich and famous, she thought, they think instant gratification is their birthright. She would see if it was worth her while. She disliked translations. They took too much time and usually paid badly. Her executive English classes, on the other hand, could be fitted into her schedule at the newspaper and were more lucrative. They required some preparation, but a good accent, a willingness to listen and the knack of giving constant encouragement satisfied most of her students. Some of her male students were a little too keen on that drink after class but since a promotion or a pay rise depended on an increased proficiency in English, coming on to the teacher could be counterproductive.

When she arrived at Chateau Ville, the guard at the entrance waved her through; odd since usually she had to sign a book, have her car trunk checked and leave an official identification. On Avenida Chaumont in front of the García's house, an Audi with tinted windows and three official looking Fords were parked. Power breakfast, she speculated as she maneuvered her ten-year-old blue Jetta behind them. Their chauffeurs and body-guards were crowded into a speck of sunshine near the large iron-work entrance to the house.

"*Buenos días, Señores*, cold morning," she said pressing a button on the interphone which was no doubt connected to a TV moni-tor. "*Sí, Señorita*," they chorused, smiling as they not very subtly looked her up and down.

As the gate opened, Humberto García Borresen came down the front steps. Alma smiled as he shook her hand and gave her a light kiss on the cheek. What had Jessica María seen in this tall, chubby, disheveled man? Dark brown curly hair, lightly tanned skin, bright blue eyes and an intelligent face drew you to him but his shambling walk, heavy midsection, stooped shoulders and baggy clothes would certainly disqualify him as a leading man in any soap opera. Of course, his father was the wealthy governor of the state of Tepetlán which might have counted for something. She thought of Jessica whose flawless bronze skin, green eyes, long shapely legs and spectacular figure not only turned heads but drew stares of admiration.

"*Gracias, Licenciado,*" she said as Jessica's husband held the front door open for her.

"No, for Christ's sake, call me Beto. *Licenciado* sounds like I should be pushing papers at the Ministry of Finance." When they entered the living room, three corpulent uniformed middle-aged men and a fourth seemingly younger, slimmer man greeted her. As she shook hands with the federal, state and local policemen, she noticed that it was only the expensively-suited civilian, Beto's partner, Clyde Ramsey, who gave her an appraising look. What's going on? she said to herself. Why am I here?

Beto anxiously pacing the room, got straight to the point. "We've asked you here, *Señorita* Jaramillo, because we need your help." He stopped for a minute and took a deep breath. "Jessica, my wife, hasn't been seen since your English class on Saturday morning. We need to know what happened that morning." He stopped again and then seemingly distracted said, "Can I send for some coffee or tea?"

Shocked into silence, she shook her head. Looking again at Beto, she saw now that his shirttail hung limply down the back of his trousers and that he hadn't shaved. There were purple bags under his eyes, and he kept clasping and unclasping his hands. She looked around the perfectly decorated room where not a thing was out of place: no children's toys on the floor, no unemptied ashtrays. Even the large bouquet of fresh flowers had been changed since Saturday; their scent perfumed the room. What was Beto saying? How could their world seem so orderly and Jessica not be there?

"What we know is that Jessica left the house Saturday morning around eleven o'clock to see a friend; at least that's what she told Lupita, the maid. Then she vanished. Her cell phone is turned off, and she hasn't communicated with me nor has anyone else contacted me. If there'd been an accident---," his voice trailed off.

"That's what she told me too when she interrupted the class; that she had to see a friend about some problem."

"If you please, *Señorita* Jaramillo, could you tell us step by step what happened on Saturday morning after you arrived at the house?" interrupted Captain Durán from the Federal Police.

"I arrived for the class at ten o'clock sharp. Jessica's assignment was to prepare a talk on her new soap opera, you know, '*El viaje inmortal*.' She was supposed to go to Miami next week to discuss the Mexican rights with the Brazilian producers. She thought that the discussions might be in English."

"How long did the class last?"

"Please, let the *Señorita* tell the story in her own words," said Captain Durán pulling rank on the local chief of police.

"Jessica was excited about the new project because she said it would be a first for her," she continued. "She'd not only star in but produce the show and the subject, Spiritism, was important to her." Across the room, she could see Beto nodding.

"We'd been at it for about an hour and had reviewed a lot of new vocabulary when Lupita appeared. She said that Jessica had a phone call. Jessica told her to tell them to call back, but Lupita said that the person, I think she said, the man on the phone, insisted that he had to talk to her immediately, that it was important. Jessica asked the person's name, but Lupita said the connection was bad and she hadn't understood it. So, Jessica said 'Excuse me for a minute' and left the room."

After she had left, Alma had remembered standing at the living room window watching the gardener on the large front lawn, clippers in hand, trimming a bush into the shape of a peacock. She had tried to picture that peacock in the Jaramillo's small front garden, but her imagination failed her.

"So," said the local cop butting in again.

"Yes, well, she came back about ten minutes later and was kind of agitated. She said that she was so, so sorry but she had to go out immediately and see a friend about a problem. She had on her jacket and was holding a small purse. Oh, yes, she also picked up her cell phone. 'Can we make up the time at the end of the week before I leave for Miami? Same time?' I said, 'Sure' but before she left, she turned to me, 'You don't have to rush out, enjoy your coffee.' So, I did finish my coffee, then gathered up my things and probably left about fifteen minutes later. When I closed the front door, I noticed that her Mercedes was still in the driveway."

"Describe what she was wearing," demanded the local cop interrupting once more.

"She had on a black tee shirt and black jeans," Armani she wanted to say but thought better of it. "A forest green leather jacket and a pair of very high heels," Manolo Blanik, she could have added. "I thought at the time 'Gee, I hope you don't have to walk far in those heels'."

"If that's all, *Señorita*, I would like to remind you how important your total discretion is if we are to get Jessica back safely. Although as a journalist, I'm sure you're aware of that. By the way, I am putting a total news blackout on the case," said Captain Durán scowling as he looked around the room.

"Yes, of course." Standing up Alma got ready to shake everyone's hands as she said good-bye.

"Alma, could you please wait while I see these gentlemen out?"

Surprised Alma sat down again contemplating the room as she had done on past occasions. The first time she had given Jessica a class, she had received a tour of the ground floor of the house. Besides the large living room and formal dining room, furnished with *faux* French Provincial antiques; there was a family room with a 70" TV and a whole movie theater set-up. How Kurt would love that, she had reflected. Beto had an office-library on the same floor, and there were not one but two powder rooms at the end of the front hall. The kitchen had floor to ceiling hand-painted Italian tiles on three of the walls. The state-of-the-art German appliances and stainless steel counters gleamed in the sunlit room.

When they had entered the kitchen, Jessica had introduced Alma to a chubby woman in her forties with short gray hair, lively brown eyes, and a wide, welcoming smile.

"This is Martha; she runs the show here," Jessica had said giving the older woman a hug.

"This is some kitchen," Alma had ventured, gesturing towards the two dishwashers, restaurant-sized refrigerator, and professional stove.

Jessica had laughed. "Martha hates the kitchen."

"I do," Martha had said. "Every time I use the oven I have to call *Señor* Beto to come home from his office to turn it on."

"Doesn't he mind?"

"No," Jessica had said, "Martha was his nanny, and he'd walk across the Sonoran Desert for her. Right Martha?"

"Yes, *Señor* Beto is the best man in the world."

Leaving the kitchen, Alma had asked if Jessica had decorated the house. "Are you kidding? This is all nonsense. I grew up in a small house in one of Mexico City's least fashionable neighborhoods. We had a few pieces of furniture from my mother's family, but it was pretty much a hodgepodge of styles. Beto did all this with a decorator from Dallas or Houston. I didn't see it until it was finished. He said that it would be good for my image. I guess so. It did get me a five-page spread in *Hola*. I have a small study upstairs where I spend most of my time. It has my daughter's toys and family photos. Hey, before you go let me introduce you to the other love of my life, Valentina."

When she had reappeared with the little girl, the child's sleepy face was buried in her mother's neck. "Say 'Hi Alma,'" coached Jessica. A little voice had muttered, "Hi, Alma."

"She's going to speak perfect English because her daddy only speaks to her English," Jessica had said.

"I do the same thing with my son, Kurt."

"Oh, you have a child too. How old is he?"

"He's almost eight."

"No, you can't have an eight-year-old! You look like you just graduated from college."

"I'm older than you are but thanks." As the front door of the house was closing, she heard Jessica and Valentina call out, "Bye-bye Alma." Easing herself behind the steering wheel of her car that day, she could only think, was Jessica for real?

That phrase, "Was Jessica for real?" was still in her head when Beto returned. Despite the worried look in his eyes, she could see by the way he spoke and had run the meeting with the police that at heart he was a no-nonsense businessman used to being in charge.

"Sorry, that took a little longer than I wanted. You can imagine when the local, state and federal police are involved, it's complicated. Look, while you were describing your last class with Jessica, an idea came to me. I want you to help me."

"Help you, in what way? I'm a journalist, not a detective."

"Maybe you're more of a detective than you know. I read two of your articles in the El Diario de Ávila, and they were good. The story you did on the trafficking of children from Central America was full of investigative work and the other article on the corruption in the teacher's union; you had to dig deep for that." He paused looking at Alma as if he was seeing her for the first time.

"Look, I think that the police will start looking for Jessica immediately." He frowned and gazed off into the distance. "She's well-known and the daughter-in-law of a governor. But you can get information from people, particularly people close to her, stuff that they simply wouldn't tell the police. Plus, I've already had you checked out and you're clean. I don't have time to start with someone new that has to be vetted."

Alma paused for a moment. So, he'd investigated her. Of course, he wouldn't have let anyone close to Jessica María and Valentina without them being thoroughly checked out. "Yes, but I never put myself at risk with either of those stories you mentioned. If Jessica's disappearance is a kidnapping, it's probably organized crime that's behind it, and I'm not going anywhere near that kind of danger. Too many journalists have turned up dead in this country."

Beto jumped up and began to pace the room. "Does it sound like organized crime? First, why did Jessica get into that car? The cops didn't tell you, but we have footage from the security camera next door showing her entering a late model Honda Accord with what seems to be just a driver. So, she wasn't grabbed off the street. The security guards at the entrance to the compound can't remember anything. The registry shows the name, Javier Arias. I never heard her mention that name. The security people would have had to call ahead to get clearance for this Arias person to come to the house. That had to have been Jessica because no one else in the house picked up the call. We have the license plate of the car from the security camera at the entrance. It was reported stolen three days ago in Mexico City. The police found it this morning abandoned outside the city. If it is organized crime, why haven't they contacted me? Usually, kidnappers want their money in cash as soon as possible and the victim out of their hair to limit the possibility of identification."

Alma nodded her head. "Yeah, you're right it doesn't follow the mafia's usual playbook. The other thing which struck me as odd is your wife's high profile. Organized crime isn't normally preying on famous people. They want to stay in the shadows, collect their money and hightail it to safety." Now it was Alma's turn to pause. Her reporter's nose began to twitch with the smell of a story.

"But before I get involved in this, I have two questions. Is this a publicity stunt to promote Jessica's new soap opera and in a few days, some psychic is going to tell us where she's hidden? Or, sorry because this might be painful for you, is your wife having an affair?"

Beto sat down in front of her. Rubbing his day-old beard, he said. "Look I've known Jessica for five years and been married to her for three, and although I don't believe you can ever really get into somebody else's head, I can't imagine either one of those situations." Getting up again, he began to pace the room.

"When my wife was thirteen her parents disappeared. Her brother, Samuel, who everyone calls Sami, can tell you more about that but she swore that whatever it took, she would never abandon Valentina. Also, she worked hard to get to where she is, and she didn't take short cuts. So, I can't see her doing some publicity stunt now, particularly without telling me."

"The lover angle?" continued Beto running his fingers through his unruly hair. "Again, how well do I know her? It seems to me that we have a happy marriage but perhaps I'm comparing it to my parent's awful relationship. Sure, we fight like everyone. In fact, we had a shouting match on Saturday morning at breakfast, but I adore her, and she knows it. I think, too, we both decided after Valentina was born, that we wanted to build a happy family. Neither of us had that growing up, particularly as teenagers."

Alma looked at Beto, "Why did you wait so long to report Jessica missing? She's been gone almost forty-eight hours."

"On Saturday morning, I left the house at about nine-thirty to play golf. I stayed for lunch at the club then went to my office to see to some business. I came home around five. Martha informed me that Jessica had gone out to meet a friend. I changed and went to have dinner with my father. Jessica and I do lead separate lives a lot of the time, so I didn't think much about her still being out when I got home a little before midnight.

"When I woke up on Sunday morning, and she wasn't in our bed I thought she had gone to the guest room the night before so as not to wake me. At eleven that morning, I knocked on the guest room door, but there was no answer. When I entered, there was no sign of my wife. I called her cell phone repeatedly, but the calls went to voice mail. That's when I called Sami and Gloria and tried to reach her Aunt Renata. When it got to be lunchtime and she still hadn't called, I got uneasy and phoned my father. We both thought she was angry with me and had spent the night with a girlfriend, but by evening when she still hadn't called, he insisted we contact the police. They agreed that we should all meet this morning."

"What was the argument about?"

"She wanted me to ask my father to fund her soap opera, '*El viaje inmortal,*' but I was very reluctant. My father set me up in business here because he wanted me to return to Ávila. He was afraid I'd make a career in New York. He always wants to have his family close even if we don't see him much. He doesn't react well to pleas for money. So, I told Jessica that I couldn't get the money from him to back her project. She wasn't happy, to put it mildly."

Alma uncrossed her legs and waited a moment to speak. She could hear Valentina crying upstairs. "Okay, I don't know how much good I can do, but I'll try and find out what I can. I'll ask you for two things, though: a per diem to compensate canceling my other jobs and a first go at the story, really an exclusive interview, when Jessica is back."

"Fair enough about the per diem and I will be generous because for some reason although I hardly know you, I trust you. I guess it's because Jessica liked you. Also, frankly I suppose I'm buying your silence and complicity. Publicity could complicate things and even, God forbid, get her killed. About the interview, that depends on Jessica. However, if you help to find her, I think she would be very grateful."

"Who do you recommend I talk to first?"

"Several people, Sami, her brother, who is also her manager. He might be a bit difficult. He is so protective of Jessica that he's often hard to reason with. Gloria Sandoval Franco is her best friend. She has a top salon and spa in Mexico City. Then, Martha, our cook, she and Jessica are very close. She was my nanny but became Jessica's confidant when we got married. There's Aunt Renata, too who took care of Jessica and Sami after their parents disappeared. She's Jessica's mother's sister. You should probably talk to my mother, Catherine, and my step-mother, Cécile, although neither one was a favorite of Jessica's."

"Your father?"

"Let's leave him out of the picture for now. He knows that she's missing, but he likes for things to go through official channels. He's the one who insisted that the federal police be brought in. Personally, I had my doubts about contacting the police at all."

"Well, they're on the scene now for better or worse. Do all the people you want me to talk to know that Jessica has been out of touch since Saturday?"

"Except for Aunt Renata and Cécile who I couldn't reach; the rest of them know I was looking for her yesterday midday."

"I want to see Sami and Gloria first. You'll need to call them. I'll head to Mexico City as soon as I can get on the road. Also, I would like to look at Jessica's computer or did the police take it away?"

"No, they said they would send for it later. It's a Mac laptop. Let me copy the files onto a flash drive, and I'll send it over to your house this afternoon."

Alma looked at Beto and thought that maybe what Jessica had seen in him was a nice guy.

As she headed towards the front door, Alma stopped, "By the way do you have kidnapping insurance? Because if you do, the company will bring in a negotiator."

Beto looked surprised. "Funny that you should ask. Clyde who you just met convinced me to take out a policy three months ago. I called Lloyds this morning before I called you and they have someone from The Olive Group here in Mexico right now. He's getting in touch with me this afternoon."

Minutes later when Alma walked out the street door of the García's house, she could not believe she had only been there for an hour and a half. It felt as if a half a day had gone by. What had she gotten herself into? Then a small smile crossed her face. What a story and it had just dropped into her lap.

Chapter 2

MONDAY, JANUARY 4TH, MIDDAY

Alma sat in her car at the side of the highway near the entrance to the toll road to Mexico City, cell phone in hand, Starbuck's latte in the cup holder beside her. She could hear her father's voice as she took a sip of the milky coffee.

"You're such a *gringa*, Alma."

"Of course, I'm a *gringa*, Pa. You took me to California when I was a year old, sent me to school with the *gringos* and loved it when I had *gringa* girlfriends but not so much when *gringo* boyfriends showed up."

"Yes, but Starbuck's coffee? I never saw anyone so excited as you when they opened a franchise last year in Ávila. Even Kurt thought it was crazy."

Speaking of Kurt, she had better touch base with her mother before she got on the road. Sami and Gloria had agreed to see her as soon as she could get to the city. Meanwhile, she had managed to postpone her English classes until next week. Now she only had to deal with her editor and her mother. A text message with her plans for the day would do for her mother who in any case picked Kurt up from the school bus and gave him lunch. But her editor, Ricardo Nuñez Salcedo, was another story.

"Hey, Richie, it's me, Alma, checking in."

"Oh, now El Diario de Ávila has become your favorite no-tell motel." Ricardo was clearly at his congenial best. "I've been calling you all morning. I need you to get over to the State Assembly. It looks like they are finally voting on the big crime bill."

Alma cringed and waited for a fresh blast. "Richie, I'm on the road to Mexico City. It's important. I think I may be on to a really big story."

"What's your big story, Miss Pulitzer Prize? Sean Penn back in Mexico chasing the *narcos*?" She pictured Ricardo's handsome face with two angry red blotches on his cheeks.

"It's an impeccable source. I need two or three days, that's all."

"Look, Alma, you're a good journalist, but I got a newspaper to run, and, if I might remind you, these are very uncertain times for newspapers. Two days is all you get, and it had better be an exclusive."

As she wove into the fast lane accelerating towards Mexico City, she thought about turning on the radio but what would she hear? There would be the same old trouble on the U.S. Mexico border: girls gone missing from Cuidad Juárez; children from Central America denied asylum in the U.S.; cans filled with cocaine labeled as chilies.

Her thoughts turned instead to her boss. Ricardo Nuñez meant a lot more to her than just a tough mentor. He had been her guide to a Mexico she had never known and in so many ways rejected. When she had arrived at his newspaper five years ago, her eyes had blazed with defiance; her shoulders were stooped with sullen discontent. Two weeks before, after a lunch of a tasteless tuna fish sandwich on soggy white bread with Kurt's American grandmother, she had realized that her California journey was over.

But what a journey it had been! It had begun twenty-nine years ago on a cold March night on the outskirts of Nogales when a young couple from Ávila, her parents, Jesús and Sofía, had made their way at two A.M. to a break in the U.S. border fence. There were twelve passengers in the van. "No babies," said the oldest of the three smugglers as he discovered Alma wrapped in Sofía's shawl. Paying the men one hundred precious dollars more, Jesús insisted that the baby would behave. "If it cries," said the youngest pocked-marked trafficker, "All three of you will be out of here and into the desert on your own."

"We had one small bottle of water each to last us for twelve hours," related Sofía years later. "All through the night the rut-filled road bounced us back and forth on the hard, improvised benches of the old van," Jesús would later tell Alma. "Still you never cried but never closed your eyes either."

"When the sun finally shown on the distant Granite Mountains, and we saw the giant Saguaros and the Palo Verde trees blooming in the sand, I forgot the danger and wanted to get down from the van and admire the beauty of the desert," confided Sofía.

The trip took on mythic proportions as new details emerged with each recounting. Alfonso, Jesús's cousin from his hometown of Nuevo Progreso, had lent him the money for the traffickers. In Tucson, Jesús had used his last dollars to pay for the bus tickets to California. When they had arrived hungry and tired in Los Angeles, he had phoned his cousin from the bus station. "The first place we go is to your church, Alfonso. We need to light many candles to La Virgen de Guadalupe. She took good care of us."

In East Compton where they lodged in Alfonso's and Julieta's house, the Jaramillo family slowly began to learn, like small salmon swimming upstream, the shoals and deeper, safer pools of their American experience. Jesús and Sofía studied English in a no-questions-asked night school. Jesús learned to arrive at the Home Depot on North Figueroa Street at daybreak before the other laborers lined up. Here he had found work by accident with an architect-developer who mostly did million dollar remodels. Michael Harold was a perfectionist, and in Jesús he found his alter ego. "You know what, Alma?" Michael told her often in amazement. "We've never, ever had a call back on your dad's work."

When Alma was five and about to start school, Michael found Jesús a job as a super in a small apartment building in Los Feliz. He could attend to any problems with the pipes or lighting at night or on weekends and Sofía could work for any of the tenants who needed a cleaning woman. It was a basement flat, but it had two bedrooms and a back patio where her mother could fill pots with tomato, chili and *cilantro* plants.

When Sofía complained about being so far from the family in East Compton, Jesús had flatly said that they were moving for Alma and the schools in Los Feliz. "She can go to the best Catholic schools, Sofía. Do you know what that means?" And so, she did, first Holy Trinity Elementary School and then Immaculate Heart High School. When she was accepted at UCLA on a full scholarship, the pastor of the parish sung her praises from the pulpit. Yes, the Jaramillos were illegals, but in California, they felt protected.

As the miles sped by on her trip into Mexico City, Alma reflected on how different her safe adolescence had been from Jessica's seemingly rocky teenage years. Then, Alma's life began to fall apart when she was in her early twenties while Jessica's gained stability. Now the wheel looked to be turning again.

Fortunately, the Mexico City lunch hour traffic had barely begun as Alma circled the Colonia Roma at last nearly colliding with the Plaza Rio de Janeiro where Sami's apartment was located. Very cool address, thought Alma, as she gazed into the windows of the art galleries which dotted the neighborhood and admired the pocket-sized plaza where a replica of Michelangelo's David graced an ornate fountain.

A modern security system buzzed her into Sami's flat situated on the second floor of a nineteenth-century mansion. After driving for two and half hours, she bounded up the circular staircase glad for any exercise. Sami was waiting for her at the door of the apartment. As he greeted her with a formal handshake, Alma thought, Was he Jessica's twin? He certainly had the same tall, slim figure, the same green eyes and dark wavy hair, the same perfect features.

"Hi, I'm Alma Jaramillo. Thank you for seeing me on such short notice."

"It's hardly a favor when my sister, obviously, is in some trouble. Come in." As she stepped into the apartment, she exclaimed, "This is amazing. I feel as if I've stepped into *Architectural Digest.*"

The space was large, perhaps two thousand square feet. High ceilings with natural light brought in by a skylight, gave the impression of an artist's studio. To her left, she saw a modern open kitchen with a marble-topped breakfast bar. To her right was a dining area. A Knoll glass-topped table with six chairs filled that corner. In the middle of the apartment, the living area held several beige leather sofas. Those look like genuine Eames chairs, she said to herself. Woven rugs from Oaxaca in muted tones of gray, orange and black were scattered over the wooden floors. However, it was the artwork hanging on the white walls that most held her attention. Some pieces were large oils, some lithographs, some collages.

She was about to ask the names of the artists when the look on Sami's face stopped her. That's hostility, she thought. He doesn't trust me, and he doesn't want me here. Not even offering her the chance to sit down, he launched into a tirade. Why, in God's name, would Beto be using a journalist to track down his sister! That would be the last person on earth he would have confided in. He'd been up all night worried sick about Jessica, then Beto called to say he'd hired a reporter to look into her disappearance! "He's an idiot, always was and always will be."

Offering to leave, Alma started walking to the door. "Now that you're here sit down. But can you explain what's in Beto's head? What does he think you can do?" Taking a seat on one of the expensive Eames chairs, she gave Sami her most disarming smile. "I can see why it seems crazy to you, but he's desperate. Can he count on the police or some unknown private detective?" she shrugged her shoulders. "Jessica knows me and apparently trusts me. I promised Beto I wouldn't publish anything until she's back. Do you see many other options?"

Still tense as a tripwire, Sami sat down in front of her. Asking what was in it for her, he listened while she explained that if she could get an exclusive story, it would be a coup for her and her newspaper, something both could use.

"How about my sister's welfare. Is anybody interested in that?"

"For me, honestly, it's a job," said Alma.

"So, you're the hired gun," said Sami. "I guess you're looking for money and fame like the rest of us."

"*Señor* Lara, I think we're wasting time. Do you have any questions for me about your sister's disappearance or do you want to continue probing my motivation for taking on this investigation?"

"What happened on Saturday? Why has Beto moved so slowly?" Alma laid out her version of the facts. Jessica had received a call during their English class from a person who they thought was named Javier Arias. From the surveillance videos, she had gotten into a Honda Accord willingly. The stolen car had been found this morning. Beto hadn't received a ransom call. Could it be a publicity stunt or a romantic getaway? Beto didn't think so. They'd had a fight so he thought she might have stayed away for a night but not calling to ask about Valentina, that wasn't like her.

"That, I would agree with. She wouldn't just walk off and leave the baby. The fight doesn't surprise me," said Sami. "But what if this guy, Arias, is a psychopath? What if---?" He couldn't go on. He sat with his hands covering his face.

"We can't think the worst. Don't do it. It'll drive you crazy. Instead, tell me a little about Jessica's life. How might she know this Arias person?"

"Look, her life has changed since she got married and had a kid. I'll get in touch with the accountants and her P.R. people to see if Javier Arias rings a bell, but I've never heard the name before. I don't know much about her life in Ávila. She was looking forward to starting work on the new TV production. I think she was bored which is why she got mixed up with the Spiritists."

"What do you mean 'mixed up with'? She gave me the impression that the soap opera, what was it called? Oh, yes, '*El viaje inmortal*', was just a commercial venture. Was she a believer?"

"I don't know the details. I think Martha, their cook, can tell you more. What I know is that Jessica ever since our parents disappeared has been obsessed with what happened to them and why. Since neither we or the authorities have come up with an answer, she decided to try Spiritism. She knew that I thought it was *una pendejada*, so she didn't confide in me."

"Could you tell me something about your parents and their disappearance?"

"You think it might run in the family?" said Sami, his lips curling into a bitter smile. "Or are you looking for background for your exclusive? Because I don't have the time or energy for a press conference right now."

"*Señor* Lara, I don't expect you to like me or even have much respect for the press, but if I'm asking the question, it's for a reason. Jessica's disappearance is strange. I can't get to the bottom of it if I don't know more about her."

"I need a beer. Do you want something?"

"A Coke, if you have one."

When she read back her notes later that night, she thought she had captured Sami's account of their early life well. It seemed that until they were in their early teens, their lives had been normal, even boring. Their mother, Rosalba, was a stay-at-home mom, a lot younger than their dad, Juan Carlos. He was a pilot who flew cargo planes to South America. Their parents rarely left the house except to go to work or the supermarket. As children, they'd had only one brief vacation, and that was to Ávila of all places. Their parents had met while seeing their respective cars being towed away and had shared a taxi to recoup them. They were a happy, if solitary, couple who loved to dance Rock 'n' Roll and watch old Cantinflas movies on TV. Their mother had one sister, Renata, and their dad was an orphan with no family at all. When they disappeared, the children found his passport but no birth certificate. "He was vague about his past," said Sami. "He didn't look Mexican even. Everyone thought he was Spanish or Portuguese."

The day they disappeared he and Renata, Jessica's real name, had come home from school to find the breakfast dishes still on the table, no parents, no lunch. The car was in the driveway. The neighbors hadn't seen them go out. Their Aunt Renata called the police that evening. The authorities made a lot of their father's trips to South America, particularly Colombia. The airline was clean, but the authorities believed that Juan Carlos was a mule who had gotten in over his head. Jessica and Sami never bought that explanation. They'd never seen extra money or drugs.

The next years had been hell. Their Aunt Renata moved in and turned their home life into boot camp: no hugs and kisses at bedtime; late for meals, no food; bad grades, your bedroom all weekend. Hanging out at the shopping malls trying on clothes they couldn't afford was their main entertainment. Standing on the edge of a fashion show one Saturday, they were pulled into the event as models. A famous photographer had spotted Jessica, and her career was launched. Sami became her manager.

"Do you think this is a kidnapping, *Señor* Lara?"

"For God's sake, stop calling me, *Señor* Lara. We're about the same age, *Señorita* Jaramillo. But to answer your question, if Jessica was abducted, the kidnappers aren't up-to-date about Beto's finances. Jessica told me last month that his business was in deep shit, and that he wouldn't be bankrolling *'El viaje inmortal'*. He was socked with a lawsuit by some peasant movement, the Salvador something or other Front. So, if organized crime is behind Jessica's disappearance, good luck to them. They may be tapping a dry well."

"Doesn't Jessica herself have money?"

"She has investments but not the kind from which you can get immediate cash."

"What kind of a guy is Beto? How do you see their relationship?"

"More deep background for your story?" But stretching out his long legs, Sami gave her his take on his brother-in-law. He didn't dislike him, but then he wouldn't have picked him for Jessica either. He found him to be in many ways a typical rich kid, entitled, too in love with the latest expensive toy. But he had done well at university in the States and had worked for Goldman Sachs. His father had handed him the business on a silver platter, but he'd managed it well, up to now. Was Jessica a trophy wife? Maybe, maybe not. Anyway, Jessica seemed happy enough with him despite living in Ávila in that awful house. "Beto knows that if she becomes unhappy she'll take Valentina, slam the front door and walk away."

"If this is a kidnapping, Sami," she said and noticed that for the first time, a ghost of a smile, "who could be behind it?"

He leaned back on the sofa and stared at her for a moment. "I have no idea. It could be organized crime tipped off by some unhappy employee present or past or that dissident group looking for funds to finance their cause. It's hard to say. There is so much kidnapping now that it seems to be the start-up of choice. I'll tell you I'm terrified. We all know what happens to kidnapped victims whose families don't pay up, but then they often kill the victims even when a ransom is paid. In fact, they sometimes kill the messenger who delivers the money."

Chapter 3

MONDAY, JANUARY 4TH, AFTERNOON

As soon as she got into her car, Alma took out her iPhone and punched into Google, "Front, Salvador, Tepetlán." The first reference was a story from her newspaper. The Salvador Navarro Front, a group of *campesinos*, who had owned land near the Ávila airport, had taken out an *amparo* against the state government charging that the authorities had fraudulently confiscated their property. They were represented by one Gabriel Ruiz Abascal. She made a note of the names.

As she journeyed across the city, the traffic was stop and go even though the evening rush was still a few hours away. Her thoughts turned to Sami. The interview had ended better than it had begun. He seemed to have a strong attachment to his sister. No doubt those difficult teenage years had forged a bond. He had expensive tastes; original artwork and designer chairs didn't come cheap. How had he been making a living for the last three years? He might have other actors or models to manage but a star like Jessica María? No, not likely. Maybe Beto would know more about his finances.

Jessica's brother was a type she didn't run into often in Ávila: sophisticated, private, sensitive, a bit of a pain in the ass too. His apartment furnished in the most exquisite taste seemed to say to the visitor, "You're welcome for a day and maybe even a night but be careful where you put that glass and keep your feet off the furniture." She understood that. Her room at home was her oasis. In fact, the weariness which began to creep over her as the drive stretched out, made her long for the comfort of her bedroom.

She thought about how she had decorated her small space; the care with which she had selected each pillow, each poster and each piece of furniture. The centerpiece of the room was a soft wool woven blanket she had bought in Chiapas. The vibrant colors, deep purple with touches of green, blue and yellow, were picked up in the pillows and rugs that dotted the room. She had expensively framed two Diego Rivera posters: one of The Flower Carrier and another of The Weaver. Frieda Kahlo was more in fashion, but it was Diego's images that moved her.

The dresser, which had been unvarnished pine, was now the same purple as her blanket. Above it was a mirror framed in vintage Mexican tin work that she had found at a street market. There was a bookshelf painted dark green which housed her small collection of poetry and novels. Several framed photographs sat on the top shelf: one of Kurt as a baby, one of her parents on their wedding day and several of her childhood friends from Los Feliz. The walls were painted light lilac. The headboard on her bed was part of an old carved screen that an architect friend had found for her.

This room was her Mexico: the handicrafts, the artwork, the writers she loved. Cautious and discriminating were the adjectives she often used to describe her attitude to the country of her birth but if she were truthful, wouldn't timid and stand-offish better define her behavior? She recalled a recent dream where she found herself standing alone on the banks of the River Mexico, testing the waters of the great waterway from time to time with the tips of her toes. The whole population was drifting down the river. Mostly, people were swimming along happily. A few swimmers seemed to flounder but then recover while other unlucky souls were set upon by river pirates. There were a few luxurious rafts whose passengers gaily drank Champagne and danced to tropical music. Alma, poised on the shore, was dressed in a faded red, white and blue bathing suit too tight across the bottom. "Jump in," called her friends and family as they floated by but she never did. Just as she had gotten her voter's registration card, but had never voted.

When Alma reached Gloria Sandoval's business, Avant Garde Spa, it was after five o'clock. Situated on the ground floor of a modern apartment building near one of Mexico City's main parks, the spa could not have been better located. Alma opened the heavy glass door and walked up to the receptionist's granite-topped desk. One perfect orchid and a package of leaflets stood in lonely splendor on the long counter. The receptionist who was logging information into a computer ignored her for a good two minutes, a sign that the business thought she needed them more than they needed her. Finally, the perfectly coiffed young woman looked up from her screen, "Yes, can I help you?"

"I have an appointment with Gloria, Gloria Sandoval. I'm Alma Jaramillo."

The woman's cool glance said that if it were her decision, she wouldn't get to see Gloria anytime soon. When the receptionist spoke on the interphone to her boss, it was clear from her tone that the woman standing in front of her wouldn't be her choice of client for the Avant Garde Spa. While she waited, it occurred to Alma that Jessica's friend might be just as hostile to her inquiry as Sami had been.

When Gloria's office door opened, however, the owner gave a welcoming hug to Alma. The receptionist with a slight shrug of her thin shoulders went back to her computer. "I am so delighted to meet any friend of Jessica's," Gloria said smiling broadly. Oh, my, thought Alma, could there be two women as different physically as Jessica and Gloria? Gloria was barely five feet four even in three-inch heels. She was blond and curvy, favoring skin-tight tee shirts and form-fitting jeans. He voice was breathy. She fluttered her eyelashes to emphasize a point.

"We are not exactly friends yet, but as I told you on the phone---." Alma, remembering the receptionist, put her finger to her lips and waited until the door of the office was shut before speaking.

Sitting down next to Gloria on a white leather sofa, Alma resumed her introduction. "As I was saying, I just met Jessica a few weeks ago, so I don't know her that well. I'm her English teacher which is a part-time job for me. I'm also a reporter on El Diario de Ávila which makes Beto think that I'm a good detective. As you might have guessed from Beto's calls, we are very concerned because Jessica hasn't been heard from since Saturday morning."

"Oh, my God, that's terrible, awful! Have the police been called in? Did she go out in her car? What about the chauffeur and doesn't she have a bodyguard?"

"Someone who called himself Javier Arias picked her up. Did she ever mention him to you?"

Gloria looked puzzled, "No, I've never heard that name before. Jessica was choosy about her friends. I thought I knew them all. She hated to be thrown in with strangers and was obsessive about her personal safety."

"You know her pretty well then?"

"Oh, we go way back."

"Are you from here?" said Alma detecting a *Norteño* accent in Gloria's Spanish.

"No, I grew up in Monterrey. My great grandparents wandered over the border from Texas looking for work and just stayed in Nuevo León."

"So, how did you end up down here?"

That's it, thought Alma, I need to warm people up before they'll confide in me, like coaches do with pitchers before a baseball game. She needn't have worried. Gloria was a talker. She had grown up in Monterrey but studied in San Antonio where she had family. In fact, she had a U.S. passport, having spent the first week of her life in Texas. Her job in Monterrey had been to remake the image of the local weather girls. Having been successful at that, the network's Mexico City studio had hired her away. She had met Jessica when she was still Renata and had a bit part in the soap opera, "*Hasta que la eternidad nos abrace.*" "She came in to have her hair done, and our whole team was blown away. She was that beautiful."

As Renata's part got bigger and bigger, the director had the hots for her, the two women saw each other almost every day. They decided to share an apartment after too many late-night cab rides back to their far-flung family homes. Sami joined the project, and they rented a real dump not far from the studio. Their Aunt Renata went ballistic, but since her niece and nephew had the money, there wasn't much she could do.

Not long after, Renata on the strength of her performance in "*Hasta que la eternidad nos abrace*" got the lead in a new primetime soap opera. With that, the three of them had moved into a huge apartment in La Condesa, the trendiest address in the city. She also had changed her name to Jessica María, taken from the label on a fake Barbie her dad had brought back from one of his trips.

She had met Beto when she was twenty-two and starring in "*Lágrimas en el sol*" which was to be filmed partially in Ávila. The choice of Ávila was Jessica's idea. She said she had been there as a child and loved it. To thank the TV chain, the state tourism people had organized a big cocktail party in the Governor's mansion and had invited the whole cast. Jessica hated big gatherings because you usually had to stand on your feet for hours and listen to a lot of nonsense. Beto gave the welcoming speech. Thirty minutes later he had walked up to Jessica and invited her out for tacos.

"Was it love at first sight?" asked Alma cutting into the monologue.

"Not exactly, but Jessica was impressed that although he was a rich kid, she despised that kind of guy, he seemed different. He asked her about herself, the person she had been before getting famous. She liked that he understood how lost she'd felt when her parents disappeared."

"And the rest is history, and I can read it in the movie magazines. But I still have a couple of questions. First, did Jessica ever have trouble with over-enthusiastic fans?"

"It's funny you ask that because just the other day I was reading an article online about stalkers in Hollywood and it reminded me of this guy, Luis Cruz. First, he sent messages to Jessica through her fan site. Then he hacked her private email account and started sending love letters. She changed her email address, but he hacked that too. Next, the flowers started arriving, pink roses which she hated. When she met Beto, he insisted she have a bodyguard and, Jaime, the bodyguard-chauffeur, noticed that there was a car following them to the studio every morning. He had the license plate checked, and it turned out to belong to this Luis Cruz. Beto consulted his friends in the local police about a restraining order, but under Mexican law, he couldn't get one because the guy had never threatened Jessica, physically or sexually. He'd just been a nuisance. "I think that Beto must have gotten Cruz roughed up by somebody because Jessica, as far as I know, never heard from him again."

"Did Jessica have any enemies or people who were resentful of her success? Also, what about personal or professional jealousies? It must not have been easy to have a best friend who was always the center of attention?"

Gloria smiled. "Was I jealous of her success and beauty? Sometimes. My ex-husband was madly in love with Jessica before he started dating me. She doesn't have many girlfriends. She seems to prefer hanging out with guys. Perhaps she sensed that women would always be envious. What did you feel when you were around her?"

Alma thought for a minute and then spoke of how her mother and her friends were totally fascinated with Jessica. They wanted to know every single detail of her house, her clothes, her marriage. She wasn't envious of the star but friendship? No, their lives were too different. "I think," finished Alma, "that Jessica, the celebrity, would always be sucking up all the air in the room."

"Since we became friends before she was a TV star and I knew the young, non-famous Renata, I guess it's different for me. Still, I wouldn't want to get on the wrong side of her. She has toughened up since she was seventeen. You do know she owns this building and is the principle stockholder in Avant Garde Spa."

"How's that worked out for you both?"

"Oh, just fine, we're still best pals," replied Gloria innocently blinking the lids of her deep blue eyes. "But you know, what I find surprising is that Beto picked you to investigate her disappearance.

A reporter? I would have thought that he would have stayed as far away as possible from the press."

Here we go again, said Alma to herself giving Gloria the same speech she had given Sami but adding, "Beto told me to ask you to please, please not to say anything about this to anyone: family, friends, colleagues. Jessica's life could depend on our discretion. Just a few more questions. If she has been kidnapped, do you have any idea who could be behind it?"

"Look, every day there is stuff in the newspapers, on the radio and TV about kidnapping but mostly they are the children of wealthy people or plain middle-class people or even poor people, not TV stars. It's weird, but perhaps this is a frightening trend. The cartels are so powerful that they think they can do anything."

Changing tack, Alma asked, "What do you know about her interest in Spiritism. Did she tell you about trying to communicate with her mother?"

"Yes, we talked about it a lot. I thought it was cool. I'm a great believer in the Occult. I wanted to go to one of the séances, but she never invited me."

"For how long has she been attending the sessions?"

"At least for six months. She was excited about it the last time we talked because she thought they were getting near to contacting her mother's spirit."

"Then she was convinced that her parents were dead?"

"After so many years what else could she think?"

"I'm sorry to be taking up so much of your time but what do you know about Beto's financial situation?"

"Isn't that a strange question coming from someone working for him? Are you worried about getting paid?" said Gloria frowning. Then, she shrugged her shoulders and answered. "I don't know much except Jessica seemed more concerned about money lately. I thought that it was because she was only bringing in royalties from her old soap operas. It could be though that Beto was having problems, but with the father he has, that doesn't sound too likely."

"Did Jessica ever talk about an organization called the Salvador Navarro Front or a guy called Gabriel Ruiz Abascal?"

"No," said Gloria shaking her head. "That sounds like some radical group. She wasn't at all interested in politics. In fact, she would walk out of the room if the subject came up."

Alma posed her last question to Gloria. What did she know about Sami's business and personal life? Gloria fluttered her eyelashes. Sami was a mystery to her. "He's always in the best restaurants and throws the best parties, but I don't know anyone else he manages. I've never seen him with a girlfriend or a boyfriend. Jessica used to kid him that her leading men were more interested in him than in her."

On the homeward trip, Alma thought about Jessica's rise to fame and compared it to the swings of fortune which had marked her own life. At eighteen Jessica was carving out a career as a TV star and paying rent on an apartment. Alma at the same age was living at home, applying to colleges and dreaming about a career in journalism. Over the next four years, Alma thought whereas I was enjoying myself at UCLA, Jessica was becoming more and more savvy about her career and men while I couldn't have been more clueless about either one. At the age Jessica had met Beto, she had met Kenny whom she once imagined would be the love of her life.

In her mind, she started to compare Kenny to Beto and then had to laugh, talk about night and day! She had met Kenny because he was flunking out of Glendale Community College and had needed a coach to help him pass his Spanish course. A friend of a friend had recommended Alma. "Hey," Kenny had said, "you're too pretty to be a tutor." At first, they met twice a week at Starbucks in Hollywood. Then he invited her to a few gigs his band was playing in bars around the city. Kenny was the lead guitarist and vocalist for the three-man group. If a registry of Punk Rock bands in L.A. had existed, *Putrid Soul*, Kenny's band, might have been listed among the top twenty. That is if they had worked at it. But Alma couldn't believe how hopeless they were about bookings, practicing and arriving on time.

Still, she was smitten with Kenny's stylish blond ponytail, his blue eyes, and tall, lanky body. His seductive compliments were flattering. "How come your mom calls you *'flaca'*?" he asked one day when they were talking about nicknames in Spanish. "Cause I'm thin like my dad, I guess."

"Yeah, but you're not skinny where it counts," he said smiling. Alma had dated other boys, good Catholic boys, from her high school or church, and they had fooled around in the backseat of cars. But going to bed with one of them seemed almost laughable. When Kenny suggested that they move their classes to his parent's house in Shadow Hills, butterflies fluttered in the pit of her stomach. Sensing what was coming, she was more excited than apprehensive.

"Look, Kenny, I can't get pregnant. I have a semester to go at UCLA, and I'm going to make Phi Beta Kappa."

"Aren't you on the pill? Everyone's on the pill." He had laughed and pounded the pillow on his bed when she blushingly admitted that she was a virgin.

"If my parents found birth control pills, they would kill me and then kill you," she had said.

"Okay, it's condoms, *mi flaca*."

Then graduation night after a tequila and beer filled evening and naked on Kenny's bed both desperately wanting to make love, Kenny's admitted he had forgotten to go to the drug store. "Come on babe, just this once, nothing's going to happen."

How many times had she looked condescendingly on her cousins in East Compton when at barely seventeen before the baby came, a quick marriage had been arranged. Kenny said he could get the money for an abortion, but she couldn't even think about that. "Look, just give me a few months, and we'll get married," he had promised.

When she told her parents about the baby four months into the pregnancy, Kenny was on tour. Her mother had wrapped her in her arms, cried briefly and then smiled. "Oh, but we'll have a grandchild!" Her father had asked when they were getting married. "In a few months when Kenny can manage it," Alma had replied. Stalking out of the room, Jesús had shouted as he slammed the door. "*Es un cabrón!*"

She did in some ways keep her eighteen-year-old dreams alive. Two Los Angeles Times reporters paid her under the table to do leg work and sometimes let her write parts of their stories. She compiled reports for a market research firm and made-up short gossip-filled tales for a celebrity website. Kenny showed up now and then always with promises of a future wedding but never with a ring.

When the baby was born, her father paid for the hospital. Kenny's contributions were flowers and a large teddy bear. "I have the perfect names for him," Kenny exclaimed when they went to register the baby. "Kurt after Kurt Cobain and Sixto after Sixto Rodríguez. Kurt Sixto Dwyer. Isn't that a cool name?"

"Kurt Sixto Dwyer Jaramillo," Alma corrected him.

Kenny had taken her into his arms, "Look, babe, it won't be long now. The band is doing great. We have a new manager, Helen, and she's getting us a ton of work."

As the months rolled by, one day ran into the next. Work, which she liked, kept her mind occupied. A night out with her girlfriends more often than she deserved provided some fun. A mother who cared for the baby gave her freedom. Occasionally Kenny sent a little child support and stopped in to see Kurt when he was in town. She wasn't sorry that Kenny's name was on the birth certificate. Kurt, as he grew up, would need to know who his father was. She realized now there never would be a wedding. Did she have regrets? Yes, and anger too. There would be no two-parent family for her son and no easy path to American citizenship for her.

"Ma," she would say at least once a week, "I have to figure out how to get a Green Card." But then work and the baby would take over, and the Green Card would temporarily be forgotten.

When Kurt was a little over a year, a telephone call came from Phoenix from her cousin, Alejandro, Alfonso and Julieta's son. "Jesús, you got to help me out. I'm building houses like crazy here, and my electrician just got hepatitis. I need you for just two weeks."

Michael was away on vacation; so Jesús who hated to travel, agreed reluctantly. "Isn't Arizona a bad place if you don't have documents?" Sofía had asked.

"I suppose it's like anywhere you have to be careful, but I'll be working with Alex and staying in his place. It's safe. I'll be back before you even miss me."

"Anything for family," Sofía had said shaking her head.

When the call came around ten o'clock a week later, Alma was already in bed. Almost before she could say "Hello," Alex began shouting. Had Jesús called? He hadn't come home after setting out to pick up a few last-minute supplies at Home Depot. He had borrowed Alex's truck.

"Have you called the hospitals?"

"No, because he has another name on his driver's license and I can't remember it." Oh, God, Alma had thought, that old license that his boss got him years ago.

"Listen, Alex, we have to find Michael. He's the only one that can help." Sofía and Alma had stayed up all night waiting for any news. At eight A.M. Alma had gone around to Michael's office. "Thank goodness you're back. Dad's in trouble."

Jesús spent four months in a detention center somewhere outside of Phoenix. Michael got him the best immigration lawyer in Arizona, but it was hopeless. His twenty-three years as a perfect citizen, because they had been spent in the shadows, had counted for nothing; his American grandson hadn't either. One day he appeared before a judge with twenty other unlucky souls and in thirty minutes they were to a one deported. He called Sofía from Nogales. "I'll be in Ávila tomorrow night," he said. "I can't believe it."

The first months back in Ávila, he was so busy finishing the house and finding work that he barely missed them. "You won't believe it, Sofía, how everything has changed. The new foreign companies are pounding down my door. The pay isn't what it was in L.A., but we'll manage. We'll more than manage; we'll do well." He never said, "When are you coming back? I miss you."

It was Alma who finally spoke to her mother, "You got to go, Ma. It's not right that he's all alone there."

"But how can I leave you? How can you work and take care of Kurt?"

"Millions of women do it. Trust me. I'll work it out."

But she hadn't counted on the recession which hit just after her mother left. Work dried up. The owner of the building asked for the apartment back as Alma couldn't fix the clogged-up sinks or the leaky toilets. Kenny stopped by one day to say that he was sorry but he and Helen, well, had gotten together but he would still send Kurt money when he could. How could she blame him? They had hardly held hands since the baby was born. Perhaps if they had been able to rent an apartment together things might

S.B URQUIDI

have been different, but in her heart of hearts, she knew that it was more than that. What did they have in common? Except for Kurt, not much.

She lasted somehow for a year, but when she had turned to Kenny's mother for a loan of five hundred dollars, the answer couldn't have been clearer. "We so love you because you're the mother of our wonderful grandson, but you people have to understand that asking for handouts is not the American Way." Gesturing at her dismal kitchen and weedy yard, she had continued. "Phil and I did this all on our own. We worked hard, and I know you don't think so now, but your sacrifices will bring rewards."

That night she had called her father. "I'm coming back," she said. She couldn't say "home" because Ávila wasn't home. He hadn't asked why or said, "Good luck getting a visa if you want to return or where's that bastard Kenny?" He simply had said, "Sell everything. We'll be waiting for you."

Her father's words had lifted her spirits but she had felt a sense of failure. She knew that in going to Ávila she would be surrendering her independence, but there she wouldn't have to face an indifferent world alone. Anyway, did she have another choice? None that she could see at the time.

Chapter 4

DAY ONE: MONDAY, JANUARY 4TH, EVENING

As she parked in front of the house, every muscle and bone in her body ached from fatigue. It was 8:30 P.M. and she had been on the go since 6:30 A.M. Her head was so filled with information that she felt the sorting mechanism in her brain had blown a fuse. As she opened the front door and before even the "*Buenas*" of "*Buenas Noches*" had left her mouth, the barking and ominous growling started. In a matter of seconds, small sharp teeth were nipping at her ankles.

"Dulce, no," she said. Her purse and bag flew out of her hands as she tried to push the short-haired brown bundle away from her feet. At the same time, Kurt jumped off the sofa and swept the dog up in his arms. "Bad dog," he said, softly stroking Dulce's head. Her father switched his attention from the soccer game being broadcast on their newest acquisition, a 40-inch TV, and smiled at Alma, raising one eyebrow ever so slightly.

"You see what a great guard dog she is, Mom," said Kurt.

"Except I live here and I'm the only one she attacks."

"Come on, Alma. Dulce's still a puppy," said her father.

As she picked up her purse and bag, she asked Kurt, "Homework?"

"All done and checked by Grandpa and I aced the vocabulary test." Jesús turned, and he and Kurt exchanged a high five. They looked so comfortable cuddled up on the sofa, Kurt in his pajamas, her dad in a pair of old slippers. For a moment she gazed at them fondly.

"Hey, Mom, it's Max's birthday on Saturday, and his parents are taking us ice skating in Mexico City and then out to lunch in a real restaurant."

"That's pretty cool. What do you want to get him for a present?" Kurt looked puzzled. Max, the only son of the director of Ávila's biggest automobile plant, had just about everything an eight-year-old could want.

Alma suggested that they search for a gift at the outdoor markets set up downtown for the Sixth of January. This brought up Kurt's wish list for the Three Kings Day. "I most want the Nike sneakers we saw in the Mall, the ones I showed you, remember, Mom?"

"I remember you got a lot of presents at Christmas is what I remember," said Alma.

"Alma, did you have lunch?" her mother shouted from the kitchen.

"No, I'll be right there," she said passing through the ex-dining room which was now an office.

"We had *chiles rellenos,* rice and salad," Sofía said opening the refrigerator door.

"No, Ma. The whole way home I could only think of a big bowl of Coco Pops," whispered Alma.

"Alma, that is so unhealthy. What would you say if Kurt wanted Coco Pops for his lunch?"

"I would say 'no' of course, but he's a little boy, and I'm a grown woman who can give into temptation occasionally. Please, Ma, it's been a long day, and Dulce went for me again when I opened the front door. Why does that dog hate me?"

"Alma that is ridiculous. How could a little puppy hate you? She's just---"

"Just getting used to us. No, she wandered in here a year ago. She's had it in for me, and *dulce* does not describe her disposition."

"Who's the thirty-year-old here? Maybe if you played with her or walked her occasionally when you were home?" said Sofía putting the emphasis on the words "occasionally" and "home." Hint, hint, thought Alma, but am I such an absentee mom?

"Why were you in Mexico City anyway?" asked her mother.

"Working on a story."

"What story?'" asked her mother who listened for hours to the radio and could tell you the latest on the Mexican War on Drugs or the fighting in the Middle East.

"Oh, just background stuff that Ricardo wants." There was no way she was going to admit she was investigating what was probably a kidnapping.

"Hey," Alma said changing the subject as she shoveled a spoonful of Coco Pops into her mouth. "Did you see Kurt's invitation to Max's party?"

"Of course, I did," said Sofía shaking her head. "Taking those children on a long drive into Mexico City to go ice skating of all things and then to some expensive restaurant. I think it's ridiculous, but no one listens to me. It's all about showing off how much money you have."

"You've met Max's parents. I don't think they're showing off their money even if they have it. I'm sure they think it would be a fun experience for the boys."

"But what does it teach them? What's it teaching Kurt?"

Alma sighed. They had had this discussion so many times. When she had enrolled Kurt in the British Academy three years ago, it wasn't because it was fashionable or because of the contacts he would make. Well, not entirely anyway. The American, French and Japanese general managers of the automobile and high-tech plants sent their kids there as did the wealthy Mexican business people and politicians, but they were there because the school just might get them one day into Harvard or Princeton.

As for Max, she was happy that Kurt had a friend who shared his interest in space travel, computers, and Harry Potter. Her son often accompanied Max's family on their vacations, one year to Cancun and another to Disney World. "What's wrong with the *balneario* outside of town?" his grandmother would ask before each trip, far-flung vacations being at the top of her list of senseless extravagances.

"So, what happened around here today, Ma? How are sales going in Mi Premiecito?" Alma asked changing the subject to more neutral ground.

Her mother's mouth curved into a wide smile of delight. "Alma that is the best name you thought up for my store. 'My little prize' is perfect for a store in a neighborhood named after the man who won the big prize. Mi Premiecito is doing fine. My healthy snacks are not selling as fast as I would like even though I talk them up to all the mothers."

In her business, Sofía strictly limited the neighborhood children to one bottle of soda a day and constantly offered them little bags of raisins and nuts or a fresh apple. No one ever dared to tell her that they got all the chips, Cokes and cookies two blocks away at her closest competitor's mini mart. Still, her business had grown as she added grocery items to her stock. One could buy in Sofía's limited space fresh cream and milk, packets of rice, pasta and black beans, cooking oil and a few fresh fruits and vegetables. Her profits inevitably ended up in yarn for a neighbor's baby blanket or flowers for the altar at Sagrado Corazón.

Alma thought, as she often did, about her mother's unexpected journey from a poor rural village on the edge of Ávila to the freeways of Los Angeles. She had never doubted why her father was so captivated by her mother. Her straight bearing made Jesús refer to her as the "Huesteca Princess." "Her ancestors were royalty," he would joke. But it was her quiet dignity and serene features that had caused her L.A. clients to refer to her always as Mrs. Jaramillo. They conformed to her schedule and were delighted when she could spare them an extra hour. She bought her own cleaning supplies and freely gave advice to these sophisticated women on how to maintain their homes between her visits.

Although Alma knew that in many ways their interests and beliefs differed, her mother's constant encouragement and nearly blind support had been the wind that had pushed her daughter's sails out into the world. When that world had been cruel or indifferent, it was to her mother she had returned for a fresh dose of love and confidence.

"Kurt and I had a fantastic idea this afternoon," piped up Sofía breaking into Alma's reverie. "We want to open an Internet café. Well, not a café exactly, but a place where children can get on the Internet to do their homework or play those video games that your son so loves. Their parents will be able to call a friend or relative in the U.S. on Skype. We could sell school supplies too, notebooks, pens, and pencils, maybe even some little gifts."

As Sofía's plans came tumbling out, Alma looked at her mother in admiration. The wall between her store and Jesús's workshop would have to come down to make room for the computers and the new stock. They could finance the new equipment with Alma's credit card and offers from the phone company for computers. A second floor would have to be built over the garage, but the neighborhood men were skilled at that type of construction.

"I'm impressed," said Alma. "We need to convince Pa and then figure out all the details but definitely, let's do it." Getting up from the table stretching out her tired arms, she said, "Would you believe it? I have a little more work to do. Did I receive a package this afternoon?" Sofía reached into a basket on the kitchen counter and handed Alma an envelope.

"Before I tuck Kurt in. What are you putting in his Three Kings' shoe on Wednesday?"

"Those Nike sneakers he can't stop talking about. Papi and I are going to the mall tomorrow, but I hate to go to that store. It reminds me of that little boy who was kidnapped and murdered."

"Please, Ma, let's not talk about that again," said Alma whose heart lurched at the mention of children being harmed. "I'm getting him two tickets to a soccer match between our home team, who by some miracle is still in the First Division, and Cruz Azul. Of course, he'll invite his grandpa."

"Kurt," called out Alma, "Bedtime. Can I borrow your Mac?"

"Sure, but you have to close it right this time."

The computer had arrived the day of Kurt's seventh birthday, a present from Kenny, Helen and their two little girls. It was Kurt's pride and joy. As Alma walked him upstairs to his room, she thought about the gift of the computer and how things had worked out with Kenny since that last awful week in California five years ago. The purpose of the computer was for Kurt to communicate with his father, stepmother, and half-sisters in between visits. She had to admit if it were not for Helen none of this would have happened. Helen, now a successful music promoter, had steered Kenny into studio work in L.A. but it was he who mostly took care of their four-year-old twin girls. It was Helen too who sent Kurt the airplane ticket for his yearly summer visit and who made sure that the child support was deposited in Alma's bank account at the beginning of each month.

Kenny despite Alma initial misgivings had kept in touch by Skype and email with his faraway son. She didn't know if their bonding had been helped by the fact that father and son looked so much alike or if it was their shared quirky sense of humor. It doesn't matter what glues them together, just let it continue, she thought crossing her fingers.

Before she inserted the flash drive with Jessica's files into Kurt's laptop, she dialed Beto's cell phone. "Hey what's up?" she asked when he came on the line.

"Not much. The Feds were here most of the afternoon interviewing the staff and asking me about any past employees that might have left with a grudge. We did have a chauffeur that quit three years ago or rather, to be honest, he was driven away by Martha and her family."

"How so?"

"You know how it is everywhere in Mexico, business, government, households; it's feudal or tribal. Once you hire someone, it becomes his or her job to employ the rest of the family. Lupita is Martha's niece; as is Erica, Valentina's nanny. My chauffeur, Pedro, and Gerardo, Jessica's chauffeur-bodyguard, are Martha's brothers. Can you believe it? Of course, the poor chauffeur that came with Jessica from Mexico City was a thorn in her side and had to go. I love Martha like my own mother but what a system."

Alma could only laugh. "So, what else is new?"

"The negotiator from the Olive Group came by about an hour ago. Interesting guy, his name is Steven Bennet, French father, and British mom. He works mainly in Latin America and speaks good Spanish. He thinks we'll be getting a call in the next twelve hours. He wants us to get together at nine tomorrow morning. I didn't mention anything to him about your investigation, but I can't see why he'd object."

"I look forward to meeting him. My day was sort of productive but more for background than any concrete clues. But do you remember a guy called Luis Cruz?"

"Of course, I remember Cruz, that little weasel; he was stalking Jessica. I had the cops haul him in for a little talk."

Alma thought that the police probably had wasted little time on talk. "Could you see if the Feds have any idea of his whereabouts?" She said aloud.

"Sure, but I think he's out of the picture. I've got to go and eat something. See you tomorrow."

"Wait a minute. How's Valentina?"

"She's sad. She keeps asking for her mommy. It's awful. Everything is awful, Alma. God, I don't know how many days I can stand of not knowing where she is."

Before opening Kurt's Mac and inserting the flash drive, Alma studied the note Beto had sent with the username and pin for Jessica's email account. The username was predictable, elviajeinmortal17@gmail.com. Frankly, anyone could hack that with an ounce of ingenuity. But the pin was curious: ¿03octubre? It took her a minute and a look at her notes to realize that was the date of Jessica's parents' disappearance.

As she clicked on Jessica's account, she wondered if the Feds who should have the computer itself would know that someone else was checking out the account. First, she tried the Inbox. There were a couple of emails since last Monday: two from the Brazilian producers of "*El viaje inmortal*" about arrangements for the Miami visit, another from Jessica's lawyer on the same subject and a query from her accountant. It took Alma about a half an hour to skim through the last three months of emails. They were ninety percent business, mainly from Jessica's PR firm concerning fan mail, some from Sami about the future promotion of the upcoming soap opera but two perked her interest. They were both from a certain Luz María Fuentes reminding Jessica of the date and time of a Spiritism get-together at an address very near the center of the city. No one else was copied in the email. Alma wondered if the Feds were already checking her out.

She next went to the box for Sent mail. There indeed she found a big surprise and one that Gloria had conveniently forgotten to mention during their interview. Jessica's email written a week ago to Gloria confirmed a recent telephone conversation. In very plain language Jessica stated as both the owner of the building and majority owner of the Avant Garde Spa that she was very dissatisfied with the financial results of the business. It seemed that the Spa had never made a profit and that the rent the business was paying was minimal. The purpose of the email was to advise Gloria formally that if better results didn't happen in the next two months, Jessica would close the Spa. The lease clearly allowed her to do this.

The note was not harsh, but it was firm. Cancelling the lease on the business would mean bankruptcy for Gloria. She not only would lose her investment but also most probably, money from friends and family. Did Beto know about this? Why had Gloria painted her relationship with Jessica in such rosy terms? Did she think that in the chaos surrounding Jessica's disappearance, the financial problems with the business would be overlooked? Alma sent a copy of the email to herself and printed out a copy.

Before she looked at Jessica's files, she went to the email Trash box. It looked like someone had cleaned it out completely three months ago, and again the accountants, PR firm and Sami were the main emailers. Curiously there was no emailing of photos of Valentina to friends or family. Security? Perhaps.

There were a few more emails to and from Luz Maria. The most interesting one had a dark photo of four people sitting at a round table. They were leaning into one another so that all could be captured in the frame. On the far left was a middle-aged fat woman, with deep purple hair, a tone fashionable ten years ago. She was dressed in a blue pants suit and had a broad smile on her face. Sitting next to her was a large black man, dressed in a yellow Guayabera. He could have been forty or sixty. He wasn't smiling. The woman beside him looked to be in her forties. Her blond hair was carefully styled, her jacket looked to be Chanel. Around her neck was an exquisite gold necklace. Alma recognized her immediately. It was Cécile Reynaud, the Governor's second wife, and Beto's step-mother. What in God's name was she doing there, Alma wondered? To Cécile's right was a slight brown-haired man maybe in his late twenties or early thirties. Strangely he wore in the semi-dark room, aviator sunglasses. His right hand covered his mouth, a baseball cap, his forehead and hair. Was he attending the séance incognito?

Alma sent a copy of the photo to herself and then printed it out. She was about to close the Gmail account when she saw a message from amoreterno38@hotmail.com. She recognized the Pablo Neruda poem immediately:

My dearest Jessica:

I do not love you except because I love you;
I go from loving to not loving you,
From waiting to not waiting for you
My heart moves from cold to fire.

I love you only because it's you the one I love;
I hate you deeply, and hating you
Bend to you, and the measure of my changing love for you
Is that I do not see you but love you blindly.

Maybe January light will consume
My heart with its cruel
Ray, stealing my key to true calm.

> *In this part of the story I am the one who*
> *Dies, the only one, and I will die of love because I love you,*
> *Because I love you, Love, in fire and blood.*

I've never forgotten you.
LUISMI

Alma felt sick when she finished reading the poem. Those beautiful words in the hands of what could be some sicko. Again, she forwarded the email to her account and printed out the text of the message. Was this the stalker Luis Cruz? Why hadn't Jessica reported it to her husband and the police? Finally, before dragging her tired body to bed, she printed out Jessica's ten pages on Spiritism. She would read them tomorrow after dropping off Kurt at school. Now sleep was all she wanted.

Chapter 5

TUESDAY, JANUARY 5TH, MORNING

Still deeply submerged in a dream in which she was reaching for the gorgeous man beside her, Alma tried to filter out her mother's voice. "Almita, it is almost eight." Opening her eyes, she saw the morning sun spread across the room, and the man become an oversized pillow.

"Ma," she called after a one-minute shower. "What happened? Why didn't you call me sooner? Where's Kurt?"

"His grandfather took him to school. You looked so peaceful; we didn't want to wake you."

"Yes, but I have an appointment at nine in Chateau Ville."

As she rushed out the door, lipstick-less and wild-haired, wearing the first thing she had pulled out of her closet, her mother handed her an apple and a *quesadilla*. "I'll text you if I can't make lunch," she said over her shoulder.

Arriving at Beto's house three minutes after nine, she noticed there were three cars parked in front of the house today. The two official Fords and a big Nissan SUV. Beto greeted her with a light peck on the cheek.

"I think you know everyone except Steven. Alma Jaramillo, Steven Bennet."

Before Alma could extend her hand towards Steven, Captain Durán of the Federal Police stepped forward. "¡*Carajo*! What's she doing here? I remember saying very clearly yesterday that I'd put a blackout on press coverage? That's all I need, a media circus."

"Look, Gonzalo, I don't think you understand," said Beto placing a hand affectionately on the official's shoulder. "Alma's newspaper is not involved. She's working for me. You're not going to be involved in a media circus."

"I get it. That's what this is about, press coverage for your wife who wants back in the spotlight. Since there's no evidence this is a kidnapping, I think my time would be much better spent in Mexico City working on a real case."

As Captain Durán headed for the door, Alma stepped forward, calling out, "Please don't go. I'll---." But before she could offer her resignation, Pedro Ramirez, the local police chief, took her arm and put a finger to his lips. When the door slammed behind Durán, Pedro's shoulders began to shake, his hand covered his mouth, and tears began to roll down his cheeks.

"What's going on?" said Beto getting angry. "My wife's missing and you start laughing when the Feds walk out?"

"Look, Beto and Alma, can I call you Alma?" She nodded. "The Feds haven't abandoned us," said Pedro. "This is what I think just happened. Gonzalo Durán is pissed off because he was sent to a backwater like Ávila when there is a huge case breaking in Mexico City. I bet that in two or three days we'll hear that the Mexican Special Forces with the help of the Feds have captured some big capo from the Sinaloa Cartel or the Zetas or whoever. Durán didn't want to be left out of the action, and he found an excuse in Alma. Now he can go back to his boss and say, 'The García case is a non-starter. I want in on the upcoming bust'. After all, as he said, we or they still can't prove it's a kidnapping or anything else."

Beto and Alma looked at Steven Bennet to see his reaction. "Pedro's right. The big promotions, bonuses, and glory all go to those arresting drug lords. I am sorry to say that kidnapping right now isn't a priority. Of course, there are great guys in the Feds who will help us once the big bust is made, but today they're vying to see who gets their picture in the paper with the latest villain. Besides the fact that arresting big drug lords brings cheers from the FBI and the DEA in Washington and that in turn brings in money from the U.S. Congress for all those little toys that the cops everywhere love: fancy helicopters, powerful guns, electronic surveillance equipment. But it isn't just Gonzalo Durán who has a problem with Alma's presence in this meeting. The Olive Group doesn't allow outsiders to be present during negotiations."

"I can't believe what I'm hearing," said Beto. "I'm convinced that this is a kidnapping, and Alma is not working as a journalist. She's gathering information for me, and I want her privy to everything that's happening in the case."

"Look," said local police chief, "we have very good contacts at the lower levels of the Federal Police where, frankly, the work is done. I'll call them in a few minutes to see if they have anything from their interviews with your staff yesterday and from Jessica's computer. As for Alma's investigation, I think she's an asset if the information she gathers is kept out of the press."

"You know," said Alma, "Gonzalo Durán has a real nerve. Wasn't it precisely the authorities who contaminated the evidence when they staged, for the benefit of the press, the arrest of that famous ring of kidnappers? Their ineptitude got the case thrown out by the courts."

"Well, if we begin to dwell on our law enforcement's *pendejadas*, excuse me Alma, we'll be here until midnight, and we wouldn't have helped Jessica one little bit," said the policeman.

As the three men stared at Alma, the sound of the Beatle's song "*Love Me Do*" filled the air. Beto opened his iPhone. Looking at the screen, he pressed the button for the speaker.

"*Bueno,*" he said.

"Beto, I'm so sorry, I---" Jessica's voice sounded hoarse from shouting or weeping.

"What happened? Are you alright?" said Beto his voice full of anxiety.

"No, yes, pay them the money. I'm so scared. They're---"

Then a door slammed, and a stranger's mechanical voice began to speak. "She's fine for the moment, but we're in a hurry, *Señor* García, so don't test our patience. Your wife could be with you in twenty-four hours. The price is twenty million dollars, nonnegotiable. I repeat twenty million dollars. Tomorrow you'll be told how to deliver the money." The line went dead.

Steven Bennet took the phone from Beto's hand. "A Mexico City cell phone number. I bet the chip is being destroyed as we speak. No doubt they have ten similar ones ready to go."

Beto sank into the nearest chair. "She's alive, thank God, but did I hear right? Twenty million dollars? That's insane. We don't have that kind of money."

"It's a starting price, Beto." Looking at Steven Bennet, the police captain said, "He's got a lot to learn, doesn't he?"

"Beto," said Steven "negotiations at this level, take days if you're lucky and the kidnappers are desperate for their money. They can take weeks if they feel secure. If the local authorities protect them, it can go on for months."

Beto looked at them. "Jessica can't be held captive months or even weeks. She won't survive. We must get them down as quickly as possible. I can't remember, up to what amount does the insurance cover?"

"Five million dollars. We have a lot of negotiating to do. You realize of course that Lloyds will not sign off on any deal which is not private and not thoroughly negotiated," said Steven casting a glance at Alma.

"But Jessica's life is at stake," said Beto close to breaking down.

"Unless they're amateurs or crazies, they are not going to harm her. Frankly, the way it has been handled so far with the voice distorter and the quiet capture, they seem more like pros."

He knows his business reflected Alma. Challenging him, she said, "Am I still on board?"

"I have no problem with your investigation; you just can't be party to the negotiations."

"Fair enough. Then I would like Captain Ramirez to get on to the Mexico City authorities as quickly as possible about a guy called, I think, Luis Miguel Cruz. Unfortunately, even if it is his real name, there are probably thousands of Luis Miguel Cruces."

"Really Alma? Why do you think Cruz is at all relevant?" said Beto, irritation creeping into his voice.

"Look at this message," she said pulling out the discarded email. "It was in Jessica computer trash."

"If it was that creep, Luis Cruz, who sent this poem, why didn't Jessica tell me?"

Shrugging off Beto's doubts, Pedro said, "Alma's right. We need to follow this up. Does anyone have a photograph of the guy?"

Beto shook his head. "Neither Jessica or I ever saw him. We had a license plate number and Jessica's then chauffeur-body guard, Jaime Santos, and the Mexico City police dealt with him."

"I hope you are not going to tell me," said Alma, "that Jaime is the chauffeur that you fired three years ago to give Martha's brother a job?"

"Selfsame," said Beto.

"Okay," said the policeman, "give us all the information you have, Beto, on Jaime and this Luis Miguel Cruz, and we'll see what we can find out."

"Anything else?" said Steven, "because I need to call my office."

"I'm going to interview the staff myself," said Alma to the policeman. "But if you get any interesting information from your Fed friends, call me."

When the three men had left, Alma took out of her bag the photograph that she had downloaded from Jessica's computer. "I wanted to check this with you first," she said showing Beto the print. "Do you know any of these people?"

"What the hell! That's my step-mother, Cécile," he said pointing to the blond woman in the middle of the group. "Where'd you get that photo?"

"Again, it was in an email in Jessica's computer trash. She must have taken it at a Spiritism meeting. She sent it to someone called Luz María Fuentes. Did she ever mention anyone by that name? Do you recognize any of the other people?"

"No, I don't recognize anyone else and Luz María Fuentes? Never heard of her but maybe you should talk to Martha. She was as keen as Jessica on this Spiritism business. But Alma, before you talk to the staff, I want you to see my mother. I don't think she can help, but she needs to be put in the picture."

"Fine, but if your step-mother is available, I need to talk to her too and don't forget Aunt Renata."

"I'll call all three right now. Then can you come back this afternoon to talk to the staff? I need to get hold of Clyde as soon as possible to see about raising money. But twenty million dollars, where could we get that from?"

"Do you really think you'll end up paying a ransom? Don't you think there's a chance she'll be found first?"

Beto looked exhausted, and it was barely ten o'clock in the morning. "I have to talk to my father right away and have him call the Interior Minister. The Feds must get involved now at the highest level. But I think they and we will need a miracle to find her. It's like looking for a needle in a haystack. But we have to try, and I think I need your help now more than ever."

Pobrecito, Alma thought. You may not know it, Beto, but your life has changed forever.

Alma loved Santa Teresa, the neighborhood where Catherine, Beto's mother, lived. A seventeenth-century village, it had gradually been incorporated into the city of Ávila. Thanks to a group of civic-minded residents, it had maintained its cobbled-stoned streets and adobe houses. Some of the lanes were so narrow that even compact cars found navigating their unexpected twists and turns a challenge. Hidden behind the bougainvillea covered walls, were everything from multi-generational mud-brick dwellings to the most modern twenty-first-century homes. The town had at its center a twin-spired church which at most seated forty people. The eighteenth-century Baroque altar covered in gold leaf dominated the church's small interior. A tiny chapel at the one side of the altar held a life-sized statue of Saint Teresa of Ávila, arms outstretched, eyes looking heavenward.

Next to the church were several shops, a few rather good restaurants, and a crafts market. Once a year on the tenth of January, the village held a festival in honor of Saint Teresa. Bands and fireworks, Masses and parades marked the day. There were bumper car rides and drippy popsicles for the children and *tamales*, tacos and corn on the cob for the adults. People, including Kurt, Alma, and family, came from all over Ávila for the fete. Alma wondered if her family would make it this year.

Catherine Borresen de García lived a short block from the village church. Yellow flame vines covered the adobe wall which surrounded the property. Atop the wall were foot high black metal spikes which silently sent the message: intruder beware. When Alma pulled the cord that hung by the front door, a bell chimed; that in turn set off a large dog barking at the back of the house. A woman with a pronounced hump on her back opened the door. Her gray hair was neatly formed into a waist-long braid. She had a dark blue *rebozo* wound over her shoulders and a pink rather shabby apron around her middle.

"*Buenos Días*," greeted Alma. The woman mumbled an answer and beckoned Alma to follow her down a dark hallway. Opening the door to her right, she showed Alma into a sunny sitting room furnished with pretty chintz-covered sofas and arm chairs. The wooden end tables and desk looked like antiques. What drew her attention, however, were the French doors leading out into a breath-taking garden.

Surprisingly large, the garden was terraced and filled with citrus trees covered in tangerines, oranges, and grapefruit; blue-flowered jacaranda trees defined the boundaries of the land. Pink and white gardenia and azalea bushes sprouted early buds, roses of too many colors to count, thrived in the middle of the space. Large pots of bright orange, red and purple bougainvillea were everywhere. A small stream ran through the plants forming at intervals lily-filled pools. The smells of orange blossoms, gardenias, and roses filled the air. As the eye glided from plant to tree, it finally came to rest on the towering Sierra Madre Mountains in the hazy distance. A voice from behind said softly in slightly accented Spanish, "It is my pride and joy." The woman could only mean the garden.

"Oh, I congratulate you," said Alma in English. "It's magnificent. It must have taken years to create."

"Gardens are never finished. They are only as good as the care and thought you give them every day. I am Catherine, Beto's mother," she said. "You're, of course, Alma. What perfect English you speak."

As Alma greeted Catherine with a kiss on the cheek, she tried not to register her surprise. From what Beto had told her, Catherine had to be in her early fifties, but she looked ten years older. Her features were good, but her fine skin was rough and wrinkled from the sun and years of neglect. Her figure, probably once attractive, had lost its shape. If she shed 25 pounds, she wouldn't look bad, Alma reflected. The woman's clothes were dreadful. She had on a plaid skirt which did nothing to diminish her ample hips. The hand-knit sweater which covered a plain white blouse might once have been handsome but now only seemed faded and unfashionable. Her shoes were the type that gripped the tired feet of nurses. Still, her eyes were as bright with curiosity as a girl's.

"Thank you, and I congratulate you on your Spanish. I lived in Los Angeles for twenty odd years so I can't take much credit for my accent. I also give English classes."

"Oh, then, we have that in common. I help in the rural schools in the communities outside of Ávila."

"I would love to chat about your work, but I'm afraid I'm here to talk about your daughter-in-law's disappearance."

"Has she really disappeared? I was sure it was some stunt."

"We had a ransom call this morning at nine-thirty."

"Oh, dear me, poor Beto. What about Valentina? Is she all right? I must get over to see her this afternoon."

How odd, Alma thought, no sympathy or questions about Jessica's welfare. She went on to explain to Beto's mother that she had been hired to investigate her daughter-in-law's disappearance because although it might be a straightforward kidnapping, there were some details which didn't add up.

"I'm not surprised," said Catherine. "Jessica never fit in, either here in Ávila or in our family."

"Oh, how's that?" said Alma, astonished at Catherine's frankness.

"I don't want to speak badly of her but Beto's father, his sister, Lucía, and I always thought she wasn't, shall I say, the perfect match for Beto. My son had a brilliant university career and was a successful broker at Goldman Sachs. His former girlfriends were educated women from well-known families. So, when he said that he and Jessica were getting engaged, we were more than surprised. We were stunned. Humberto had a fit. He argued with Beto for weeks. He even said he would take the business away. Beto just said, 'Fine, I can get a job in any bank I choose in Mexico City, and I'll be managing director in two years.' In the end, Beto had his way. I couldn't see what they had in common and how, after the life she'd been leading, she could possibly find a home here."

"So, you think she wasn't happy?"

"Happy, who knows if another person is happy and what does the word even mean? She didn't participate in anything worthwhile here. She's in Mexico City half the time, doing heaven knows what. She didn't make friends in Ávila. She certainly didn't try to include Lucia and me in their family life. We almost had to beg to see the baby."

Alma thought better of introducing the topic of Jessica's Spiritism friendship with the Governor's second wife, better to move on to a more neutral topic. "I don't mean to pry but how did you and Beto's father meet?"

"Oh, that's a long story. Are you really interested?"

"If you don't mind. It would help me understand the family better."

Catherine settled back in her armchair with the obvious satisfaction of getting her side of the story on the record before her ex-husband gave his version. If Alma had listened only to the singsong tone of Catherine's voice, she would have heard a dull story, but the devil was in the details and what she heard instead was almost operatic. "We met," Catherine began, "at the University of Minnesota when I was nineteen and Humberto, twenty-four. We were as different as night and day."

Physically, she had been as pallid as a Minnesota winter, wispy blond hair, white skin, light blue eyes. His rich dark skin tones, chestnut hair, warm brown eyes had matched the futile soil of his home state. She was shy and religious; he, boisterous and extroverted. He spoke excellent English; she only knew text-book Spanish. She had been raised in a big family on a farm; he was the only child of a provincial shopkeeper. She was an evangelistic Christian who dreamed of being a missionary; he was a non-practicing Catholic who wanted to make his country boom. Their first encounter had been like atoms colliding; an explosion had ensued. She had hated him and been wildly attracted to him. He had wanted her but promised no commitment. She finished her first year of college with honors; he got involved in university politics and flunked out. Nine months later, without a single relative present, they had married.

They settled in Ávila thanks to a government job Humberto had gotten through friends and built the house Catherine and Lucía still lived in with money inherited from her grandmother. Remembering her younger self, Catherine said, "I was fearless then, but it came from a total ignorance of the world."

"When the children were born and I became a member of the Pentecostal Church, my parents more or less accepted the marriage. I used to go every summer to Milaca, the small town where I grew up. The children loved the farm. It was as exciting for them as it had been boring for me."

Humberto's parents she always thought would have preferred that he marry a girl from one of Ávila's wealthy older families; someone who could have helped him with his political career. In Nuevo Progeso his father had been a big fish in a small pond, but he had wanted more for his son. "Humberto was their golden boy, too handsome and intelligent to run a general store," Catherine concluded with a sigh.

"Have you been divorced for a long time?" asked Alma fearing she might be stepping on the older woman's emotional toes.

Pointing to the jacaranda trees in her garden, Catherine said with surprisingly little emotion, "They were half that size when I learned about the other women. If I'd found him so attractive, why didn't I think other women would too?" Humberto had risen quickly in the government. In ten years, he had become Tepetlán's Minister for Agriculture, then he was elected first to the National Congress and later to the Senate. Fifteen years ago, he had started a new regional political party. With each new responsibility, there had been a new woman. Catherine had found solace in her church, her children, and her garden. She had never considered leaving Ávila; it was her home. They had agreed not to divorce until Lucia, their daughter, went away to college. He kept his promised. Then a few months after he had met Cécile and just before he had become governor, they had divorced quietly. "However, no matter how estranged we became, Humberto never lost interest in the children. He wasn't the most hands-on father, but I know he deeply loves his children. That's what I admire most about him," she concluded.

"Hasn't the conversation made you thirsty? I think we both could use a cup of tea," Catherine said rising from her chair. While she went in search of the maid, Alma looked at the walls of the sitting room. There were several rather dark landscapes, pastoral visions in oil of eighteenth century rural Mexico. On the far wall, Alma studied the words of a needlepoint sampler which had been framed with care.

Love is patient; love is kind. It does not envy; it does not boast, it is not proud. It is not rude; it is not self-seeking, it is not easily angered, it keeps no record of wrongs. Love does not delight in evil but rejoices with the truth. It always protects, always trusts, always hopes, always perseveres. Love never fails. **Corinthians 13:4-8**

Returning to the sitting room with a tray, Catherine said, with pride in her voice, "I stitched that sampler myself as a present for Humberto. I meant to say that I could be forgiving, that I could overlook a lot. When we first met, he was so idealistic, so anxious to improve things here but then a few years into our marriage, he changed." She still loves him, thought Alma. Despite everything, she'd be a willing accomplice to anything.

As Catherine poured the tea, she began again, "Where were we? I think I was telling you about the children. Lucía and Beto were such different children. He was always a leader, organizing the neighborhood children into games, hikes, bicycle trips. In high school, he was president of his class at the British Academy, valedictorian too. He made friends so easily. Lucia was different. She was such a fearful child, always clutching my hand. She was, is so beautiful but she seems to frighten off boyfriends and girlfriends."

A figure suddenly appeared at the door. "She's a bitch. Jessica's a bitch. We hate her, don't we Mommy?" A young woman with the doll-like face and clothes of a young teenager walked into the room.

"Lucía, please your language," said Catherine rising from her chair. "Come meet, Alma, she's a friend of Beto's." Alma could see that Lucía, as she drew closer, was no adolescent, but rather a striking woman in her late twenties.

"I heard her say that she's trying to find Jessica." Turning to Alma, Lucía almost spat out her words. "Don't try too hard. She's not welcomed here. She's a selfish bitch. Beto used to visit us all the time. He used to care about us. Now it's 'Jessica says, or Jessica wants.' He can't think of anything else except Jessica. Mommy won't admit it, but she hates her too."

"Lucia, Jessica is one of God's creatures and God loves all His creatures."

What a strange way to refer to your daughter-in-law calling her a "creature," Alma reflected. That made her sound like an exotic animal, but perhaps that's the way Catherine thought of Jessica, as a predatory leopard or tiger, and Beto, no doubt, as her prey. Poor guy, caught in the middle of an emotional tug of war, she thought as she closed the front gate.

Chapter 6

TUESDAY, JANUARY 5TH, MIDMORNING

S itting on an iron bench in the square in front of Santa Teresa's village church, Alma made a mental list of her afternoon appointments. She was most anxious to see Cécile Reynaud, the Governor's
second wife. Then Aunt Renata if she could be found and, of course,
Martha and the García's other employees. Afterward, she wanted to
check out the address where the séance had taken place. Perhaps it
held the key to Luz María's whereabouts. It was just twelve o'clock,
but she could have used a thirty-six-hour day.

She dialed Beto's cell. "Did you get hold of Cécile?" she asked.

"I spoke with her secretary, and she's due back from Mexico
City at four-thirty this afternoon. Do you know where they live?"

"Don't they live in Governor's Mansion?"

"No, that's just for official business and big receptions. My
dad bought an old hacienda near the city center about ten years
ago. When he married Cécile, they completely renovated it. It's

several blocks north of the Cathedral, just on the edge of the historic part of the city, Avenida Benito Juárez."

"Got it. I'll be there before four-thirty. But don't hang up, have you had any news from Aunt Renata?"

"I spoke with Sami. He called one of her friends; she's in Acapulco where she has a timeshare. She goes once a year to enjoy the beach. Renata's bad about keeping credit on her phone. He thinks she should be back in Mexico City tonight late. Listen, I would like you and me to get together with Steven later in the day. We need to convince him that your investigation could be very useful to Lloyds."

"Fine with me. Where do you want to meet?"

"I'm going to be downtown. Could we meet at seven o'clock at Steven's hotel? He's staying at the Camino Royal."

She was glad he had not asked about her interview with his mother and sister. She supposed their hostility to Jessica wouldn't be news to him, but she needed time to make sense of the encounter. Catherine who seemed at first glance so friendly and pious was, in fact, passive-aggressive. She'd be a slave to any plot which her ex-husband dreamed up and Lucia, what a hothead! Did they know more about Jessica's disappearance than they were letting on? Could be.

She punched in Jessica's home number next. When Martha answered, she asked if she might come by in the early afternoon to talk to the staff. "Then you might as well come to lunch," said the cook.

After texting her mother that she wouldn't be home until late evening, Alma opened her bag and took out the files on Spiritism she had printed out last night. It's now or never, she thought, with a sigh looking at the weighty texts. In an hour she had read the material once straight through. After reviewing most important parts of the mishmash of information, she got out her notebook and began making a few random notes.

Stopping, she began to imagine herself in front of a giant cauldron like the witches in *Macbeth*. But instead of throwing in the eye of a newt or the toe of a frog to make Jessica's Spiritism brew, she would toss in a pound of the practices of an ancient tribal shaman, a few doses of medieval lore from clairvoyants and seers, two large cupsful of stories from laying-on-hands healers, and many verses from the Hindu *Bhagavad-Gita*. When it got to a rolling boil, in went the experience of the New York's Fox sisters, who communicated with a spirit that haunted their nineteenth century home. Then, little by little, the Frenchman Allan Kardec's *Spiritist Codification* could be added. Finally, she would mix in the writings of Arthur Conan Doyle and Mexico's Revolutionary hero, President Francisco Madero.

The startling toll of the church bell brought Alma's thoughts back to earth. What would she have done if her parents had suddenly vanished one morning when she was thirteen: their coffee cups still half-full on the kitchen table, their jackets still on a peg at the front door? Wouldn't she have tried to communicate with them no matter how faint the hope? Wouldn't she have grasped at any straws to find out what had happened to them?

Ashamed of her flippancy, she agreed with the more sympathetic voice in her head; yes, of course, she would have pursued any path, talked to any medium to solve the mystery. It was also comforting to think that we are essentially immortal spirits who temporarily inhabit physical bodies over multiple incarnations. Who could resist a second or even third chance to get life right?

Then, too, healing through spiritual power was as old as time, popular long before the Spiritists practiced it. Hadn't *The Hummingbird's Daughter* by Luis Alberto Urrea been one of her favorite books? His heroine, Teresita, born in 1873, had possessed a supernatural gift for curing the sick. A female Christ-like figure, she had risen from the dead to perform miracles and consequently, almost started a revolution.

As she tucked away her papers, a cool breeze stirred up the leaves around her feet. She wrapped her scarf a little tighter around her neck. Suddenly, although she knew that the square was empty, she felt she wasn't alone. An image of Jessica in her Armani jeans and green jacket popped into her head. Alma hurried towards the warmth of her car.

When she walked into the García kitchen, the first thing Alma saw was a table set with bright blue straw mats, yellow cloth napkins and blue and yellow hand-painted pottery from Puebla. "Oh, how cheerful," she said, but there wasn't even a hint of a smile on the three faces in front of her.

"*Bienvenida, Maestra*," said Martha politely, belying the atmosphere in the kitchen which was anything but welcoming.

As the four women seated themselves at the table, Martha leaped into battle mode saying that if Alma had any accusations to make against her brothers, the García's chauffeurs, her nieces or herself she should state them right now.

"Accusations?" said Alma looking baffled. "I thought I was here to have lunch and later, a little chat. Can't I eat my soup before it gets cold?". When they had finished the creamy *Flor de Calabaza* soup, a treat since squash blossoms were out of season and started the second course of *Pollo en Mole Verde*; the atmosphere relaxed a little.

"Jessica loved to eat here in the kitchen with us," Martha said, the lines around her mouth sagging.

"Yesterday the police acted like we were behind her disappearance," said Erica, Valentina's nanny. "They treated us like criminals. I bet one of us ends up in jail, whether there's evidence or not." Martha and Lupita, looking scared, made the sign of the cross.

"How did you learn to cook, Martha?" asked Alma hoping that a little diversion might dispel the anger in the room.

"I don't feel like telling stories," said Martha clearing the dishes from the table.

"In the family we call my aunt, Martha *La Valiente*," said Erica. "She came to Ávila all by herself when she was only fourteen and asked Catherine for a job. Can you imagine? She used to go to Mexico City to explore the markets all alone too. Now she says she's going to Paris to visit a friend."

"I've been lucky," said Martha as she put an orange-scented *flan* on the table. She had grown up in Nuevo Progreso. Her mother had been the cook for the Governor's parents; her father, the gardener. She'd been the oldest of six children living in a three-room shack at the end of the garden. She had liked the *Señora* Catherine right from the beginning when she had come as a bride to meet Humberto's parents. She had saved her pennies, got on a third-class bus and appeared at Catherine's door right after Beto was born. She'd become the children's nanny, gone to school in the evenings, watched cooking shows on TV and taken several courses on how to make "foreigner's food" as her mother had called it.

"What were the Governor's parents like?" asked Alma. "Were they rich?"

Martha didn't think they were rich after seeing some of the homes in Ávila, but they'd had a big refrigerator, the first color TV and a car that wasn't old. Humberto had been their only child, and his mother had spoiled him. His father wasn't a good man; he was cruel. He had paid her parents almost nothing and had expected them to work all day, half the night and seven days a week. "I didn't cry at his funeral," Martha said finishing her story.

"She's wasted here," said Erica. "Jessica is always on a diet and lives on salads and Beto is never on a diet and only eats *tacos, tamales,* and *sopes,* except when Jessica gets after him and makes him eat salads."

"Beto and Sami both told me that it was you who got Jessica interested in spirits and mediums," said Alma finishing the last drops of her *expreso.*

Martha took her by hand and led her to the back door. Just inside the entrance, carved into a niche in the wall, was a shrine which contained a foot-high statue of La Virgen de Guadalupe, several candles, a small vase of fresh flowers and a framed, faded photograph of a young man. She picked up the picture. "This is my saint, El Niño Fidencio. He has helped me through every problem I've ever had, and I told Jessica that I thought he could help her too."

"Who was he?"

"You never heard of El Niño Fidencio? His real name was José de Jesús Fidencio Constantino Síntora. He was Mexico's most famous *curandero*. Even Presidents consulted him. He operated on people with a piece of glass without causing any pain and used only plants and herbs for medicine. He communicated with spirits who helped him in his healing."

"Where and when did he live?"

"He was born not too far from here in Irámuca, Guanajuato. There's a shrine to him in Espinazo, Nuevo León. I think he died young. He became famous after the Revolution. Some of his followers believed they could enter a trance and receive his spirit; so that, through them, El Niño could continue his work. They called themselves his 'little boxes.'"

"You thought," said Alma, "that if Jessica prayed to him, she would feel better about losing her parents?"

"No, no that's not it. When I need help, I go to the Fidencista Christian Church. I go to the Catholic Church too, just in case. But a couple of years ago, after Valentina was born and Jessica was so sad that her daughter would never know her grandmother, I went to the priest at the Fidencista Church and asked if he could help Jessica. He said we were very lucky in Ávila because one of El Niño Fidencio's 'little boxes' lived here, and she could help her."

Alma's heart started to beat. "That person was Luz María Fuentes, right?"

Martha looked surprised, "How do you know about Luz María? Do you have those powers too?"

"No," said Alma smiling, "but I wish I did sometimes. I saw an email from Luz María to Jessica. But I don't know anything about Luz María. I have an address in the center of the city where the séances were held but nothing else. Do you have a phone number or can I get in touch with your priest?"

"The priest only comes for the service on Sundays. I have no idea how to contact him, and I gave Jessica Luz María's phone number. I didn't think to keep a copy."

"Don't worry. I'll be downtown this afternoon anyway. I'll stop by the address I have and see what I can find out. Do you know Luz María?" said Alma, taking the photograph of the séance out of her bag.

"I never met Luz Maria but I recognize that woman from church," said Martha point to the purple-haired woman in the blue pants suit. "But what's *Doña* Cécile doing there?"

"I hope to find that out this afternoon, but I guess we can assume that *Doña* Purple Hair is Luz María."

Chapter 7

TUESDAY, JANUARY 5TH, LATE AFTERNOON

To get to the Hacienda San Ignacio, Governor García's seventeenth-century home, Alma took the ring road that skirted the city's historic center. Small by comparison to the colonial cities nearby, the heart of Ávila's historic center had been turned into a pedestrian zone about ten years ago. Founded in the late fifteen-hundreds by Spanish merchants connected to the silver trade, Ávila was sometimes called, Alma thought indignantly, the poor man's Querétaro because of its relative lack of imposing Baroque buildings.

However, the churches, convents, and museums we do have are magnificently preserved, argued Alma, and then laughed at her new-found civic pride. How she had hated the city when she had first arrived five years ago. Its slow tempo, its old-fashioned stores, its snail-paced nightlife, it had seemed after L.A. as if she had been sent to an island prison. Slowly in her writing classes at the state university, she began to meet a few women and men whose friendship had transformed her dull existence. Ávila, too, began to change rapidly with the arrival of new industries and new residents. There was a big shopping mall now on the edge of town, new hotels and restaurants also.

Her first friend Sarita had laughed when Alma told her she had never taken the pill. "You're the only woman I know who doesn't," she had said. "Are you planning to have a baby with every guy you fall for? *Chulita*, it's the 21st century."

About the same time, she became friendly with a group of painters and sculptors who were doing work which was twice as much fun as anything she had seen in L.A. Another new friend designed clothes with fabrics woven by local indigenous women. A group of architects took her for tours of the nearby colonial cities. Slowly, as her stories for the newspaper began to be published and as she found friends who surprised and delighted her, she began to see that Ávila offered her opportunities that in her old life she might never have had.

Still the feeling deep down in her bones of being an outsider never quite left her. She and her new Mexican friends had had such different childhoods. Their TV heroes had not been hers, the books they read, the movies they watched, the pop stars they idolized, the sports they played seldom had a familiar ring. She quickly learned the slang they used, but it never felt entirely comfortable on her lips. Sometimes, not so often anymore, she longed to be dropped back in that Starbucks in Los Feliz where she used to gather with her high school girlfriends to laugh for hours over their *Quince Años* celebrations or their hundreds of other shared memories.

Concentration, Alma, she reminded herself, you're supposed to be looking for Benito Juárez Street which should be right where the stone aqueduct ends. She parked a block away from where she calculated the Hacienda San Ignacio ought to be. Before the shutting the car door, she bolted her steering wheel to the brake pedal with a steel lock. What a way to live, she thought, always checking and rechecking around us to see what danger lurked.

Immediately, as she walked into the pedestrian zone, she spotted to her right what was unmistakably a seventeenth century hacienda. The two-story building, painted a tomato soup red with windows and doors outlined in bright blue, looked as if it occupied a good part of the city block. As she looked up at the ironwork balconies on the façade, she was reminded of old movies showing pretty *señoritas* being serenaded by Mariachi bands; a cliché perhaps but then there wasn't a wedding or religious feast day in her neighborhood which didn't include a brass band.

As she approached the massive wooden front door framed by a carved stone archway, she wondered if this was the real entrance to the hacienda because the door looked too big to open. A discrete twenty-first century interphone was embedded in the wall next to the stone frame. It was answered promptly by a soft-spoken man who identified himself as the *Señora* Reynaud's private secretary.

The uniformed maid who opened a hidden door in the massive entrance showed Alma into a large central courtyard. A hexagonal fountain lined with Talavera tiles occupied the center of the courtyard. Large blue and white ceramic pots from Puebla filled with red carnations surrounded the fountain. There were eight perfectly trimmed miniature Kumquat trees planted around the garden. Carved wooden pillars supported the covered corridor which ran the length of the buildings surrounding the courtyard. Each pillar appeared to represent a different real or mythical animal.

Alma could see, as the maid led her down one side of the courtyard towards the back of the hacienda, into a formal living room furnished with a mix of modern and antique furniture. A grand piano occupied a quarter of the room. On the wall facing the door of the living room were two Rufino Tamayo paintings: one of his famous watermelons and the other of what looked like a dog howling at a half moon. Someone's a wealthy art collector, she thought.

As they approached Cécile's office, the size of the rooms became less intimidating. "Madame's study," said the maid, opening a carved wooden door. As she sat down on one of the off-white sofas, upholstered in soft Irish linen, Alma gazed at the paintings on the walls. It wasn't Cécile who collected contemporary art she decided. But that could be an original Degas pen and ink, she mused gazing at a sketch of a young ballerina. There were several nudes that looked like Renoir wannabes and one large oil that could be a Joaquin Clausell landscape.

"The Clausell is an original," said Cécile breezing into the room with a small white dog tucked under her arm. "It was a gift from my husband on my forty-fifth birthday."

Rising, Alma extended her hand. "Thank you so much for taking the time to see me when you're having such a busy day and what is his or her name?" she said trying to stroke the dogs head while thinking I hope you're nicer than Dulce.

"This is Belle," said Cécile putting the tiny dog down on the sofa. "I could hardly refuse to see you. Jessica's kidnapping is just so shocking, and Humberto told me about the problem with the Federal Police this morning, which is also very shocking. He says he has them back on board now."

Sitting down opposite Alma and crossing her elegant legs at the ankle, Cécile looked her guest up and down and then glanced at her watch. "I am pressed for time, but please tell me how I can help you."

Alma extracted the photograph of the séance from her bag and handed it to Cécile. As the governor's wife studied the copy, Alma, in turn, examined the older woman. If perfection could be measured in dress, manicure, hair styling and a trim, fit figure, Cécile would get a ninety-nine point nine out of a hundred on Alma's scale. She was about five feet six and weighed less than a hundred and ten pounds. Her shoulder-length light brown hair was streaked with auburn highlights to hide the encroaching gray. She was not in any way beautiful, not even pretty; but despite eyes which were a bit small and a nose which was a bit large, she was a handsome woman. Cécile only had the slightest trace of a French accent indicating that she must have learned Spanish very young or else she had a great ear.

"Where did you get this awful picture?" said Cécile.

"In the trash bin of Jessica's computer. It would be helpful if you could identify the other three people at the table."

Cécile leaned back on the sofa and sighed. "That was one of the ghastliest days of my life. You cannot imagine how much I hated going to that place and having to sit and talk to those horrid people about the most dreadful drivel. I told Humberto when I got home that it didn't matter how disturbed Jessica was, I was never going to be involved in that kind of nonsense again. Excuse me, do you mind if I smoke?" she said, taking an electronic cigarette out of the drawer of the small table next to the sofa.

"No, of course, not. But even if it wasn't a pleasant experience, can you remember who the other people were?"

"First let me explain about my relationship with Jessica. I don't have children of my own, and truthfully, I never wanted any. I don't think that I'm the motherly type, but Humberto was worried that Jessica was getting in over her head with this Spiritism business. My husband didn't want her getting mixed up with a bunch of, what I can only call, charlatans. So, he sent me along to check things out. It should have been Catherine, Beto's mother, who accompanied her, but that's the most oil and water relationships I have even seen. Well, as I said, I participated just once and found the whole thing weird. Yes, weird, very weird."

"Did the people around the table introduce themselves?"

"Yes, of course. The busty woman was named Luz María. Jessica seemed to like her. I thought she was incredibly naïve. The big black man was Brazilian and was touring around visiting those churches--- what are they called?"

"The Fidencio Christian Church."

"Yes, he was the medium in the séance. He was Leandro something or other. Yes, I think it was Sousa. The other guy was a cousin or something of Luz María's. He was very quiet. Maybe he thought, as I did that it was all very strange. Luz María called him something like Harvey. But that doesn't sound Mexican, does it? I can't remember."

"Was there an actual séance?"

"Oh, yes. The medium was the Brazilian gentleman. First Luz María pulled the curtains so that the room was completely dark, and then she lit four candles. She asked us to put our hands on the table, close our eyes and to concentrate very hard. The room was in total silence for about ten minutes, and then this Leandro person began to speak in a totally different voice. It was a high-pitched, squeaky voice, very unpleasant, silly almost. What was curious and creepy was that when he spoke in his voice, he constantly mixed Portuguese words into his Spanish but when the high-pitched, squeaky voice spoke, it was accent-less Spanish."

"What did the new voice say?"

"Leander told Jessica that it would be better to ask the spirit questions with just a yes or no answer. After about five minutes, Leander spoke. 'There's a spirit present!' Jessica shouted, 'Is that you Mama?' The squeaky voice said 'Oh, my dear Renata.' I couldn't resist. I opened my eyes and looked at Jessica. She was reaching out across the table towards the voice. 'Mama, what happened to you and Papa?' Then the voice said, 'He found us.'

'What do you mean, Mama?' Jessica asked but right then Leandro's head jerked forward, and he said in his normal voice that he had lost 'the signal.' Jessica wanted him to try and find her mother's spirit again, but Leandro said that there was some interference in the room, a resistance that the spirit felt and that it was useless to continue."

"Do you know if Jessica went back to meet with them?"

"If she did, she didn't invite me. She did mention last week that she thought that Leandro was coming back to Ávila soon and that she expected Luz María to contact her."

"The place where the séance was held, was it Luz María's apartment?"

Cécile thought for a moment. "It didn't look like anyone lived there, but I don't know. That Luz María person talked incessantly, so it was hard to figure out anything about anyone."

"Just a minute more of your time. Can I ask you how you met the Governor and how you learned your perfect Spanish?" said Alma smiling charmingly.

Cécile sighed and looked once more at her watch. "It will have to be the two-minute version because I am expecting a very important call. I'm French as you know but from the area around the border with Switzerland. The village is called Barcelonnette, and in the nineteenth century for some reason or other, many of the entrepreneurs in the new Mexican textile and retail businesses came from that town. My great-grandmother and grandmother kept in touch with our cousins in Mexico City, and when I was a teenager, I came here for a school year."

After taking a long drag on her cigarette, Cécile continued, "When I graduated university, I joined the French bank, Société Générale, and was eventually sent to Latin America to negotiate loans mostly in the energy sector. I soon learned that ambitious women are not prized in the French banking world, and after I was passed over several times for promotion, I left the bank and formed my own consulting company. I mainly gave advice to very rich people on asset acquisition, and I must say I did well. In fact, I still have a few special clients. I met Humberto at the World Business Forum in Mexico City about eight years ago. He asked me out to dinner and the rest, I'm sure, would not interest you. And now I must go. I'll ask Álvaro, my secretary, to show you out."

With Belle under her arm and a slight nod to Alma, Cécile swiftly left the room.

A few minutes later, Álvaro Jiménez appeared at the door. A slender man in his forties with horn-rimmed glasses and peppermint breath, he asked Alma if she would like a brief tour of the hacienda.

"The Hacienda San Ignacio was built, we think, in about 1640 by a family from Puebla which is why we have all these marvelous tiles." Álvaro said. What Alma realized as they headed towards the rear of the building was that only the front of the structure had two stories. The other three sides of the hacienda, although with probably thirty-feet ceilings, had only one floor.

The entire back section of the building was devoted to a hotel-sized kitchen and storerooms. The upper part of the walls and the *bóveda*-style ceiling of the kitchen were entirely covered in cream colored tiles. On the counters, in the niches and around the windows, the architect had played with three or four different designs of authentic seventeenth century Talavera tiles. The brick floor, interspersed with blue and white tiles of different motifs, was original.

The only word that came out of Alma's mouth was, *¡híjole!*

The third side of the hacienda housed rooms for the live-in help which consisted of a maid and cook. The other employees, like gardeners, security staff, and secretaries, were dailies. After the servant quarters, the rest of the space on that side of the courtyard seemed to be Humberto's. First, there was a state of the art gym with a lap pool and every exercise machine known to modern man.

Alma commented dryly as Álvaro closed the door of the exercise room, "The Governor must be an Adonis with that kind of help."

"He is very health conscious," said her guide with a totally straight face.

As they walked along the covered corridor, Alma asked, "Where are the bedrooms?"

"Up there," pointed Álvaro to the second floor over the front entrance. "There's a master suite and two guest suites."

"I suppose *Señora* Reynaud is resting. She seems to have had a very exhausting last few days."

"Poor woman," said Álvaro, "her favorite cousin, Louisa Michel, is having treatment for cancer. Cécile is upset about it, naturally. She lived with Louisa and her family when she came here as a young student."

The final room on the tour was Humberto's library and study. "You saved the best for last," said Alma admiringly. As she gazed down the long expanse of the room, she thought that the bottom floor of the Jaramillo house could probably be wedged into the same space; there might even be space for a small patio.

The floor to ceiling window at the front of the study projected sunlight across the large inlaid mahogany desk. Above the desk was a portrait of Humberto García de León looking very majestic, hands folded in his lap, silver gray hair lending him great dignity. "Juan Soriano painted that," said Álvaro. "It's one of his most famous portraits." Bookshelves, from floor to ceiling, lined the rest of the wall. There were not one but two wooden ladders of different heights to reach even the most inaccessible volumes.

However, what took Alma's breath away were the twenty-four lighted niches of different sizes which adorned the other two walls. Each niche had an exquisite piece of pre-Colombian art. There were six round Olmec heads whose smiling faces were almost Buddha-like. Other niches held small painted pottery figures, some of women, one of a child perched on a swing. There were ancient bowls and jugs with intricate designs painted in a rust-colored tint. Finally, there were tiny indigenous faces carved in jade.

Alma felt a sense both of awe and anger. All this for one man's pleasure. Shouldn't these pieces, some more than fifteen hundred years old, be in a museum? But then again, she thought perhaps one should congratulate the Governor for preserving the ancient art of the region. As she said good-bye and thanked Álvaro for the tour, she inquired if she might have his cell phone number. "Just in case I need to speak to Cécile again." As she walked towards her car she thought, hasn't our Governor been lucky! No doubt he too is a winner of our national lottery like so many of our politicians these days.

Standing in front of her car, Alma took out her phone to check on Google maps the location of Luz María's address. The apartment was in the twentieth century commercial center of the city, not to be confused with the more elegant, much older historic center. There would be no parking in that part of town now she reflected. It would be better to take a cab there and back and keep her present parking spot.

The taxi that picked her up had the back seat covered with a clean but battered throw rug. The car's springs and shock absorbers were long gone. The driver, however, was young and bright. She gave him the address and sat back ready for a chat.

"So, you like Justin Bieber," said Alma, wishing he would turn the music down just a touch. "Are you from here, Juán?" she asked, getting the driver's name from the identification card posted on the windshield visor. Nice face, she thought, despite his shaggy hair and three-day-old stubble.

"Yes and no," he answered. "I was living in Chicago for the last ten years, but ICE caught up with me nine months ago, and here I am back in Ávila. My wife and two kids are still in Chicago."

"What work were you doing in Chicago?"

"Working in a nursing home taking care of old guys. I washed them, dressed them, played cards with them. They liked me. I liked them. They reminded me of my grandfather. My wife works at the same home. She says my old guys keep asking what happened to me. Our kids are three and four. She had to move back in with her parents. I send money from here every month, but it doesn't go far. Funny, huh, money going the other way."

"What are you going to do? Can she come here?'"

"She could but she's American and doesn't speak Spanish, and my kids only speak a little. Anyway, she wants the kids to grow up in the States despite the gangs in Chicago. You know unless I can get across the border again and that's dangerous now, or she agrees to come here, I may never see my kids again."

"I'm sorry, I know how you feel. I'm frightened my son will choose to live with his father in L.A. and then what would I do?" Or she thought Kenny might one day just not send him back. Kurt was after all his only son and Kenny was legally his father. She once had looked at the U.S. visa application. It said you had to show your school diplomas. Hers were all from California. The stamp "application denied, undocumented alien" was the only possible outcome she could imagine.

When they reached her destination, she patted Juán on the shoulder and left him a big tip but what could she say? Politics, she thought, what chance do we have?

The four-story building at 16 Avenida Revolución looked to be nearly a hundred years old. The stucco decoration around the door and windows showed its Art Nouveau influence. The bright pistachio paint which covered the outside of the building was in perfect condition, a pleasant change from its graffiti-scarred neighbors. Alma rang the bell for apartment number four. No answer. She rang again. Silence.

She walked to a newspaper stand on the corner of the street. The daily tabloids clothes-pinned to the roof of the kiosk broadcast the country's latest tragedies to a scandal-weary public. Alma bought three Mexico City dailies to see if there was any mention of TV stars who had dropped out of the sight. Jessica María seemed to be off the gossip radar. So far, so good, she thought.

Wondering what to do next, she saw a small roly-poly man wearing a smart Panama hat approach the pistachio-colored building. Producing a key, he started to open the door.

Hurrying up to him, Alma called out, "Wait up!" She could see that, although he was quite elderly, his gray eyes were inquisitive. "Can I hold your cane while you open the door?" she asked politely. He nodded to her but held on to his cane.

"I'm looking for Luz María Fuentes. The woman in apartment four."

A whisper left his mouth which if Alma had caught it right said, "She doesn't live here. Just uses the place as if it were a bordello."

"Really?" said Alma now very interested. "She's a madam?"

"No, no," said the small man. He hesitated a moment sizing her up, and then shrugging said, "Come in, and I'll tell you all about *Señora* Fuentes, but I like that you called her a madam." He chuckled as he led her to one of the two apartments on the ground floor.

"Who are you anyway?" He asked taking off his Panama hat revealing a perfectly bald pink head. Waving a hand, he offered

Alma a chair in the cramped, musty-smelling living room. Not a thing has been changed in this room since 1930 she said to herself. She wondered if he even had electric light and a telephone.

"My name is Alma Jaramillo. I need to contract Luz María about a business matter."

"Glad to meet you. I'm William Craven Padillo. She owes you money, I bet."

"Are you British?" said Alma reluctant to reveal her real interest in Luz María.

"My father was. He came here in forty-five, met and married my mother. He was a mining engineer from Yorkshire. My mother was from here and an art teacher at the British Academy."

"My son goes to the British Academy."

"I'm glad it keeps going," said William.

"Was this your parents' apartment?"

"The building is mine; my grandfather built it. I grew up here and moved back in after my parents died."

"I guess that's why it's in such better shape than its neighbor's."

"It helps that I was an art restorer," said William and started to chuckle again. "Sometimes being short is very helpful. I was the only one on the team who could squeeze into the corners of the Cathedral ceiling." And paint the cherubs that you so closely resemble, thought Alma.

"You were telling me about Luz María," she said aloud.

"I am not fond of those meetings she has with a lot of peculiar people. They bring the tone of the building down. She even had some so-called movie star here the other day. Great tall woman with too much hair," complained William. "The apartment originally was rented to Luz María's ex-husband who wasn't such a great tenant either, liked the ladies of the night a little too much. He died three years ago, although not in bed with some tart as I had predicted. Then Luz María took over the place. She holds the lease so there was nothing I could do."

"Does she live here?"

"No, just has those séances or whatever you call them here every once in a while."

"Would you have an address or phone number for her?"

"I have both of course, but I'm afraid the information is in my lawyer's office which is closed now and will be closed tomorrow for Three King's Day. You should know, as well as I do, that this country practically shuts down from December 12th to January 7th. Guadalupe-Reyes they call it. But it's simply an excuse to slack off if you ask me."

William sat down at an old desk in the corner of the room. "I think I have a cell phone for the blasted woman somewhere." He opened a drawer and took out several scraps of paper. "Here's the number she gave me years ago; in case there was a problem with her ex."

Alma opened her bag and took out the photograph of the séance. Holding it out to William, she asked, "Is this Luz María?"

"Yes, indeed but her hair is different now. She showed up last week with brown hair. She looked a lot better. She's lost weight too."

"Do you know the man with the sunglasses?"

"Don't know his name but he came knocking at my door about a month ago looking for Luz María. Said he was a distant cousin. I didn't like the look of him, so I didn't give him her number, but I guess he found her because he turned up here with her the day the movie star came."

"Thank you, William. I appreciate your help. Could you call me on Thursday as soon as you can locate Luz Marie's address?" said Alma handing him her card.

As she walked out the door, William said with his now familiar chuckle, "I wouldn't count on seeing your money again."

Chapter 8

TUESDAY, JANUARY 5TH, EVENING

Born as a sixteenth-century convent, the Camino Royal Hotel now, if structurally unchanged, was in terms of comfort, a totally different proposition. The rooms, formally monastic cells, had become luxury suites. The Sisters would have been scandalized, Alma thought: king-size orthopedic mattresses instead of rough planks; Jacuzzis instead of a buckets of cold water; sweet smelling organic shower gel instead of caustic soap.

She was to meet Beto and Steven at the bar located at the back of an enormous partially covered patio. They say, she thought, that the Spanish built these enormous patios so they could simultaneously convert hundreds of indigenous people. How confused and afraid the Indians must have been when those Spaniards, with their firearms and horses, obliged them to kneel and worship an unknown, unpredictable god.

Alma could see Steven in the distance sitting alone at a table intently reading something on his iPhone. Although they had hardly spoken in the morning, she had noticed that he was an attractive guy. A little older than her with light brown hair and eyes. He was tall and slim, with a pleasant if not handsome face. Yes, definitely her type. Too bad he seemed such a nitpicker for protocol.

Steven stood up as Alma approached. "Beto called. He's going to be a few minutes late. Look, I'm sorry I gave you a hard time this morning. I do want to work with you, and I would like to be in on any information you come up with. It's just that Lloyds is a stickler about confidentiality in the negotiations. In fact," he began his face turning quite pink, "I think if we are going to discuss our current problem it should be in my room."

"In your room?" said Alma smiling. "Is that part of Lloyds' protocol too? Does your company's manual say to conduct all confidential conversations with females in a bedroom?"

"No," said Steven laughing, "It's just that there are too many employees and customers in the bar. Any part of our conversation overheard by the wrong people could be dangerous for Jessica. I have a suite. We won't be sitting on the edge of my bed."

"Okay, lead the way but will Beto be able to find us?"

"Yes, I sent him a text."

When they were seated in the ample living room of Steven's suite with a Margarita from the mini bar in their respective hands, Steven explained why the negotiations had to be secret. "You cannot imagine the number of people who would try and jump on the ransom bandwagon if they knew about the kidnapping."

"Sure, no problem. We're both here to get Jessica out of this mess as soon as possible and at the least possible emotional and financial cost."

"I'll drink to that," said Steven. Then looking at her with a quizzical expression, he asked "Has it crossed your mind that Beto might be implicated in this business? I know that's probably a very indiscreet question because you're working for him but---."

"What makes you think that?"

"Well, first, it wouldn't be the first time I've come across a family member who's hard up for cash looking for a quick buck from their insurance company. Beto seems very upset and concerned, but I've also come up against a desperate husband or wife who could've won an Oscar for the phony misery they conjured up. Then as we always do because fraud is such a reoccurring problem, we checked him out, and his financial situation is dicey. Most of his capital and that of his company is tied up in the land deal for that new industrial park on the outskirts of Ávila. He has lines of credit, of course, and his father is very rich indeed."

Alma took another sip of her Margarita and turned her attention again to Steven. "Look, I definitely don't have the experience you have in these kinds of crimes. I do have a bit of experience interviewing people, and I think I've developed a kind of sixth sense for liars. There is just something about Beto that makes me think he is on the up and up, but before I put my hand in the fire for him, I think I need to know a lot more. To back up what you're saying, both Jessica's brother, Sami, and her friend, Gloria, mentioned that they had heard that Beto and Jessica were having money troubles."

"I guess we have to proceed as if we believed it's all legit and keep our eyes open. The other possibility that we should consider is the home-grown terrorist angle. That's where most of my work in Colombia has come from."

"Yes, Sami mentioned a man called Gabriel Ruiz Abascal who's a lawyer, I believe. He seems to have gotten a judge to issue an *amparo* which prohibits Beto's company from developing the land they bought a while ago from the state government. The self-same government had originally seized the land under the pretext of Eminent Domain.".

"But what's an *amparo*?"

"It's a Mexican legal maneuver which allows a plaintiff to stop, for instance, the purchase of land or the construction of a building if fraud or something else illegal has taken place. Of course, it has to be approved by the courts."

"So, if I understand it correctly," said Steven. "The state government claimed that it needed private property for a civic project and bought it at a ridiculously low price. Then after a while, they sold it at a nominal price to a developer. In this case, it's the governor's son who intends to develop it as an industrial park for a substantial profit."

"You got it. So Beto's company is stuck in the middle. They've paid the government for the land, but the *amparo* stops the whole project dead. It could go on for years. Of course, as Beto's father is the governor, the chances are that the problem will be solved in his favor sooner rather than later."

"It seems then that Beto has a cash flow problem rather than bankruptcy on his hands."

As if called up by a medium in a séance, Beto knocked on the door of the suite.

"Sorry I'm late," he said slightly out-of-breath, "but I was yet again meeting with our lawyers about the *amparo*. It is just so stupid. We have gone back and offered to pay a fair price to the villagers whose land is affected but that Ruiz guy just will not budge. He says that the only way to proceed is to return the land and start the negotiation process all over again. That's crazy. How could the government even do that? If we want to create the jobs we need in Ávila, we've got to move as soon as possible on this new industrial park. San Luis Potosi and Querétaro are breathing down the necks of the companies we've already signed up, just waiting to grab them."

Steven raised one eyebrow ever so slightly and said, "Okay, let's see where we all are in the investigation. What did our police friends find out, Beto?"

"The first piece of information we wanted to check out was the name, Javier Arias. They've run the name through their database and come up with a blank; so if that's the guy's real name, he isn't a known criminal. The cell phone used for the ransom call this morning was, as you predicted Steven, lost by some thirteen-year-old kid in a Montessori school in Mexico City. His mother was shocked when the police called. But the big news is that we have tracked down Jaime Santos, Jessica's ex-chauffeur-body guard. That's the good news. The bad news is that he can't come to Mexico City until Thursday midday because, of course, tomorrow is *El Día los Reyes Magos* and his kids would kill him if he wasn't there to cut the *Rosca de los Reyes*."

"Can't we email the photograph that I have of the séance to see if he recognizes Mr. Shades?" asked Alma.

"So, sorry," said Beto, "he doesn't have email or access to a computer and begged not to be taken down to the local police station. He has an illegal taxi, but better that I don't go into that long, boring story. Anyway, we want him to check out Luis Miguel Cruz with the local police in Mexico City where Cruz was taken into custody, don't we?"

"Anything else?" asked Steven.

"The Feds interviewed the staff at my house, Martha and her whole gang, and don't think there is any past criminal behavior. They are putting a tap on our home phone, but I can't see what good that will do since they all have cell phones."

"What about Erica's ex, the traffic cop?" said Alma.

"He's living in Aguascalientes, working as a security guard in an automobile factory and doesn't seem to have left that city in the last few months."

"Did they mention Jessica's computer?" asked Steven.

"If they did find the poem or the photograph," said Beto, "they haven't told me."

"So, Alma, what news do you have?" asked Beto.

"You know that I saw Sami, Jessica's brother, yesterday and her friend, Gloria. Both gave me a lot of background on Jessica's life which I'll be glad to share with you, Steven, if you need it, but

Beto, I'm sure knows it all. The big tragedy in Jessica's and Sami's lives was the disappearance of their parents when they were young teenagers; a mystery which still haunts them and apparently, what got Jessica mixed up with Spiritism."

"Spiritism?" said Steven.

"We can talk about that in a minute. There was another interesting email in Jessica's computer, Beto, which I didn't mention this morning because we were rushed for time, but I wonder if Jessica talked to you about it." Alma reached into her bag and handed the email over to Beto. "She advised Gloria that if the financial results of the Spa didn't improve in two months, she was going to close it down. I find it odd that Gloria didn't mention a word about this when I saw her yesterday."

"Jessica's emails are full of surprises. No, she never mentioned a word to me about closing the Spa."

Alma brought Steven up to date about Jessica's interest in Spiritism showing him the photograph from the séance.

"This morning," she continued, "I saw your mother, Beto, and briefly, your sister." Beto raised his eyebrows. "In the afternoon, I interviewed your stepmother and checked out the apartment where the séances were held. Concretely, Cécile furnished me with the name of the medium at the séance, Leandro Sousa. I would like to have him checked out by the Feds and the immigration authorities. Could you call them tomorrow? I met a man at Luz María's apartment, well, her séance apartment because she doesn't live there. He's going to get me her address but again not until Thursday when his lawyer's office reopens."

"What did you think of Sami?" said Beto out of the blue. "Could he need money because he's being blackmailed?'"

"You mean because he might be gay?" asked Alma. "I'd say that's a long shot. Being gay today in Mexico City might mean that some people drop you, but there are so many pop and TV stars that have come out of the closet, that most people couldn't care less. Plus, it's Jessica who's the star. I don't think the press cares about Sami's sex life. More to the point where's his income coming from? He's got expensive tastes and his main client, your wife, hasn't worked in three years."

Beto looked blank. "I haven't a clue about his finances, but you're right. Maybe he's broke. Then there's Gloria. We've just seen that she's in financial trouble. She's facing bankruptcy and could lose all her savings."

Alma felt Steven's shoe tap her right ankle as if to say, look who's talking.

"The kidnappers are asking for twenty million dollars," said Steven. "How much is Gloria in the hole for?"

"Maybe two hundred fifty thousand or three hundred thousand dollars," said Beto.

"The amounts don't jibe," said Alma, "but she does know about Jessica's movements and her interest in Spiritism. I think it is worth checking her out and digging more into her personal life. She mentioned an ex-husband to me."

"I'll mention Gloria and Sami to the police tomorrow," said Beto, making a note on his phone.

"Finally, there's Cécile," said Alma.

"No," said Beto, "what about your interview with my mother?"

Alma paused and thought for a minute. "Your mother and your sister seem to be very devoted to you and Valentina. I didn't feel the same affection for your wife." She wanted to say but thought better of it: your family detests your wife and would be all too happy to see the back of her.

Beto shrugged his shoulders and looked at his watch. "I got to go. I haven't gotten Valentina a present yet for tomorrow."

"Just a minute," said Alma, "did you ever met Cecile's cousin, Louisa Michel, you know the one who's ill?"

"She must have been at our wedding with the other sixteen hundred people, but I don't remember her. Why?"

"Could you get me her address? Also, I need to speak to Aunt Renata. Any word from her?"

"Sorry, yes, she will be here tomorrow afternoon, but she's not staying at the house. I'll let you know where she's staying when I hear from her."

"Sit down again for a minute, Beto," ordered Steven. "You need to be prepared for the negotiations tomorrow. Alma close your ears."

Beto sat down and looked from one to the other. "Why? What's happening?"

"I had a conference call with The Olive Group and Lloyds this morning, and I don't want you to be shocked when we start negotiating the ransom tomorrow with a very low figure?"

"How low are we talking about?"

"Fifty thousand dollars."

Beto jumped out of his chair. "Are you trying to get her killed? They asked for twenty million, and you are offering fifty thousand? That's insane."

"Look Beto, we have years of experience in this, and the first move is always to sound out the kidnappers. Neither you nor I have any idea who they are. They could be some jokers who just got lucky and have dreamed up an amount of money because they heard it in the movies. They might be overjoyed to get a hundred thousand pesos and be rid of Jessica tomorrow. I told you that this is a long process and it takes time to feel out the kidnappers."

"I don't know," said Beto wringing his hands. "I'm so afraid that the slightest wrong move could get Jessica killed. I keep picturing her in some cell-like room, alone and terrified."

"I know this is very difficult," said Steven, "but you have to trust us."

"I have another suggestion," said Alma. "I can think of least fifteen people who know that Jessica is missing and that's not counting the authorities. I also think that soon her P.R. people, fans, or someone else is going to notice that she's not around and start asking questions."

"What can we do?" said Beto his eyes darting between Alma and Stephen.

"I think we should invent a story that Jessica has gone into seclusion. How about this? We, I mean her P.R. people, put out on Facebook and Twitter that she has gone on a spiritual retreat to prepare herself for her new role in *'El viaje inmortal.'* She will be in total seclusion for a week. You know a spiritual cleansing."

"That's a fantastic idea," said Steven. "We can't take even the remotest chance that the news of the kidnapping gets into the press."

"I'll call Sami tomorrow," said Beto. "He can deal with her P.R. people."

"One final point for me. Tomorrow morning I am devoting to my son. I'll contact you both in the early afternoon."

As Beto left the suite, Steven said "Hey, how about another drink?"

In her heart, Alma said yes to the hopeful face sitting on the sofa. She rose, however, and gathered up her purse and bag. "Maybe another time, Steven. I haven't been home all day. Do you have children?"

"No, but not to mind. Fly home to your kids."

"Kid," said Alma. "He'll be eight soon and is very independent. Still,"

Steven finished her sentence. "He needs his mom," and smiling said, "Go on, get home to your family."

As she walked to her car, Alma reflected on what her mother called her "partner problem." In fact, her mother would have been the first to say: Almita, you should have accepted that second drink and gotten to know the man. What's the matter with you? Indeed, what was the matter with her? Both her parents not only encouraged her but pushed her to date, to get out into the world and find a boyfriend or even better, a husband. At least once a week her mother would lament her unfortunate relationship with

Kenny. "You were both too young, but Alma you need to put it behind you and find a good man. Don't you think your father and I have been happy? You won't have a full life if you don't share it with someone, and what will happen when we're gone? I can't think about it. It's too sad. You won't have Kurt forever, either."

So why at thirty when all her cousins and most of her friends were married, was she still living with her mother and father, and worse still, not even actively seeking a relationship? "Go online," said both her L.A. and Ávila friends. "You'd be surprised. There are some great guys out there." Then all the stories would emerge of Graciela who found the man of her dreams on Mexican Cupid and Andrés who believe it or not found a wife on Date Hookup.

It wasn't as if she had been disappointed by the men she had been involved with over the last five years. Pedro was a wonderful lover. Whereas Kenny had had the enthusiasm of a twenty-year-old, Pedro had the soul of a true romantic. When she visited him, there was always dinner and a good bottle of wine, flowers, and candles in the bedroom. The sex was prolonged, sensual and satisfying, but the relationship never went beyond his bedroom. She loved to listen to his dream projects and admire his innovative houses. He, however, showed no interest in her newspaper work and seemed to think that raising Kurt was like training his dog.

After that, there had been José Manuel, an engineer, who had a great job at the G.E. plant and was desperate to get married. He had courted Kurt more assiduously than he had courted her. He was so nice but so boring that at the end of the evening she had felt almost suicidal. She had endured the relationship nine months and then broken it off. He had married his patient secretary six months later. Finally, a year and a half ago, there had been her bad boy, Sebastian. He had a motorcycle and bought her a black leather outfit for cruising down the highway. Her helmet had wings of fire painted on each side. Kurt thought he was the coolest guy he had ever met. Her father had only raised his eyes to heaven every time the motorbike was parked outside. Sebastian wasn't boring. He was a talented industrial designer and a great reader, but his idea of the perfect vacation was gambling in Las Vegas. When he learned that Alma wouldn't be able to accompany him on his dream trip, he drifted away. He hadn't asked for the black leather suit and helmet back, but Alma had dropped them off at his apartment one day when she was sure he wouldn't be home.

No, she hadn't been disinterested in men, just unlucky. When the Jessica business was over, maybe she would try one of those dating sites. He had to be out there, the man of her dreams. But then she had to laugh because she still had very little idea what she wanted in that dream man.

Chapter 9

WEDNESDAY, JANUARY 6TH, MORNING

As Alma came abruptly awake, she found a small shoe in front of her nose, a loud voice in her ear, a slight hand shaking her shoulder, a dog barking noisily and sunlight pouring into her eyes. Unquestionably, it was morning.

"Mom, Mom wake-up. Look what the Three Kings brought me," cried Kurt as the shoe got perilously close to her nose. "Also, two tickets to the big match next week. I'm going to invite Grandpa." Then conscious stricken, "Next time I'll invite you, I promise. You got to get up. Grandma says the *chiliquiles* are almost ready," he shouted as he left the room.

Her mother had put her best embroidered tablecloth on the round kitchen table. There were four glasses of freshly squeezed orange juice, a dish of *papaya*, scrambled eggs a *la Mexicana*, a bowl of refried black beans and a plate of her mother's famous green *chiliquiles* which were dotted with chunks of succulent chicken, fresh white cheese, thick cream, onion rings, cilantro and slices of red radish.

Alma's father pulled out a chair for Sofía and instructed Kurt to do the same for his mother. After the women had served themselves, Jesús pasted the serving spoons to Kurt and then took an ample portion of everything for himself.

"Sofía," he started to say, and then Alma and Kurt joined in, "these *chiliquiles* should grace the table of the president of Mexico."

Sofía acknowledged the compliment with her usual answer which her family could have repeated in unison too. "You have to toast the *tomatillos* and the chiles; if you boil them, it's not the same."

Everyone ate slowly and silently savoring the different flavors. "This is the best Three Kings breakfast ever," said Kurt giving his grandmother a hug.

"The coffee," said Sofía, "I almost forgot."

While they sipped their coffee, Sofía said, "Another late night last night that seems like a very big story."

Before she could answer, Kurt interrupted, "Mom we didn't get Max his birthday present. Can we go this afternoon?"

"So, sorry, *mi amor*. Of course, we'll go this afternoon."

"Can I be excused?"

"Go ahead but, Kurt, those new Nikes are for school; when you go out to play, wear your other sneakers. And take Dulce upstairs with you," said Alma keeping a suspicious eye on the dog.

"But why can't I wear my new shoes, Mom?"

"Because, just because they're new," said Alma but thought it's because they're show-off shoes and we don't want jealousies springing up in the neighborhood.

"Kurt," said his grandmother, "we're cutting the Three King's *Rosca* at six; so, if you go out, don't be late."

Alma, Sofía and Jesús settled back to enjoy a second cup of coffee.

"So, what's so hush, hush, Almita," said her father. "Where were you yesterday?"

"I'm working on several stories that Jessica María is going to use to publicize her new soap opera *El viaje inmortal*, getting a little background on her private life. I interviewed Catherine Borresen, her mother-in-law and the governor's second wife, Cécile Reynaud. Catherine's garden is amazing, but the Governor's private residence is unbelievable!"

Alma turned to Sofía. "You wouldn't believe it, Ma. Oh, my God, it's an old hacienda with a kitchen that you could fit our whole house into or maybe the whole block. It's tiled floor to ceiling, Puebla-style, with the most fantastic antique hand-painted tiles and the Governor's study has the most incredible collection of Olmec art." Turning to Jesús, she said, "Why didn't you ever tell me that you and the Governor were from the same town? Also, your mother's name was García, are you related in some way?"

Her father arose abruptly from the table. Throwing his napkin down, he said, "Excuse me I have some work to do."

When he was safely out of the room, Alma looked at her mother, "What's that all about? I seemed to have touched a nerve, but I have no idea why."

"*Aye*, Almita it's a long story, but I think it's one that you should know. Let me talk to him." Sofía was gone perhaps fifteen minutes, and when she returned, she said, "Your father is in the garden out back, I think it's time you two had a talk."

She found her father sitting near the lime tree on a wooden bench that he had made himself. Alma sat down next to him, "What is it Pa? What did I say that upset you so much?"

"Almita, it isn't what you said; you know you couldn't make me angry. It's a long story and a story I try to forget."

"*Por favor* Pa, we're a family, and I should know what's going on," she said, clasping one of his rough hands.

"You never knew my mother, María; she died when we were in Los Angeles. She was an incredible woman. You look a little like her."

"I remember you used to call her every Sunday, and I would always say hello. Mama said you sent her money every month and paid for her funeral."

"That was the least I could do."

Jesús took a deep breath and rubbed his eyes with his free hand. He looks older than fifty-two, thought Alma. He's still trim and muscular, but working long hours in the sun, has etched those deep lines into his face.

"As you know there were four kids in my family. I was the only son. My mother was always saying, 'Jesús, you're going to be somebody.' My father was a *campesino*. We were poor, Alma. You have no idea what real poverty is. My sisters and I shared one blanket and the nights can get cold here in the winter. Our clothes were hand-me-downs, and mostly we went barefoot. Meals twice a day were tortillas and beans. Sometimes there was a little chili to flavor the beans, and sometimes my father came home with a few avocados or mangos. Once a month there might be chicken or meat, but I was always hungry.

"Our family worked a small farm that was owned by our Governor's father. My mother was distantly related to him. My parents tended the animals, planted corn and vegetables. Even if they couldn't read or write, they were smart in the ways of the land and hard workers.

"The six of us lived in an adobe hut near where they kept the animals. The floor was hard dirt. Water came from a well, and the toilet was a hole in the ground surrounded by a few stalks of bamboo. When I was five, my father cut his foot badly with a machete. My mother ran to a large hacienda nearby to get help. The foreman of the hacienda telephoned José, Humberto's father. He sent them to some rundown clinic on the edge of town where the doctor stitched up the wound, poured some alcohol over it and sent him home. When the wound didn't heal, my father went back to the clinic, but it was too late; he died a few days later from the infection. José did offer my mother a small pension. I think *Doña* Clara, his wife, made him do it.

"We moved in with my grandmother. My mother worked cleaning the public baths in Nuevo Progreso which kept us fed. She took me every Sunday back to José García's farm to collect her pension. He was supposed to show up after Mass, but usually, we had to wait two or three hours and then listen to a speech about his generosity. Sometimes there would be Humberto's old clothes for me. They were a godsend and made it possible for me to go to school."

"Did you ever meet Humberto?".

"In person, no, but I knew who he was. I used to see him around town when he came back for vacation. People said he was very intelligent, but then he didn't have much competition in Nuevo Progreso. I always felt funny wearing his old clothes. They were mostly school uniforms, but occasionally there would be shoes which were always too big. When I started to work the first thing I bought myself were a pair of shoes that fit. I can still remember how good they felt." Jesús released his hand from Alma's grasp and taking a handkerchief out of his pocket wiped the sweat off his forehead.

"How did you get to the Tech in Ávila?"

"I wanted to be a plumber or an electrician. A favorite teacher convinced me to apply. I took an exam and was accepted; the whole village turned out to see me off. I had a scholarship which covered the tuition and lucky for me, my mother's sister, Alicia, lived in a small village, El Rosario, not far from the Tech. She was a childless widow. She had a cow, about twenty chickens, a small corn field and a few fruit trees. The house had three rooms; the adobe had started to crumble, but the floor was cement, not dirt. In the back garden, she had a small hut where she kept a tin bathtub. We had to heat water on an outdoor stove, but the luxury of a bath in hot water amazed me," said Jesús rising from the bench to stretch his legs.

"Then you met Mama, got married and went off to Los Angeles."

Jesús turned to Alma, his eyes narrowed. His voice now was a husky whisper. "What I am going to tell you, you can't ever repeat. You can't reveal it to anyone, and I mean no one. Alma, I am talking about something that's very, very dangerous. Your mother knows but no one else. It's the reason we went to Los Angeles."

Alma stared at her father. "I don't understand. What are you talking about?" Her father seated himself next to her again. This time it was Jesús who took Alma's hand.

"You work for a newspaper, Alma, so you must be following the problem that Beto García is having with an organization called the Salvador Navarro Front?"

"I didn't know about it until, well, someone involved in the story I'm writing mentioned it to me."

"Salvador Navarro was my friend," said Jesús.

"You knew him?"

"He was our neighbor in El Rosario. He was five or six years older than me. People were attracted to him. He was very---"

"Charismatic?" said Alma

"Yes, Salvador was like a bolt of lightning. He was always charged up; he could talk the angels out of heaven. You just wanted to be around him to absorb some of that energy. When he wasn't furious with the authorities, he was laughing at his own jokes. I guess what I want to say is that he was like a tornado. He was El Rosario's own tornado." Jesús paused for a moment and said, "Alma could you get us some water?"

When she returned with a pitcher and two glasses, Jesús swallowed his water in one gulp.

"It was November 1982. I had finished at the Tech that summer and had a job working for a small construction company, not getting paid much, but my life was good. I had just met your mother and was falling in love with her. I was also attending a lot of Salvador's meetings as was everyone in El Rosario. For almost a year the town had been battling the state government over the village land. The authorities wanted it for Ávila's new airport which they said would bring many new jobs to the city. They had offered to resettle us way on the other side of town in some new apartments. But what would happen to our animals, to our corn, to our fruit trees? How would people earn a living? We weren't city people."

As Jesús downed another glass of water, Alma felt that if she moved it would break the spell.

"The government saw Salvador Navarro as our chief troublemaker. He had opposition politicians on his side as well as several Mexico City newspapers. One morning several men from the state government showed up to make their last offer. They would give each family a small apartment, some land to farm several miles away and two thousand pesos. Many people in the village wanted to take the offer. No one ever had any money, so it seemed like a fortune. Salvador said it was ridiculous that our land was worth at least five times that amount and maybe more since they couldn't build the airport without it.

"That same night around midnight three cars pulled up, and about a dozen men ran through the village to Salvador's house and took him away. Aunt Alicia and I could hear his mother and his sisters screaming. In the morning, his family went to the police to file a complaint, but they were turned away. I had to go to work, but when I got back, my aunt said the authorities had been there again and wanted an answer. Everybody was scared because of what had happened with Salvador, but they were angry too. People met through the night, but there was no decision. Some farmers were just stubborn and refused to move; others couldn't decide, many wanted to take the offer."

Jesús sat back on the bench and sighed. "I left for work early the next day. It was the twelfth of November. We didn't have cell phones then and there were no landlines in the village. It was still daylight when I finished work and headed home. I was hurrying because although still a kilometer away, I had seen a huge cloud of dust rising in the distance. As I neared the village, a caravan of cars, trucks and several bulldozers came along the road. The caravan stopped. A young man got out of the lead car and approached the bulldozers. I hoped that no one was paying attention to me, a nobody dressed in dirty workman's clothes. The driver and the young man exchanged a few words. When he turned to get back in the car, I recognized him immediately. It was Humberto García. He looked exhausted; his shoulders slumped, the expression in his eyes was that of a dead man.

"When the caravan moved on, I peddled as fast as I could down the road. What I found was total devastation. The village was gone. People were milling around, holding on to a clay pot here, a blanket there. The animals had mostly been run off or bulldozed under. I found my aunt sitting on the ground, holding her dog. She wasn't crying; she looked as if she had turned to stone."

Alma looked at her father. Tears were running down his cheeks. "They didn't have to do it that way. They didn't have to take Salvador away. If the authorities had just been more patient and found a place where the people could have rebuilt their village, it would have worked out. It was so unnecessary."

"What do you think happened to Salvador?"

"There were so many stories and so much confusion for months afterward. He's dead, of course. I don't know who killed him; probably, we'll never know. I also don't know who ordered the destruction of El Rosario, but I do know who the hatchet man was, and I see him almost every day smiling for the cameras as he leaves the Governor's Mansion."

"Aunt Alicia? What did she do?"

"Most of the people from the village moved into the government apartments and took the money. Aunt Alicia refused. I took her the next day to Nuevo Progreso to stay with my mother. She only lived a few months. She stopped talking and eating. Then she died."

"Pa, that is the most horrible story I've ever heard," said Alma now crying herself.

Jesús put his arm around her shoulder. "You see, don't you, why I've kept the secret. I have no proof that Humberto was involved. It would be my word against his, and who'd believe me? I found out later he'd been in his job in the Ministry of Industrial Development for only a few months. I guess he was trying to please the people who could help him in his career. I have a feeling he got in way over his head."

"Were they government vehicles that you saw?"

"Those people with him whoever they were, were goons, thugs from the *brigadas blancas*. They did what the government couldn't or didn't want to do. They're still around offering their services to the highest bidder, or maybe they're *narcos* now."

My God, thought Alma, are the sins of the father visited on the son? For whom am I working? But worst still, to whom am I related?

Chapter 10

WEDNESDAY, JANUARY 6TH, MIDDAY

After her father had gone back to the quiet of his workshop, Alma sat by the lime tree trying to sort out her feelings. Did she have any obligation to the García family now that she knew Jesús's story? She didn't think so. But more important, did she have an obligation to Jessica? She wasn't a friend, but Alma felt that she might be a pawn in a much greater game. Last Monday morning Jessica had been merely a client. But now she saw Jessica's life had been as filled with turmoil as her own. Of course, as Steven had hinted, it could be an inside job, a plot by husband and wife to milk the insurance company. But if it wasn't, Alma couldn't imagine what Jessica must be going through. The terror of captivity; the anguish of not knowing if you would come out of the ordeal alive. The ache of being separated from your child and your husband. No, thought Alma, I need to continue not only for the story but also for this woman I hardly know.

Who's still out there that I haven't spoken to? she asked herself. There's Aunt Renata who I should try and contact right now.

Neither had she spoken to Clyde Ramsey, Beto's partner; perhaps she could glean some information from him on Beto's real financial situation. Most of all, she had to talk to Gabriel Ruiz, the lawyer for the Salvador Navarro Front.

First, she called Beto. "Hey, how did the negotiation go this morning?"

"A disaster," said Beto. "Steven says he knows what he's doing, but when he said we could offer fifty thousand dollars for Jessica's return, *Señor* Metallic Voice went ballistic. He started talking about cutting off Jessica's little finger or worse."

"How did it end up?"

"That we'd get back in touch tomorrow with a better offer. The guy was not happy. He said they were getting fed up with our *mierdas*."

"How are you doing with raising the ransom money?"

"Clyde gets back from New York tonight, and we'll see what he could do."

"Beto, do you have Aunt Renata's address? Also, I really would like to talk to Clyde tomorrow."

"Renata is staying at the Hotel Central downtown. I have no idea why she would pick such an awful place, but Jessica always said she was strange. Why do you want to talk to Clyde?" he asked sounding annoyed. "He doesn't know anything about Jessica's life or at least he only knows her through me. This isn't about checking up on my family, is it? Because that is not part of our deal."

Testy, thought Alma, but possibly with good reason. "Look, being a reporter has shown me that information often comes from the most unexpected sources. If I'm to do the job you hired me for, I should talk to everyone, and that includes your father, Beto," she said with a new note of toughness in her voice.

"Okay, have it your way. I'll send you Clyde's info by email, and I'll see if you can talk to my father tomorrow."

Taking a deep breath, Alma punched in her editor's number. When Ricardo picked up, he was not happy. "Well, well, well if it isn't Miss Pulitzer Prize finally checking in. I thought we said forty-eight hours. Will you be gracing us with your presence today?"

"Richie, I need more time. This has become so complicated I won't even try to explain it to you."

"You might give it a try."

"I need to get hold of a lawyer named Gabriel Ruíz Abascal. Do you have a phone number or an address?"

There was a short silence on the line. "He's a Human Rights lawyer, Alma. What have you gotten mixed up in?" said Ricardo, the concern obvious in his voice.

"Look, I just want to talk to him about an aspect of the story. Do you know him?"

"Yes, I know him well. He's a very decent guy, but the stuff he deals with can get dangerous. Are you in over your head? Because if this story is going to put you at risk, I want you to drop it right now. I don't need to remind you that three journalists have been murdered in Tepetlán so far this year."

"Look, Richie, there's an element of danger in the story but not for me. I'm on the sidelines. I did hear something very interesting yesterday. There's going to be a big drug bust in the next couple of days. I don't know where or when but the Feds are on their toes."

"Thanks for the tip but it could only have come from the cops. So, it doesn't make me feel much better about your safety. Here's Gabriel's number but Alma, be careful. Report back to me tomorrow. Don't go silent on me."

She dialed Gabriel's number, and to her surprise, he picked up immediately.

"*Licenciado*, my name is Alma Jaramillo. I work with Ricardo Nuñez at El Diario de Ávila, and I wondered if I could talk with you?"

"When did you have in mind?"

"I know it's short notice but could you see me today?"

"Be at the entrance to the University cafeteria at three o'clock. I don't have classes today, but I have appointments with students most of the afternoon." The line went dead. He's at least decisive, thought Alma.

She called Renata Rivera, Jessica's aunt, next. The operator put her through to room twelve.

"*Señorita* Rivera," she said in what she hoped was a friendly voice, "I'm working for Beto García in the search for your niece. My name is Alma Jaramillo. I think Beto mentioned that I might be calling you."

"Yes, he did mention your name. How can I help you?"

"Could I come over to see you, say in the next twenty minutes or so?"

"If you can come by before 1:30, I'll still be here."

"Kurt," she called from the bottom of the stairs, "I'm going out for a while, but I'll be back by 4:30 so we can find Max that present. Did you hear me?"

"Yeah Mom," came the answer.

"How about coming to the top of stairs so that I can see you?" A head peered out of his bedroom door. "What are you doing this afternoon?" she asked.

"I'm going to play soccer with the guys."

"Okay, but remember what I said about those new shoes and don't forget your cell phone." The head disappeared. "Did you hear me?"

"Sure, I did," came a voice from inside the bedroom as the door closed. I can hardly wait, thought Alma, for the teenage years. Then sending him to Kenny might look appealing.

The Hotel Central was in the commercial district of Ávila four or five blocks north of William Craven's place. Featureless, neither old nor new, the white building served as a perfect canvas for the endlessly creative graffiti artists of the city. Right above the front door of the hotel in purple flowing script, someone had written *ANARCHY IS LOVE*. A budding philosopher, Alma observed to herself. I wonder what other thoughts he or she might have on modern life?

Entering the rundown lobby, she imagined the rooms. I bet they're basic, a double bed with a washed out blue rayon bedspread, a bedside table with a Bible prominently displayed. The curtains would not even try to block out the morning sun, and the bathroom would smell of Clorox and bug spray. She pitied Aunt Renata before she even met her.

The only person in the lobby was a middle-aged woman sitting on a tired looking sofa reading a leaflet about tours of the city. She doesn't look unpleasant, thought Alma. Her gray wavy hair was well cut; her trim figure held the outlines of a good shape. Her features were regular; her face, free of make-up except for a dash of pink lipstick.

"*Señorita* Rivera?" asked Alma extending her hand. The scent of lilies drifted off the older woman's tweed jacket.

"Yes, hello, you must be Beto's friend." The stern dignity of the woman stopped Alma immediately from using the informal "*tú*." We'll always refer to one another as "*usted*" Alma decided and no first names either.

Seating herself in the equally tired armchair next to the sofa, Alma spoke quickly. "I know that Beto has told you about the kidnapping. The details are still confidential, but I wondered if you could shed some light on who might be behind it?"

"Why don't you think that it's a criminal gang?"

"Jessica appears to have gotten into the car willingly. She wasn't grabbed off the street, and since she didn't take the bodyguard with her, it would seem she knew the person who picked her up."

"Before I answer your question, and I am not sure I can tell you anything useful, perhaps I should tell you about myself and my relationship with Jessica and Sami."

Why don't I work with a tape recorder? thought Alma taking out her small notebook.

Rosalba's children had been very close to their parents, particularly to their mother. When Renata had moved into their house after her sister and Juan Carlos had disappeared, she was completely unprepared to raise teenagers. She was forty-five and unused to caring for anyone else, didn't even have a cat or a dog. She had hated the way her overbearing father had raised her but that was the only parenting she knew. Going on autopilot, she tried to raise Jessica and Sami as she had been raised. It was, of course, a disaster. The more they rebelled, the stricter she became.

She took ninety percent of the responsibility for their unhappy household. In the end, both children moved out. But even for someone prepared to manage teenagers, Jessica would have been a handful. Rosalba had filled her full of ideas that she was destined to become a celebrity. What she was to be celebrated for was never explained. Jessica's head was bursting with dreams about movie and TV stars. The children in many ways were as amoral as their father. The only goals they had were to make money and become famous. They were like a gift box that has a beautiful wrapping but nothing inside.

"You don't seem to think much of Juan Carlos," said Alma interrupting Renata.

"I know I shouldn't badmouth the dead, but truthfully I never liked him. He was all charm and good looks but devious. I blame him for my sister's death."

"You're convinced they're dead then?"

"It's been fifteen years. I always thought he was mixed up in some shady business because of those flights to South America, and because he seemed too good to be true. No family, indeed!" said Renata opening and closing the clasp of her purse.

"Were you happy when Jessica met Beto? He seems like a responsible person and certainly comes from a wealthy, prominent family."

Renata looked at Alma for a second or two and then said, "You live here in Ávila. Do you think that wealthy and prominent mean that the Garcías have any integrity? The father is a crook, a big crook. Perhaps Beto isn't an out and out crook like his father, but he seems happy to take the money which mysteriously rolls in. Does he have any backbone or what we old-fashioned people call principles? How would he react if the props of wealth and power were knocked out from under him? Yes, he seems to be a nice person, or so Jessica thought. But, no, I wasn't happy when Jessica met Beto although he wasn't any worse than her other boyfriends."

"Excuse me for changing the subject but why are you staying in this hotel?"

"Because, young lady, I have no money. Beto didn't offer to put me up anywhere either. Like many rich people, he seems to think that everyone can throw away hundreds of pesos on a night in a hotel. I continue to work as a secretary which pays badly and with computers I am very rapidly becoming obsolete. I hope I can continue to work for at least five more years but it may not be possible. Jessica told me at Christmas that she was selling her parents' house and gave me two months to move out. I inherited a little money from my father, but I counted on having that house to be able to retire with some comfort. I see now a bleak old age."

"Still you're concerned about your niece, and you came all this way to see your grandniece."

"I believe, *Señorita* Jaramillo, in supporting one's family."

"One last question, do you have any thoughts on who would have a motive for the kidnapping if it's not organized crime?"

A bitter smiled crossed Aunt Renata's mouth. "I can think of more than few people including myself."

At a little before three, Alma pulled into the parking lot nearest the University cafeteria. The Autonomous University of Tepetlán had been founded in the 1950's. Insufficiently maintained, it sadly showed sixty-five years of wear and tear. The still vibrant mosaic murals on the main administration building illustrated scenes from the Mexican Revolution, but the poured concrete structure had turned an ugly, blotchy gray. As she walked towards the cafeteria, she played her favorite game: imagining what a future acquaintance might look like.

Licenciado Gabriel Ruiz, hum, he would be slightly shorter than her, around 50, bald on top but with a comb-over of brownish-gray hair. He'd have a little pot belly too and be wearing rimless eyeglasses and a suit, yes, a rumbled black suit. His striped tie might show a few hard-to-remove stains from yesterday's soup. She was so amused by her profile of Gabriel Ruiz that when she neared the entrance to the cafeteria, she discarded immediately, the tall, handsome man about her age standing at the door.

"Alma?" said the man greeting her with a kiss on the cheek.

"Gabriel, how lovely to meet you," said Alma blushing. She noticed his light brown eyes, neatly trimmed hair and square shoulders. Oh my, she thought.

"Have you had lunch?" asked Gabriel ushering into to the buzzing food hall.

"No, we had a big breakfast for the Three King's Day, but if you have something, perhaps I'll have a salad."

"Let me get a tray, and I'll be right back." She had to admit to herself that *Licenciado* Ruiz's jeans and sport's shirt were a great improvement on the crumpled black suit which she had pictured. He moved his six-foot slim body easily through the crowd of students.

Alma sat down at a Formica table and looked around her. The cafeteria was filled with all sizes and shapes of young people: short, tall, thin, chubby with every color skin imaginable from paper white to coal black and every tone of brown in-between. She had also forgotten how much college kids ate. Their plates were piled high with *enchiladas*, rice, black beans, salad and slices of bread. It could be too that this was the one good meal they'd have all day. The universal dress was jeans on the bottom but on top was everything from hand-embroidered blouses from Chiapas to tee shirts with a picture of some soon-to-be-famous Mexican rapper.

When Gabriel returned with her simple salad and his sandwich, he said, "Your salad looks like part of a starvation diet. Are you sure you don't want to share my sandwich?"

"No, it's fine."

"So why did Ricardo Nuñez send you to talk to me?" he said before taking a bite of his lunch.

"He didn't send me; I asked him for your information. I'm working on a story and your name has come up several times."

"*Aye*, let me guess? It wouldn't be about the *amparo* we filed over the state government's land seizures which now mysteriously aren't going to be used for public projects but for a new industrial park in which the governor's son stands to make a fortune?"

Alma stared at Gabriel whom she had known for all of five minutes. Although it was pure intuition and if Beto found out she would lose her precious story, she decided to trust this new acquaintance anyway. "Yes, the land deal might be part of the story, but it isn't the main part." She gave him her most serious look and said, "I'm going to ask you to promise not repeat this to anyone, anyone at all."

"Look, lawyers are used to keeping secrets."

"Jessica María, Beto García's wife, has been kidnapped, and he has hired me to investigate, along with the police, of course."

Gabriel crumpled his paper napkin and threw it on the table. "The same old story, I can see the headlines now. 'Homegrown Terrorists Strike at the Heart of Prominent Businessman's Family.' Give me a break."

"Hey, I'm not saying that the Salvador Navarro Front is behind this or that you are personally. I'm a journalist, and I want to have your point of view."

Still annoyed, Gabriel began, "How old are you? Haven't you seen---" but he was interrupted by the bouncy ring of Alma's phone. Her first instinct was to silence the phone and let whoever it was go to voicemail, but then she saw it was from her mother who never called her.

"Excuse me." Feeling embarrassed, she walked a few paces from the table.

"Hello," she managed to say before a torrent of words came tumbling out of the phone.

"Kurt's been kidnapped, I think, but I'm not sure. It all happened so fast." Her mother was crying now, uttering her words in short gasps. "I had one of those calls. You know the extortion calls and the man said they had Kurt, and I needed to deposit ten thousand pesos or they would kill him."

"Ma, we've talked about these calls. They're coming from the state prison, and everyone is receiving them. These criminals have a recording of a child crying. They hope that when a family member answers and hears the cries, he or she will shout out a name. Once the extortionists have that, they use it to blackmail the family. Is that how it happened?"

"I don't know. I was so surprised that I can't remember if I mentioned Kurt's name or not but I can't find him. I ran to the football field; he's not there. The other children said they hadn't seen him. He left the house forty-five minutes ago."

"And his cell phone, did you call his cell phone?"

"Of course, I did, but he doesn't answer."

"Where's Pa?"

"He went to look for some tools or something and isn't answering his phone either."

"Okay, I'll be right there. If you get another call, tell them we are trying to raise the money and to call back in an hour."

Alma turned back to Gabriel. "I'm so sorry. There's a problem with my son. Can I call you again tomorrow?"

"Look, I overheard your conversation. It's one of those extortion calls, isn't it?"

"Yes, I don't think it's legitimate but my mother is hysterical, and my son is not where he should be."

"Let's get going. Where's your car?"

"But you have students to see."

"My students, I can see another time. Driving while upset is a bad idea. Come on, we're wasting time."

Chapter 11

WEDNESDAY, JANUARY 6TH, AFTERNOON

As they pulled out of the university parking lot, Gabriel turned to Alma, "So where to?"

Still, in a daze, she said, "We live in the eastern part of the city, Colonia Alfonso García Robles. Do you know it?

"Sure, I've got some clients over there. Look I hope this doesn't sound silly but as a kid when I would get upset my father, to take my mind off my troubles, would tell me stories about his childhood. So instead of us sitting here silently worrying about your son, Kurt, isn't it, I'm going to tell you about my childhood, and then you're going to tell me about yours," said Gabriel.

Alma as she fidgeted with her bag thought of Aunt Renata clasping and unclasping her purse. "Okay, go ahead," she said aloud. But she didn't want to hear about his childhood or be distracted in any other way either. She was sick with worry, and Kurt was the only thing she could think about.

As he began his story, she realized that this wasn't the first time he used the technique on a frightened female. Pretty smooth, she thought. Born in Ávila to a single mother, Gabriel was an only child until he was six when he discovered he had three half-sisters. "We weren't always as great friends as we are now," he said glancing at Alma to see if she was listening. His mother was an anthropologist who used to teach at the U. but now lived in San Cristobal de las Casas where she worked among the different indigenous people. His parents had never married. His mother had been forty when he was born, and his arrival had put her free and easy lifestyle on hold, at least temporarily.

His father? He wasn't sure he ever had completely figured out his father. He had died two years ago. He'd been a well-known lawyer in Ávila. When his parents had met at the University, his father was married with three kids and a great wife. In fact, Gabriel found Maria Elena a lot easier to be around than his own mother. His father had loved both his wife and Gabriel's mother and couldn't bear to part with either one. He was lucky that they'd put up with his nonsense.

As he weaved in and out of the traffic, Gabriel turned to Alma and smiled. "So, can you top that for a confusing childhood?"

"I don't think I can top it, but maybe I can match it," said Alma with little enthusiasm still thinking about Kurt's whereabouts. The story she related was the bare bones version of her childhood, just the necessary facts. What it had felt like to be illegal and on that emotional rollercoaster for so many years, she kept to herself.

"No, you win," said Gabriel, "your story is international, and that always beats a local one. So, you went to UCLA on a full scholarship, impressive. My dad footed the bill for my master's degree at the University of Texas."

Suddenly it all seemed meaningless to Alma, she turned to Gabriel her features contorted with worry. "Why do we live this way? Why does fear have to be buzzing around constantly in our heads? I know all about the crime in Chicago, in Paris, in Rome. But it's different here. People vanish and no one does anything about it. If my son suddenly disappears, who cares? Who can I turn to? He'll become a number, a vague memory in the minds of a baffled public and an ache in our hearts forever."

Gabriel pulled the car over to the side of the road. He grabbed Alma by the shoulders. "You're right. I'm sorry. You didn't need a meaningless conversation right now. But you must pull yourself together; you have to be able to function for your son. Take ten deep breaths."

They sat for three or four minutes in silence, then Gabriel said, "We're a few blocks from your neighborhood. Do you want me to go directly to your house?"

Alma took one last deep breath and punched in their home phone. "Ma, is there any news from Kurt?" she said as her mother instantly picked up the call.

"No, he hasn't called, and the neighbors haven't seen him either. Your father is on his way home. Alma, I'm really frightened."

"I know, Ma. We're going to drive around the neighborhood to see if we can spot him. I'll call you in fifteen or twenty minutes."

"Who's we?"

"I'm with a friend. I'll be back in touch as soon as I know something."

"Let's try a shortcut that I know Kurt sometimes takes to the football field," she said to Gabriel pointing to a half-hidden turn to their right.

They were silent, each looking intently out of the car windows as they drove on the dirt road. Suddenly she shouted. "There he is," pointing to a small figure in the distance sitting by the side of the road.

As Alma dashed out of the car, Kurt jumped up and ran to her. "Mom," was all he managed to say hugging her for dear life. She immediately noticed that he was shoeless and his face stained with tears. She also noticed that the tires of his bicycle were flat. Before releasing him, she dialed her mother's number. "He's safe. We just found him. We'll be home in a little while."

Gabriel, sensing that this was a conversation best left to mother and son, stayed by the side of the car. "So, what happened?" she asked sitting down on the grassy bank drawing her son close to her.

"There were three of them, Mom. They were big kids, teenagers. I think they followed me off the main road, but I didn't notice the car until one of them shouted out of the car window, 'Look at those shoes! My little brother would love them. The rich kid's mommy will get him another pair. Won't she, *Güerito?*' Then they jumped out of the car and surrounded me.

"I said 'we're not rich, we're just like you' but they laughed and pushed me off my bike. One kid pulled off my shoes; another one started looking through my pockets. When he found my phone, he shouted 'bonus!'. The third guy took out a knife and slit my tires. 'So, you don't run home to mommy.' Then they backed up their car and drove off back down there." Kurt pointed to where the dirt road ran into the main street.

"Why didn't you come home right away?"

"'Because you told me not to wear the shoes and I felt bad, Mom. I'm sorry." The tears began to flow again.

"Okay, what's important is that you're safe; Grandma, Grandpa, and I were so worried." She decided not to mention the bogus kidnapping call. When he got older, they might learn to laugh over the whole improbable story.

"Hey, come meet my new friend, Gabriel," Alma said leading him back to the car.

"Hi Kurt," said Gabriel "let's see how we can get your bike into the trunk of the car."

When they arrived at the house, Kurt got a hug from his grand-mother and a "we need to talk" look from his grandfather. After Gabriel had been introduced, Sofía said, "We could use some cheering up. Go upstairs, wash your face and put on clean clothes, Kurt. We're going to cut the *Rosca de los Reyes* right now. Who needs to wait? I hope you can join us, Gabriel?"

"Gabriel needs to get back to the University," said Alma.

"No rush," he said, " I never pass up a *Rosca* because I might not get another offer." I bet you get plenty of offers and not only to share *Roscas* commented Alma to herself.

When Kurt appeared in clean clothes, his face scrubbed clean of tears, and in his old sneakers, each person around the table cut a large piece of the oval-shaped cake decorated with pieces of red and green dried fruit. Gabriel hit one of the tiny plastic baby Jesus figures immediately and swore he would reappear with *tamales* on February second. When her father's fork hit another doll, her mother lifted an eyebrow as if to say, can we count on two men to provide *tamales*?

While Alma, her mother, and Kurt drank a cup of *atole* with their *Rosca*, Gabriel accepted the offer of a beer from her father. This is just so nice, thought Alma as Gabriel listened attentively to her mother's plans to expand the store and her father's latest carpentry projects. The only person who was unnaturally silent was Kurt. No matter what fancy shoes he gets in the future, thought Alma, he'll never forget those sneakers.

Finally, her mother piped up with the question she had been dying to ask ever since he had walked in the door. "So how did you meet Alma, Gabriel?"

"Alma and I have a friend in common, her editor, Ricardo Nuñez. He asked me to help Alma look up some information in the University library."

Thank you said Alma to herself breathing a sigh of relief. "Yes," she said aloud, "It was very kind of Gabriel to drive me home. He was right. I was too upset to drive back alone and by the way did you get a call back from the extortionist?"

"I took the call and told him where he could go, but the guy hung up before I got out half of what I wanted to say," said Jesús.

"Gabriel's a lawyer so let me ask him the question that everyone asks me all the time. Why can't the authorities stop these calls?" said Alma.

"They have tried. They do try all the time, but it's the system. The phones get smuggled in by family members or corrupt guards or in a million other ways. Some prisons have tried cutting off the cell phone signal entirely. But, Mr. Jaramillo,"

"No please call me, Jesús."

"Jesús, I strongly suggest you change your number as soon as possible. They know Kurt's name now, and they'll try again."

On the way back to the University, Alma concentrated on her driving while Gabriel and Kurt chatted about the British Academy, their losing-prone soccer team, and what books Kurt would recommend for Gabriel's five-year-old niece; a conversation which seemed to help Kurt win back some of his self-respect.

When he was getting out of the car, Gabriel said, "We have to finish that conversation. I'm busy most of the day tomorrow. How about dinner? Give me a call when you can this evening, so I have your cell."

After Kurt had settled himself in the front seat, Alma asked if he felt up to braving the street market or would he prefer the bookstore? Sensing few bargaining chips, he answered "bookstore" and was rewarded with a big smile. When they were nearing their destination, Kurt asked, "Mom, shouldn't we go to the police to report those boys?"

"You know the police are so busy; I'm not sure they'd pay much attention to us."

"I'm never going to see my shoes again, am I?" She certainly wasn't going to give him a Pollyannaish answer that some poor boy would now be the happy owner of his shoes. Stealing is wrong, and Kurt knew it. "You know, Mom, what made me feel worse?"

"What, sweetie?"

"I felt terrible when they took my shoes and my cell phone and slashed my tires, but it made me feel worse that I couldn't defend myself. It made me feel like a baby, all helpless."

"I think you and I need to talk more about what's safe and not safe in the neighborhood. Maybe some karate would make you feel better, not that I want you to take on three big boys." But feeling helpless, they had to fix that. There were already too many citizens in Tepetlán who knew that feeling.

As Alma was about to get into bed at the unaccustomed hour of 10 o'clock, the phone rang. It was Beto. Not even a hello, just, "The meeting tomorrow has been moved up to eight A.M.," and he hung up. The second call at ten fifteen was from Catherine Borresen. Alma recognized her voice immediately.

"I'm so sorry to bother you, but I'm so worried," she said in a tired voice.

Anda, thought Alma has she changed her tune. But the call was not about Jessica, Beto or Valentina. "Lucía left this morning before I woke up and I haven't heard from her."

"Has this happened before?" Alma asked.

"Yes, but Beto has always known where she was and brought her back. Tonight, he practically hung up on me. I wondered if you could help find her?"

"Look, I have my hands full looking for Jessica. But I'm going to see Beto in the morning. Maybe he'll give me an idea where to look. I'll call you as soon as I know anything."

Chapter 12

THURSDAY, JANUARY 7TH, MORNING

B eto was a wreck. His clothes looked as if he had slept in them three days running. His hair without its weekly trim looked wild, his eyes had large bruise-like circles under them, and the skin on his jowls sagged as if he had lost ten pounds in the space of a few days. The room now looked very lived in. The smell of cigarette butts and dead flowers permeated the air. A box containing a half-eaten pizza sat open on the coffee table. In one of the arm chairs were seated a teddy bear and a naked plastic doll.

Not in a mood to tolerate fools, Beto glared at the two cops when they said that they were sure that the ransom calls were coming from Mexico City since all the phones had either been lost or stolen in the Federal District. "That's brilliant," said Beto, "We've narrowed it down to twenty-two million people instead of one hundred and ten million. Bravo!"

The Federal Police captain was back, very quiet, his tail between his legs. Apparently the big drug bust had been put on the back burner. Beto turned to him. "What have you found out about Leandro Sousa? Is anything from immigration or the local police in Mexico City?

"We checked with immigration. Sousa entered the country on a flight from Miami on December third. He listed a Mexico City address, the Hotel Colonial located near the Zocalo, but he checked out a few days later, and we lost track of him. It would help if we had a photograph."

Alma took out the photograph of the séance from her bag. "This was in the trash box of Jessica's computer," said Beto shaking his head in disbelief. "Have you checked the computer? You've had it for a couple of days now."

"Who are the other people?" asked local police chief, Pedro Ramirez.

"The woman on the far left with the purple hair is Luz María Fuentes. She lives here in Ávila. I'm getting her address today and would like to see her before you guys swoop down on her. The other woman is the Governor's wife, Cécile Reynaud, who you must recognize. The tall black man is Leandro, and the man on the far right is supposed to be some relative of Luz María's. We have also speculated," she said looking at Steven and Beto, "that it could be Luis Miguel Cruz who was stalking Jessica a few years back."

"Where was the photo taken?" asked the captain from the Feds.

"At a séance held in an apartment that Luz María rents downtown."

"I have another question for you two," said Beto glaring at the policemen. "Have you found out anything about this Luis Miguel Cruz?"

Alma passed around the email with the poem. "I suppose you never saw that either," said Beto.

Alma retrieved both the photo and the poem from the policemen as Beto beckoned her into the front hall.

"You're not needed here. Steven is doing his thing which is tortuous but let's see what today brings. I want you to go into Mexico City and pick up Jaime Santos, Jessica's old bodyguard-chauffeur. Show him the picture and then check out what happened when the police took Luis Miguel to the police station four years ago. I'm going to send you in one of my cars with Gerardo, Jessica's bodyguard."

"Beto, I got a call from your mother last night."

"I know. I was fed up when she called. She has never expressed one single word of concern about Jessica, and she professes to be such a devout Christian. It's always Lucía, Lucía, Lucía."

"Do you have any idea where Lucia might be? I gather she goes into Mexico City often."

"She's with Sami."

"Sami? I thought he was gay."

"No, it's not a romantic thing. She trusts Sami. They're good friends. My mother doesn't know because Lucía wants to keep that part of her life to herself."

As Alma sat in the backseat of a Mercedes being whisked into Mexico City, she thought how easy it would be to get used to the

Gracia's lifestyle. The leather seats smelled delicious; the ride was so smooth she barely felt the road. Lulled by the luxury of the ride, she let her thoughts drift to Gabriel. No doubt in her mind, she had been attracted to him.

What were the mysterious elements that made sparks fly between two people and then, for the lucky ones, kept them together? Take her parents: they had had a dream of making a new life in L.A., dreams for Alma too that had bound them together through the hard times. They were their biggest supporters and gentlest but most honest critics. Kenny and Helen? They had music in common. Also, Helen had been clear about what she wanted from Kenny. Alma had never been. But she would never do that again, wait around until a guy made up his mind. Beto and Jessica, the relationship that no one except themselves had wanted. They couldn't be more different, but they shared the experience of scarred adolescent years. They knew that the simplest comfort, that of peace of mind, could be snatched away at a moment's notice. What they sought in the rela- tionship was a feeling of security. If that were to disappear, Alma wondered what would happen to the marriage?

Suddenly her mood lightened. "Gerardo," she said turning her attention to the driver, "isn't it the most magnificent day? Don't we have some of the most incredible weather in the world? It's January, okay, it's a little cold in the morning and the evenings can be chilly, but there's sunshine every day. Doesn't that make the world so much more cheerful?"

"You're in pretty good spirits this morning, *Señorita* Alma. I don't know if we're lucky with the weather since I've never lived anywhere else. Still, don't forget that it gets hot here in April and May and then for five months it rains," said Gerardo playing the role of the weather devil's advocate.

"Yes, it's hot but usually only for a couple of weeks, then the rains come, and it's lovely. It rains mainly in the afternoon, and the sun shines the rest of the day. Everything turns green and lush. That's my favorite time of the year. Hey, aren't we almost to the airport? How are we going to find Jaime?"

"I'd recognize him anywhere, and I have his cell phone number. I'll tell him to meet us outside the terminal."

When Jaime jumped into the front seat of the car, he reached into the backseat and shook Alma's hand. Then he grabbed Gerardo around the neck with one large arm and gave him a friendly shake. "Good to see you, *buey*, even if your family's *babosadas* lost me my job." Laughing, he pulled the seat belt over his ample stomach.

His grin is irresistible and menacing at the same time, mused Alma. Those damaged front teeth encased in small silver frames make him look like a James Bond villain. "So, what's up? Beto was all hush, hush," said Jaime. "I understand that that *mierda* Luis Cruz might have surfaced again."

"Maybe," said Alma pulling the photograph of the séance out of her bag and passing it to Jaime. "Is this our friend Luismi?" As they headed out of the airport, Jaime studied the four people in the print. "I mean," said Alma "the guy on the far right."

" No, it's not our friend Luismi unless he's had a facelift and sandblasted his skin. Although whoever this guy is, he's sure trying to cover up his face."

"Maybe, it would be worthwhile tracking down Luis anyway," said Alma. "He's sent at least one crazy email to Jessica recently. Where did the police take him four years ago?"

"To the *delegación* near the Cuauhtémoc metro station."

"Was he booked or some charge brought against him?"

"I doubt it," said Jaime. "Beto gave me a wad of *pesos* and told me to hand them over to the sergeant in charge. The police were supposed to give Luismi the treatment, leave him *bien jodido* which I guess they did because he disappeared for a long time."

"Do you remember the sergeant's name?"

"Yeah, I do because I'd never heard it before. Froylan, Froylan Pérez but I doubt he's still there. Those cops either quit or are fired every few years."

When they walked into the police station, Jaime laughed and pointed to an officer talking to two women who looked very angry. "We're in luck," he said. Froylan didn't look very pleased either. He kept rubbing his stomach as if constant massage could cure chronic indigestion. There's a guy who lives on Tums, thought Alma.

When the two women had finished berating the policeman, Jaime sauntered over and slapped him on the back. Froylan smiled and shook hands with Beto's three representatives. In answer to Alma's question, he shook his head saying that they had never booked Luis Miguel Cruz but that they certainly did work him over. He smiled with the memory of a job well done.

"The only way we might trace him is through his license plate. I do have a friend in the Mexico City's Ministry of

Finance who could check his car registration." A smile spread across Jaime's face as he drew a piece of paper out of his pocket. "I remembered that I'd kept Cruz's license plate number, so I brought it along."

The policeman disappeared into a small office at the back of the building as Alma took in her surroundings. Folding chairs lined the bare walls on either side of the large hall. There sat some of the sorriest souls Alma had ever seen. Mostly poorly dressed older men and women who were no doubt at the precinct to report a robbery, find a lost relative or try to get someone out of jail. A weary secretary was writing down the details of each case.

"We got lucky," said the sergeant. "At least this is the address he gave on his registration form. It's in the Colonia Escondón."

"Shouldn't we have given him something for his trouble?" Alma whispered to Jaime as they left.

"The first time around he got more than a month's salary. I'd say we still have credit in his personal bank. We'd better leave the Mercedes in a parking lot where it won't attract attention. I don't think we want Luismi's neighbors taking an interest in us."

When the taxi stopped in front of Luis Miguel's building, Alma checked the buzzers, and there was the name: L.M. Cruz.

"How do we get in?" asked Jaime.

Alma thought for a minute. "How about the old trick of a delivery from Fed Ex. No one can ever resist that. You say that he has an invitation to a special event at *El Palacio de Hierro*. He's the type of guy who would have a credit card for the fanciest department store in town even though he never bought a thing there."

When Luis Miguel buzzed them in, Alma and Gerardo waited in the stairwell until Jaime got his foot and considerable bulk in the door. As the three of them let themselves into Cruz's apartment, they heard a loud protest.

"¡*Por Dios*! Who are you?" demanded Luis. "Is this a robbery? Here take all the cash I've got on me." He said as he pulled a wallet from his pocket.

"Please sit down, Mr. Cruz," said Alma. "We're not here to rob you. In fact, you must remember Jaime Santos who you met about four years ago when you had that little problem with Jessica María." He's certainly not Mr. Shades she reckoned staring at Luis Miguel's sallow acne-scarred face and puffy body.

Cruz plunked down on the old sofa. Jaime eased himself in next to him; Alma and Gerardo moved two wooden chairs in front of the pair. The apartment was sparsely furnished. A 40" flat screen TV occupied the only table in the room, and a newish computer sat on the desk. To one side of the computer was a photograph of Jessica María cut from a magazine and mounted in a cheap aluminum frame. The walls of the apartment were dingy green. Old flowered bed sheets covered the windows. There was a rancid smell in the air as if the drains were blocked or the kitchen garbage hadn't been emptied. I bet the neighbors would love to see the back of this guy, thought Alma.

"Mr. Cruz, you had an agreement with the police to stay away from Jessica María," she said in the most conversational tone she could manage. Cruz shrugged his shoulders. "Did you send this poem to her?" Taking the email out of her bag, she read the first few lines.

"I do not love you except because I love you;
I go from loving to not loving you,
From waiting to not waiting for you
My heart moves from cold to fire.

"That's from a guy who calls himself Luismi and uses the address, amoreterno38@hotmail.com. I find it hard to believe that there could be two of you."

Luis Miguel was silent until Jaime moved a little closer to him on the sofa. "I may have sent that poem, but I never meant any harm. She didn't have to open the email, did she?" said Cruz. "I never went near her. That was the deal. I promise I won't send anything else." He started to rise from the sofa to see his guests out as any polite host would do.

"Sit down, Mr. Cruz. You're lying. If you lie to us, we will notify the police, and they won't be nearly as considerate as we are."

Jaime moved again so that his hip was touching Luis Miguel's. "I might have wanted to see where she was living. You know I wanted to make sure she was okay. I saw the story they did on her house in *Hola*, but I wanted to be able to picture her neighborhood. That's all. I never went near her."

"You're lying again, Luismi." Licking his lips like that, reflexed Alma, is a dead giveaway. "You were there last Saturday, weren't you?"

"No." This time Jaime put his hand on Cruz's knee and pressed until the man winced. "Yes, okay, I was there."

"The whole story, right now, no lies, no omissions and then we'll decide what we do with you," said Alma, her eyes unblinking as she stared at him.

"When I went to Ávila, and I only went a few times, I liked to wait for the big Mercedes to pull out. I loved seeing Jessica in the back seat, like royalty, like the princess she is. So, last Saturday I wasn't paying too much attention when a Honda Accord pulled up to the guard post. Then, I noticed Jessica in the front seat and it surprised me. I thought maybe the Mercedes was in the shop or something. I didn't mean to follow them, but something made me pull out behind them.

"When they'd gone about three blocks, the Honda pulled over to the curb, and two people stepped out of the shadow of a wall and got into the back seat. The front door on Jessica's side opened, and she started to jump out, but she was pulled back into the car. Then the car took off with the four of them. I followed for perhaps a mile, but I lost them in traffic."

Alma took the photograph of the séance out of her purse. Pointing to the young man on the right, she asked Luis, "Was this man the driver?"

"I'm sorry. I'm not lying. The sun was hitting that side of the windshield. I never saw the person clearly, but he or she was wearing sunglasses."

"The two people who got into the car?"

"They were wearing hoodies and had scarves over their mouths and noses, but one looked like it could be a woman, not a young one either. The other person was probably a guy. I saw on Twitter that Jessica is on a spiritual retreat. So, was what I saw a rehearsal for the new soap opera?"

"You got it, Luis. It's one of the first scenes in the script. She wanted to practice it before she left on the retreat."

"Now we need to talk about you, Luismi," said Jaime getting up from the sofa. "The minute you send another email or go anywhere near Ávila, we will contact the authorities. The police were kind the last time. This time you'll go straight to prison, and you know what happens to guys like you in prison."

When Luis Miguel remained silent, Jaime grabbed him by the collar of his shirt. "Answer me you little shit," he said pushing the man backwards.

"That's enough, Jaime," said Alma pushing the bodyguard towards the door.

Standing on the threshold of the flat, Alma turned to Luis Cruz. "Why did you pick that poem to send to Jessica?"

He looked at her with such hate in his eyes that she took a step back. "I love poetry. Pablo Neruda is my favorite poet. You people think you know me. You haven't got a clue."

Chapter 13

THURSDAY, JANUARY 7TH, AFTERNOON

"Beto is going to be grateful," said Alma as Jaime climbed into a taxi for the airport.

"Anytime," he said laughing, "as long as it isn't the sixth of January. You guys should pay me a visit in Puerto Escondido; the beaches are fantastic. Good luck with finding Jessica."

Alma felt that he really wanted to say. "If I'd been on the job, this would never have happened and if you'd let me slug that *mierda*, he might have learned his lesson."

Alma climbed back into the Mercedes and dialed Beto's cell. It went immediately to voice mail, so she left a message to call her as soon as possible. She called Sami next.

"Hey, is Lucía with you?"

"Yes, she just got up, and I'm fixing her a late breakfast. I suppose you're on a rescue mission."

"What do you think?"

"I think it's time she went home. Let me talk to her."

On the drive, over to Colonia Roma, Alma's cell phone rang. "*Señorita* Jaramillo?" said a soft voice. "It's William, William Craven."

"Oh, William, did you find the address?"

"Yes," he said sounding proud of himself. "It's in the north of the city, Colonia Independencia, where the park is, the park with the statue of Miguel Hidalgo and all the canons. I think she might live in one of those townhouses which they built about fifteen years ago when they remodeled the old brickworks. Could you get her on the phone?"

"No answer but the address will be very useful."

"I hope you get your money back," said William and then chuckled, "but I seriously doubt it."

Alma glanced at her phone, three o'clock. She had forgotten her mother and lunch again. "Sorry, Ma, see u tonight." She pegged a sad-faced emoji at the end.

When Sami opened the door of his apartment, she could see Lucía sitting at the Knoll table picking at some scrambled eggs. She could also see the face she made when she saw Alma. "It's time, Lucy," said Sami. "I'll call you tonight. Be good."

Lucía slammed the back door of the Mercedes and sat with her arms crossed over her chest. Beto's sister was certainly beautiful: naturally blond wavy hair, the face of a porcelain doll, long legs, and great curves but with the disposition of a petty dictator, thought Alma. How in the world would she find any common ground with this woman?

"So, have you and Sami been friends for long?" asked Alma in English.

"Why do you care? Do you think I can't speak Spanish?" asked Lucia in a tone which could not have been ruder.

"No, I think I would like to have a confidential adult conversation with you about a serious matter: the kidnapping of your sister-in-law. Believe it or not, I would like to have your opinion," said Alma gesturing with her head towards the front of the car.

"No one ever wants my opinion. I'm the crazy sister. So, what do you say to that?"

"I'd say you were looking for an audience for another production of *Lucia, La Loca,* like the one I witnessed at your house the other day. Unfortunately for you, I don't find your performances amusing or even believable," said Alma bracing herself for the fury that would follow.

Instead, there was silence. Not daring to look at her fellow passenger, Alma waited. When she did turn her head, Lucia was holding a hand over her mouth trying to contain what looked like a grin. Then the smile became a loud laugh. "Where did Beto find you?"

"I'm a journalist in my everyday life."

"Your English is perfect. Beto and I have always had a slight accent in our English that makes people in the States look at us and think that maybe we're Swedish. No one ever believes we're Mexican."

"I grew up in the U.S."

"And you came back here by choice?"

"No," said Alma, "five years ago I had to repatriate."

"Oh, so my problems must seem petty to you."

"No, I think we might share some of the same problems."

Smiling Alma made a gesture as if she was wiping a slate clean and said again, "So how did you and Sami become friends?"

Lucía leaned back on the leather seat. Phew, thought Alma, she's going to cooperate.

"We met at Beto and Jessica's horrible wedding, one thousand six hundred people in a sea of tables. The only people I knew were my mother and father, who I didn't want to hang out with, and Beto. Beto wasn't going to be hanging out with me; so he promptly handed me off to Sami. We liked each other immediately, abandoned our stuffy table, took two bottles of Champagne and headed over to a bench in the garden. We spent the whole evening talking about our terrible relatives. His stories almost made me like Jessica, almost but not quite."

"So, what is your story, Lucía? I know something about your family but nothing really about you."

"If this is the definitive history of the Humberto García de León family, I guess I should put in my two cents. Did my mother give you her version of her angel-devil children: Beto the perfect and Lucía," she sighed audibly "the PROBLEM? I hated that story, but I never hated Beto. He was the only person that made my childhood half palatable.

"He was all my mother said he was. Always at ease with everything and everyone. He used to come into my room when there was a particularly gruesome fight going on between my parents, fall on my bed and laugh while I would be crying my eyes out. 'Aye Lucy,' he would say 'they're idiots, try to find it funny.'

"When he went away to university in the States, I felt abandoned. By then my father was a distant memory. He was traveling most of the time. I was stuck with my mother. Her perpetual evangelizing and anxiety over my father's affairs drove me crazy. I learned that a little pot took the edge off things. It's like this, Alma, and I've thought about it a lot. I don't seem to belong anywhere. I'm Mexican, but I don't look Mexican. People constantly speak to me here in broken English. When I went to the U.S., they saw my name was García and wanted to treat me as a Latina, but since I didn't look or act like they thought Latinas should look and act, I never found a place there either."

"I know a little bit about that," said Alma ruefully. "When I came back here, I was the only Mexican journalist in the country who couldn't write in Spanish. I had to teach English for a year and go back to college to learn to write in what was my native language. But I'm curious about your parents. Didn't your father participate in your lives at all?"

"When we were little, I remember him taking us to the park and playing silly games with us but when we started school, we found it hard to gauge his moods. He would either be overly solicitous which usually meant showing us off to his political friends or get all heated up because we got a B in gym. Beto said to me when he was fifteen, 'I love my father, and I know he loves us, but I wish I could have just one real, normal conversation with him.'"

"That seems to have changed."

"Superficially, maybe," said Lucia. "They talk about money a lot. I don't think they talk about much else. My father adores Beto and would do anything for him, but Daddy has become from his head to his toes 'the Governor,' a caricature."

"But haven't things improved since your father settled down with Cécile?"

"Let me tell you a story. Two or three months after Cécile and my father married, he was inaugurated very ceremoniously as governor. That night, there was a ball. My father looked incredibly distinguished in tails with his gubernatorial sash across his broad chest. Cécile, oh my God, no one in Ávila had even seen an evening gown like that. It was an original Galliano from his latest Dior collection. The top of the dress was black as was the skirt but the front of the skirt cut away to show yellow silk tulip petals spreading out to the floor. Conservatively, it must have cost thirty thousand dollars. She had amazing shoes on too. Her evening bag, she told me, cost ten thousand dollars. They were a handsome couple. The rest of the guests must have felt shabby. But it had nothing to do with the way we live here. Ávila is a backwater. Cécile seemed to think she was at the Élysée Palace at the inauguration of the president of France.

"Your phrase 'settled down' implies something homey, like one of my mom's old sweaters. But there doesn't seem to be anything very homey about either of them. She lives as if she had been Marie Antoinette in a previous life. I must tell that to Martha; she would appreciate it. Their marriage seems to me like a display in a department store window, two mannequins posing in fantasy roles.

"So 'settled down' maybe is an exaggeration," continued Lucía. "You know what Sami told me a month or two ago? My father called him one morning and asked him if he managed a young model named Ana Carolina something or other, and Sami asked him why. He said he had met her at a TV award's party and that she was I quote a 'spectacular piece of ass' and could Sami fix him up with her? Ana Carolina is younger than Jessica! Sami told me that it was the first time anyone had asked him to pimp for them."

"What did Sami do?"

"He said 'he would check her out' and never took a call from the Governor again. Look, Alma my father is *un pendejo* plain and simple," said Lucia staring out the window at the traffic speeding by.

"Are you okay now? I don't want to pry, but your mother hinted that you'd had a tough time in Minnesota."

"Yes, I went off the deep end. I was like a little raft that was set afloat in a big sea. Beto was a distant buoy, but he had his friends, and I had never been good at creating my own life. So, I fell in with a party crowd, and it just seemed natural to try what they tried, waiting for the next big high. The Mexico City clinic they put me in after I totally wigged out, helped me a lot. For the first time, I saw a competent shrink and began to understand some things about myself. But I know I'm still at times a brat," said Lucía and an impish smile spread across her face.

"Before we get to your house, do you have any idea who could be behind Jessica's kidnapping? Can I show this photo?"

"Well, well, well," said Lucia "if it isn't my dear step-mother all cozy with Jessica. What are they up to? What an odd group."

"It's a séance. Didn't Beto tell you about Jessica's interest in Spiritism?"

"I guess, maybe a little, but I didn't take it very seriously. But what surprises me is to see Cécile there. It definitely isn't her type of scene."

"No, she was pretty impatient with the whole thing. So, what does she do in Ávila? It sounds like she gave up a good career to marry your father."

"I'm not sure how good a career it was. She wasn't wearing Dior until she married Daddy. She loves being a big deal with the old families here. She goes to all the charity affairs, cuts all the ribbons for new buildings and smiles at all the poor children. She buys a new designer outfit for every event."

"You don't sound as if you like her very much."

"She's okay. Better she's doing all that stuff than me."

"Do you think she knows that you father has other 'interests'?"

"Maybe, he's always had a lot of other 'interests' as you so delicately put it."

She handed the photograph back to Alma. "Apart from Cécile, no one else rings a bell?"

"The guy with the sunglasses looks kind of familiar, but it probably is that he's just a type I've run into at the gym or somewhere."

"Do you have any theories about who could have engineered the kidnapping and why?"

"It definitely could be political. My father has many enemies."

"Do you mean groups like the Salvador Navarro Front?" asked Alma.

"No, I mean members of his old political party, the PNR, and his new party, the PIYS. When he was in the state government of Tepetlán, he quickly realized that the PNR was skimming off a lot of the profits from the government businesses here. He saw that this state and the whole region was going to become a powerhouse of new industry: cars, aerospace, high-tech and he reasoned that the profits from land deals and other phony expenses should stay right here. It took them years to form the party. When a new president was elected in 2000, the traditional political system seemed to be unraveling. My father and his buddies saw their chance to gain recognition for a regional party which Humberto García would head and which they called the Party of Independence and Solidarity, PIYS. They've done well. They have about thirty representatives in the National Assembly and three senators from this region in the Senate. The PNR never forgave my father for being a traitor."

"But what do they gain by kidnapping Jessica?"

"They weaken my father financially and politically. This wouldn't be the PNR doing the kidnapping itself but some obscure faction that answers to someone who wants a hand in the local pie. We all know that it's my father's money that is going to have to bail Beto out of this. I have a second idea also" said Lucia warming to the topic, "Clyde Ramsey."

"What does Clyde have to gain and how could he have carried it out?"

"Clyde has one interest in life, and that's money. Fifty percent of the capital for the new industrial park is his, and it's all leveraged. He owes the bankers in New York and Houston millions, and he's frantic because of the delays due to the *amparo*."

"But Clyde is an American citizen. I don't see him organizing something so complicated as a kidnapping in a country and culture he doesn't know that well."

"Oh, but he does know both the country and the culture. He's also a Mexican citizen. He grew up in Mexico City, and for eight years he worked at the U.S. Embassy in Mexico City for the DEA. You've got to believe that he knows a lot of mafia guys who just might owe him a favor."

Alma sat back and looked at Lucía with new admiration. "Lucía, don't keep wasting that brain. You need to put it to better use." When they arrived at Catherine's house, Alma gave Lucía her card. "If you think of anything at all, call me."

She's smart enough, thought Alma as Lucía stepped out of the car to dream up a kidnapping plot, but is she stable enough to carry it through?

When Alma picked up her car at Beto's house, it seemed even crummier than she remembered. She had memorized every detail of the Mercedes A600 for Kurt. She could hear him say after she described the ride. "The first thing I'm going to do when I grow up is buy you a Mercedes, Mom." She would reply, "I wouldn't expect anything less."

Checking out her WhatsApp messages, she saw there was one from Gabriel. "Sushi Mex @ eight?"

She texted back. "The 1 on Calle 4?" Within two minutes she received back an emoji of a smiling face. Next, she tried Beto's number again and still only got voice mail. She punched in Steven's cell. "What's up, Alma?" he said coming on the line.

"I can't reach Beto; what's going on?"

"He's been tied up all afternoon with Clyde and his father looking at the financing for the ransom."

"What happened with the negotiations today?"

"I'm not telling you this. You heard it from Beto. We're down to fourteen million dollars. I think we're going to arrive at ten million dollars with five from us and five from the Garcías although Humberto is finding it hard to part with five million. Hey, how about the second drink I owe you. Are you free tonight?

"Sorry Steven, I'm working tonight. How about tomorrow night? If you speak to Beto, could you tell him I really need to talk to him?"

"Okay, but what kind of guy asks you to work in the evening?" said Steven.

Chapter 14

THURSDAY, JANUARY 7TH, EVENING

"I wonder what the Japanese think when they see a restaurant called Sushi Mex?" asked Alma as she sat down at the table in front of Gabriel. She had insisted that they pick a table as far away as possible from the other diners.

"Probably the same thing we thought when we saw nachos in the U.S. with all that gummy yellow cheese poured over the top of fried tortillas."

"Should we order just a drink first and then if you get mad at me again, we won't have to pay for a lot of uneaten food?"

"Well, for starters, I'm paying, and if you up and leave, I'll eat your food too because I'm starving. I didn't have any lunch."

"*¡Ah, Caray!* I didn't have lunch either. So, I'm not walking out. But if we run into trouble we can finish our sushi while checking our phones which many people do without even being mad at one another."

"How's Kurt today?" asked Gabriel.

"I saw him early this morning, and he seemed resigned to his perfectly good non-brand sneakers."

"When I was nine, I lost a watch which had been a gift from my grandfather. I never found a watch which I liked as much."

The waiter appeared and Alma ordered a Margarita and Gabriel a Dos Equis. "And bring us the two biggest plates of Sushi you have," said Gabriel and then, continued in a low voice. "So, someone thinks that the Salvador Navarro Front is mixed up in Jessica María's kidnapping?"

"Let me start from the beginning because you might be able to help me sort out the information I have in my head. This whole saga started last Saturday morning. Apart from my work on El Diario de Ávila, I teach English to pay for Kurt's school. Jessica María who needs no introduction is my newest pupil. Halfway through our last class, she got a call supposedly from a friend who needed her help. She left the house immediately and was picked up by someone named Javier Arias driving a Honda Accord. The car was found Monday morning abandoned. It had been stolen as have the cell phones used in the ransom negotiations. None of Jessica's friends, family or business acquaintances that I've interviewed so far have heard the name, Javier Arias.

"Beto didn't realize she was missing until midday on Sunday because they often have different schedules. I was called on Monday morning to Beto's house to give information to the authorities. Beto then hired me to investigate the kidnapping because it didn't look as if it was the work of organized crime, and he believed that people would be more inclined to talk to me than to the police.

"So far, I've interviewed different members of her family, his family, their servants and her best friend. I went through her computer and found an email from a stalker, a man who had been warned four years ago by the police in Mexico City to stay away from Jessica. I also found a photograph of a séance which Jessica had attended. She is very interested in Spiritism. The kidnappers started out asking for twenty million dollars but have come down to fourteen million. There is a professional negotiator from Lloyds who is doing the actual negotiating.

"Here are the different motives for the kidnapping that have been suggested to me. Beto and Jessica could have arranged the crime themselves. Both are hard up for money. Her brother Sami might be gay and subject to blackmail. He also has expensive tastes and may be broke. Jessica and her best friend have a money-losing business which Jessica might be closing down. Her Aunt Renata is being tossed out of the family home because Jessica needs money to finance her new soap opera, 'El viaje inmortal.' Jessica's father-in-law is our controversial governor, and the kidnapping might be a payback for leaving his old political party and forming a new one. Clyde Ramsey, Beto's partner, is being pressured to repay his loans and all his money is tied up in the land deal which your *amparo* has frozen.

"Beto's mother and sister can't stand Jessica. The García's servants appear to be loyal and have no criminal records but ---? And finally, there's the Salvador Navarro Front which might have gotten tired waiting around to have the land dispute settled in their favor and want their money now.

"Some things you should know. Jessica's parents disappeared from one day to the next when she was thirteen, and her interest in Spiritism seems to have sprung from that trauma. We found and interviewed the stalker, Luis Miguel Cruz, and he gave us some interesting information about the day of the kidnapping. I don't think he was involved.

"The fat woman with the purple hair is Luz María Fuentes," said Alma taking a breath and handing the photo to Gabriel. "I hope to track her down tomorrow. The other woman is the Governor's second wife who found the experience of the séance dispiriting, sorry about that. The large black man is a Brazilian medium named Leandro Sousa. We are on his trail but haven't found him yet. The youngish man with the sunglasses is who I want to identify. He may be the mysterious Javier Arias, as well as a relative of the fat woman. And please can I have another Margarita?"

"You certainly deserve one, and you've barely touched your sushi," said Gabriel calling the waiter over. "I assume that the police are in this up to their eyeballs."

"Yes and no. We had a little problem with the Feds, but they are back on board now. They don't seem to have discovered much so far, but they might not have told us everything either. Does anything I've told you make any sense?"

"It's very complicated, but I agree that the séance might hold the key. What did this Luis Miguel tell you about the day of the kidnapping?"

"The guy had started stalking Jessica again and saw her leaving *Chateau Ville* in the front seat of the Honda. He couldn't identify the driver, but he or she appeared to be wearing sunglasses like ninety percent of the population. A few blocks later the Honda picked up two other people, a man and a woman. Jessica tried to jump out of the car but was pulled back in and then Luismi, as we call him affectionately, lost the car in traffic."

"I think the political angle is also interesting," said Gabriel while signaling for another beer. "For corrupt politicians, Ávila has been like hitting the jackpot; it's been a rich vein to mine. All the new industry pouring in needs a large supply of land, water, and other services. But for legit businesses too the profits have exceeded expectations. The thing is that everyone is fed up with our corrupt Governor."

"You know what I'm learning from this investigation, and don't laugh, is that it's so hard to see into people's hearts. Everyone talks such a good story. Take Lucía, Beto's sister, whom I spoke with today. We hit it off after a rough start. She turned the spotlight on the Governor's political friends and enemies which was useful, but what's she hiding? What's she capable of? Everyone I've interviewed points the finger far away from themselves. Even if it's to be expected, it's frustrating. Also, there is so much violence and frustration just under the surface; so much hate and bitterness over money, over past wrongs.

"You've only been involved in this story for four days! Even God needed six days for his creation. Give yourself a break."

Alma had to laugh. "Yes, but God was his own boss. He didn't have Richard Nuñez breathing down his neck."

Putting the few remaining sushi on Alma's plate, Gabriel said, "Now it's my turn to confuse you more by defending the Salvador Navarro Front. Do you know about Salvador's disappearance and the destruction of El Rosario?"

"A confidential source told me the whole story not long ago. But who's involved in the movement today?"

"The movement has about two hundred and fifty people, about two dozen people from El Rosario participate. They were children when their village was destroyed. There are about fifty people involved from El Milagro, the community which has taken out the *amparo* against the García's land deal. The rest come from small communities who feel that their land might be menaced next. I want you to come meet the group tomorrow afternoon."

"What's the problem with El Milagro? Beto says that his consortium is now willing to negotiate a fair price."

"Come with me tomorrow and let the villagers tell you their side of the story. Hey, I think I'm neglecting my duties. Do you want another Margarita?"

"No, I have to drive home, better a Coke."

"Sure, but I think I've had enough of the García's for today. Tell me more about your work at the newspaper."

The conversation drifted from Alma's work to Gabriel's family. He had three half-sisters: Carolina, a psychologist living with her husband and two children in Mexico City; Rosalia, with whom Gabriel had lived while studying at the University of Texas, was a lawyer, married no children; finally, there was Esther. As a child, Esther had been his worst nightmare. When he had started at five to stay weeks at a time with his father's other family, she had put dead birds and scorpions in his bed. She had pinched him under the dinner table until his legs were black and blue. Still worse, she taught him a slew of *groserías* and told him to repeat them to his father. "When I go to her house for supper now I always carry a spider or two."

"Wait a minute. Is Esther a writing professor here at the U?"

"Yes, why?"

"Because I took two semesters of her course the first year I came back. She's great."

Laughing, they both said, "Small world!"

After a brief silence, Alma ventured the question she had wanted to ask all evening. "No one ever got you to the altar?"

"Yes, I was married for three years, but we divorced two years ago. You're sure you want to hear the long, sad story?"

Glancing at her watch, she said, "Got all the time in the world."

"Linda, my ex, is an American. We met in Austin the first month I was there for grad school. I went out to dinner with a friend, and while we were waiting for a table, we struck up a conversation with two pretty girls. Soon the four of us were exchanging phone numbers. Linda was finishing a B.A. in Art History, and wouldn't you know it, Frida Kahlo was her favorite artist."

"What was she like?"

"She has dark red hair and freckles. She was full of enthusiasm about her studies, films, books. She's a very alive person. Her parents are rich Texans; her father is a corporate lawyer. They're the kind of people who speak of George and Barbara and expect you to catch on that the last name is Bush. Linda had been on lots of vacations to the beach in Mexico. She'd studied but never visited the Colonial part of our country. She was in love with the idea of Mexico. You know the color, the music, the food, the art. She was crazy about horses and would say she could picture herself riding across the 'Pampas' in Tepetlán. I told over and over that the pampas were in Argentina, not in Mexico, but she's a real romantic. My sister Carolina said that 'I was Linda's post-adolescent rebellion.'"

"What did her parent's think about you?" said Alma remembering Kenny's mother's, "you people."

"They're educated people. Linda's father has many wealthy Mexican businessmen as clients. What he couldn't get a grip on was my interest in Human Rights law. 'How will you make a living?' He asked me more than once, but then my father was always asking me the same thing. Instead of a big wedding, Linda asked her parents to put a down payment on a house in Ávila where she could board her horses. Did I mention she had three horses?

"What did you think of that plan?"

"I had grown up with a father whose maxim was 'let the women have their way because you'll suffer until they do.' I was twenty-five and totally crazy about her. Linda came down with her mother, and they chose a house in one of the golf clubs. Frankly, I had no idea how I was going to make the mortgage payments."

Taking a last long sip of beer, Gabriel suddenly looked tired. "We moved into our country club house, and Linda rode every day. I opened my small office and started teaching at the U. Linda was happy for about six months. She didn't speak the language.

I mean she was studying Spanish but felt frustrated that she couldn't work or communicate with people. She joined a thing called The Newcomers Club which she liked. In fact, she met Jessica there which I'll tell you about in a minute. Her friends at the Club were mostly wives of the corporate executives in our new industries here. When they invited us to dinner, they soon learned that I was one of the local troublemakers, and we were almost never invited back. Linda wanted to get pregnant, and that didn't happen either.

"She began to spend more and more time alone, and gradually the lively girl I had married, became a sad and depressed woman. I suggested a trip to see her parents. After a visit lasting for months and a return to Mexico postponed three or four times, the truth came out. She flatly refused to come back. When I went up to see her, she said 'I can't do it. It's too hard. It's nothing like what I expected.' She kept saying that if I loved her I would move back to Austin and do my human right's thing there. She would repeat over and over, 'You love your work more than you love me.' I kept explaining that it wasn't that I loved my work more. It was that my work was part of who I am, but she couldn't understand that. We were divorced quietly a year later. For months, I would wake up wondering why she wasn't curled up next to me."

"Do you still hear from her?"

"She sent me an invitation to her wedding last September. She married a lawyer in her father's firm whose name is López. That made me laugh."

"What happened to the horses and the house?"

"The house went to the bank, and one day a truck from Texas and took the horses away. It was as if Linda had never been here but wait, let me tell you about Jessica. One day when I arrived back from the office, Linda was very excited because her club was having a tea at the Governor's Mansion, and Cécile said that Jessica was going to be the guest of honor."

I bet Jessica hated that, thought Alma.

"All the woman assembled in their best dresses and stood around too afraid to speak to Jessica, but Linda who was still in her enthusiastic mood started talking to her about Houston, her hometown. Jessica asked her for the names of the best trendy boutiques which was totally up Linda's alley. She said that Jessica was even more beautiful close up than in photos. 'Ethereal' was the word she used. Finally, she asked Jessica how she kept her figure so perfect, and Jessica answered: 'diet, exercise, liposuction and breast implants.' When Linda looked shocked, she said, 'I'm a brand.'

'I'd never met anyone,' Linda said later, 'who was on the one hand so sensitive and, even, mysterious and on the other hand, as hard as nails'."

Gabriel looked at his watch, "Hey, do you know what time it is? Let me pay the check before they throw us out."

As they were walking to the car, Alma said, "Weren't you in school with Beto? Does that ever come up in your meetings?"

"I meet with their lawyers, not with the partners. But, yes, Beto and I were in the same class all through school but in high school, he hung out with the kids who were headed to the U.S. or

England to university, and I hung out with the kids who were into heavy metal and graffiti."

"I don't see any piercings or tattoos; you must have been a very timid heavy metaler."

"My mother was a lot scarier than my friends."

Arriving home after a brief good-bye kiss on the cheek from Gabriel, Alma sat in the car for moment brooding about the evening. I like him, I like him a lot, she thought but is that heart that Linda broke ever going to mend?

Chapter 15

FRIDAY, JANUARY 8TH, MORNING

As she punched in his number at 7:45, Alma half expected the call to go yet again to voice mail. "Beto," she said more concerned than annoyed when he did pick up on the fourth ring, "I've been trying to reach you since yesterday early afternoon. Didn't you get any of my messages?"

"Sorry, Alma. I've had a million things going down here. My father, Clyde, the police, Valentina, Aunt Renata, Steven. I feel as if I should cut myself up into little pieces so I can attend to everyone. I did talk to Jaime, so I know about creepy Mr. Cruz. Thanks so much for all that work and for bringing Lucia back."

"What's happening now?"

"Steven's here. We're waiting to hear from Mr. Metallic Voice. Ten million dollars is our final figure. I'm anxious to settle today because of all the bank stuff which I'm not sure can be arranged over the weekend."

"Listen even if you're close to reaching a deal, I think it's important to find out who these people are so you can try, even if it's a long shot, to recover your money afterwards."

"Maybe," said Beto sounding totally unconvinced.

"I have an address for Luz María. I'm going over there right now. I hope to get a bead on Mr. Shades."

"Good luck," he answered but his voice was tired, disinterested.

Her father had again volunteered to take Kurt to school. As he practically danced out the front door, her son reminded her of the birthday party on Saturday. "Mom, tomorrow we have to be at Max's house at eleven sharp and can I stay over at his house tomorrow night, please?"

"Sounds good," she said only half listening.

On the road by eight thirty, Alma hoped that Luz María would be an early bird. When she reached the old brick factory, she sat in her car after she turned off the engine. *What am I doing? Where am I going? Beto isn't even that interested anymore. I have the per diem. Shouldn't I just put my tail between my legs and confess to Ricardo that the story is a dead end? If I can't find Jessica, what will she owe me? Nothing. If they release the story at all, it's going to be to one of the celebrity gossip magazines that have a huge mass circulation. I can see the headline now, "How I survived" or "I Owe My Life to my Fantastic Husband." Who could blame them? It's a business and Jessica is the brand.*

Just then her cell phone buzzed. "Sami? What's going on?"

"Hi, look I just want to apologize. I'm sorry I was such a *pendejo* on Monday. I was angry that Beto hadn't done a better job in protecting Jessica and I was scared too, still am. I've checked out all my sister's business associates, and no one has ever heard of Javier Arias. Also I just talked to Beto, and it seems that they're getting to the end of the negotiations. Jessica should be released this weekend."

"Yes, I'm sitting here and thinking maybe I should hang up my detective boots and call it a day. Beto doesn't seem to be interested in who's behind this and frankly, I know now I'll never get the story."

"No, Alma, I know I'm a fine one to talk but don't give up. I know my sister; she'll never rest until she knows who's done this terrible thing to her. Who's separated her from her family, who's put her life in danger, who's stolen their money and worst of all who's made her fearful, probably for the rest of her life. Believe me; she'll want you to chase this down no matter how long it takes. I know she hasn't shown much concern about where the García's money comes from, but kidnapping, no, she'll never let this go."

Alma sat silently for a minute. Finally she said, "I get it, Sami. It isn't just about who gets the glory. It's about nailing these bastards."

"But Alma be careful, don't take any chances. I don't have to remind you about all the journalists who found out too much or the judges that went against the mafias. If I can help in any way at all, call me day or night."

Alma could only sigh. He seems so nice, so helpful now. But who is he really? So many masks behind masks.

When Alma entered the old brick factory through a large archway, most of the stores and restaurants which occupied the left side of the large plaza where still closed. To the right were several small cafes that had tables in the open air protected from the sun by large colorful umbrellas. The tables were filled by patrons drinking coffee and consuming what looked like crispy croissants. Though a smaller arch she could see behind the principal patio ten or so two-story townhouses. How well this was done, she thought. All the fronts of the stores, restaurants and the townhouses had been constructed with hundred-year-old burnished bricks. The design of the buildings was modern but not in your face contemporary. The construction was light, airy and very livable. Somehow this cheerful and inviting place put a bounce in her step.

She found house number four and rang the bell. Almost immediately a rather high-pitched fluty voice, called out, "Who's there?"

"Alma Jaramillo, I'm a friend of Jessica María's."

"Oh dear, let me find my keys. Yes, coming." A very short, very busty woman in her mid-forties opened the door. Luz María's hair was now a discrete dark brown and, no, she wasn't fat just very top heavy. She was wearing the same light blue pants suit she wore in the photograph, but now it seemed a bit too big for her.

"Is Jessica sending me a message through you? I saw on Twitter that she's on a very hush, hush spiritual retreat. That is so exciting." Luz María's eyes beamed as she clapped her two little hands together. "I'm so sorry; come in, come in. Would you like some tea? I have the most delicious green tea I just brought back from San Francisco."

"Oh, that's the reason I couldn't reach you, you were traveling."

"Yes, I left last Thursday and just got back late last night. I go every year to the Eternal Light Expo. It's the best, and I should know because I have been as far as England to attend these Spiritism conventions. Eternal Light has the best speakers, and this year I took a workshop with a man who curled my toes with the things he told me about my past lives. Green tea, then?"

"A glass of water would be fine," replied Alma. "I don't have a message from Jessica for you but Beto, her husband, has asked me to talk to you about the séance or séances to which you invited Jessica."

"Why would he be interested?" asked Luz María somewhat crossly as if to say interfering relatives are not welcomed in our private affairs.

"Luz María, you're going to have to give me your word that you will not repeat this to anyone, and you must promise not to post it on social media or contact the newspapers because you would be endangering Jessica's life."

"Oh, dear, what's happened to her?"

"She's been kidnapped," Alma stated bluntly.

"But when, how?" said the little woman collapsing onto a bench in the hallway.

As she recovered and they moved into the living room, Alma offered to get them both water. In the kitchen, she found the big bottle of drinking water on a stand in the pantry. When she returned, Luz María was in the living room somewhat recovered. How feminine, thought Alma looking around the room. There was a Victorian loveseat upholstered in delicate pink velvet, and two rosewood chairs covered in a floral silk fabric. The coffee table was an inlaid oak chest. There were several lamps which might have begun as oil lamps. Three floral motif tapestries hung on the walls. The room smelled of dried roses and lemon-scented polish. "What a pretty room," said Alma as they now calmly drank their water.

"I am so glad you like it," said Luz María. "These are my grandmother's pieces. My grandfather was a doctor in Monclova, and my grandmother loved her furniture. There were dozens of grandchildren, but she gave her things to me. I guess she knew I would take care of them as she did."

"Can you tell me how you came to be involved in the Fidencista Christian Church?"

"I spent a lonely childhood in Monclova, mostly in the care of my grandparents. My father was an auditor for Altos Hornos and traveled all over the country usually with my mother in tow. Monclova is very near the small town, Espinazo, where El Niño Fidencio lived and performed his miracles. My grandfather's gardener, Ignacio, who I loved dearly had been one of El Niño's 'little boxes;' men who had been given Fidencio's powers to communicate with spirits and to heal.

"Ignacio was quite old when I was a child, but he said that he saw in me the same powers that El Niño had. Before he died, he put me into a trance and pasted his powers over to me. I became a 'little box.' My grandfather, a man of science, was appalled at any mention of El Niño Fidencio. I moved to Ávila about fifteen years ago because of the Church here. I have property up North so I can live on the rents and do what interests me most, being a medium and a healer."

Alma knew it was none of her business, but she asked anyway. "William Craven mentioned your ex-husband, was he from Monclova too?"

"Oh, I get it," said Luz María. "It must have been William who gave you my address. I see William in his past lives sitting with a group of old women, knitting and telling tales. No, he hasn't conquered his love of gossip, carries it with him from rebirth to rebirth. I met my ex-husband here in Ávila, but I discovered too late that he was possessed by evil spirits." She gave a shudder remembering her marriage. "I saw taking care of him, despite the misery, a way to improve my future lives." This time Luz María smiled as if thinking of some glorious reincarnation.

Alma reached for her bag and extracted the now rather soiled, crumpled photograph. "Yes, Jessica took this picture just before we started the séance," said Luz María lifting her gaze.

"Do you know how I can contact the two men?"

"Leandro," said Luz María pointing to the Brazilian medium, "is in the south of Mexico. I think he said he was visiting Oaxaca. He might be back here this week."

"Can I reach him by phone?"

"Yes, let me get you his number." After entering the number, Alma pointed to Mr. Shades as she always thought of him. "Is this man a relative of yours?"

Luz María sighed, "My great-grandmother on my father's side had fourteen children, twelve of whom were boys. My grandmother had seven, only one of whom was a girl, my mother. My mother only had me, but still each one of my first, second and third cousins have had at least four children. Do you know how many Coutiño's that is? Hundreds. When he," she said pointing to Mr. Shades, "showed up at my door about a month ago, and introduced himself as my third cousin Javier Arias Coutiño, I just assumed that he must be one of the Monclova Coutiños. He talked about my aunts and seemed to know some family history. He said he had come to Ávila specially to meet me because he was a devout believer in El Niño Fidencio. He said he believed that he too had a gift, and he wanted to learn from me."

"Do you know where he's staying or do you have a phone number for him?"

"He said that he was staying in a boarding house downtown. I'll get you the address and his cell number. Why do you want to speak to him and Leandro? I'm sure they can't have anything to do with Jessica's disappearance. They're both spiritual men."

"It's just routine. But could I ask you a favor? Can you call a few of your relatives in Monclova to see if anyone knows Javier? Did you agree to see him when you got back from your trip?"

"He did say that he would be visiting some of the other Fidencista Churches for a few weeks so you might not find him in Ávila right now."

"What kind of a person is he, Luz María?

Again, Luz María paused and thought for a few minutes before answering. "Javier struck me as a new spirit; perhaps this is his first life. You know we believe like the Hindus in reincarnation. We think that spirits, as they are perpetually reborn, can by their actions either get stronger or suffer a decline. Those who decline are in the hands of evil spirits who tempt them to leave the path of good deeds."

"Why do you think Javier is a new spirit?"

"He's impatient, immature. He's too interested in acquiring gadgets; always admiring late model cars, fancy watches, and he loved fashion. He's a real smart dresser. It surprised me because he spoke about gaining knowledge of our philosophy, but in truth, I don't think he ever opened our Bible, 'The Spirits' Book.' Still, I liked him, he was *simpatico,* lots of fun."

"Can you tell me what he looks like? It's hard to tell from the photograph."

"I'd say he's in his late twenties: about your height, small boned, brown eyes and hair, fair skin. He sometimes has a stubble, the unshaven look that you see in the fashion magazines. He's not a very robust person. Now that you mention it, he seemed very different from my cousins' children. I wouldn't call them exactly refined. They're muscular with loud voices and big feet. Javier appeared to be, I know this sounds odd, delicate. He didn't seem like someone who grew up in the rough and tumble of a ranch."

"How did he speak? Did he have a Norteño accent?"

"He said he had lived in Mexico City for many years and had lost his accent. I'll call my aunts and see if anyone knows him. Now I'm frightened, Alma. I love Jessica, and I can't bear to think that I could have introduced her to someone who wanted to do her harm."

"We're following many leads, Luz María. However, if you could make some calls, I would appreciate it. Here's my card. Telephone me whenever about anything that occurs to you."

"Do you have any other photographs of your cousin? Something on your phone perhaps?

"No, he said that he hated to have his picture taken. He believed that cameras rob your soul. But we always do a recording of the séances. Sometimes, we pick up noises from the spirits: odd sounds, rustling or bumping sounds. I left the recorder on by mistake after we finished the last session, and I think he's recorded on the tape. Let me get it for you."

Alma knew no one would have ever heard of Javier Arias at the address he had given Luz María. The phone also surely was long gone, but the recording now that was interesting.

After checking out Javier Aries's supposed address and finding that no one had ever seen or heard of the man, Alma decided that it was time for a heart to heart talk with her editor, Ricardo Nuñez. He would not be happy. She had wasted five days of valuable newspaper time in pursuit of what now seemed like a story which they would only get to publish at best secondhand. As she entered the second floor of El Diario de Ávila, she could see Ricardo reading on his computer a page from a newspaper. Knocking, she said trying to sound upbeat, "Oh hi, sorry to interrupt."

"You've got the story written up?" said Ricardo without taking his eyes off his computer. "I haven't seen it in my email Inbox."

Her voice betrayed the anxiety she felt. "No story, I'm afraid, Richie."

"Okay, time to come clean. *¡Qué diablos,* Alma*!* What the hell is going on?"

"It's about Jessica María, Beto García, the whole García clan, Jessica's family past and present, Beto's business associates and to add a little zest, the Salvador Navarro Front could be involved. Oh, I can't forget Spiritism, and El Niño Fidencio has a part too."

"I think you'd better start at the beginning," he said turning off his cell phone and pulling down the shade on his office door.

Alma left nothing out; no detail was too small, no person too insignificant to mention. She finished her account of the events of the week with the comment, "You see the story was a natural. I thought I was in the perfect position to write it from an insider's perspective. I can see now that Beto is resigned to paying the ransom and letting the police find the culprits, if they can, after Jessica is safely home. The only person who has given me any encouragement is Sami because he said Jessica would want to know who's behind it."

"I'm going to second Sami's opinion," said Ricardo. "As you say the story is odd. It doesn't fit the way organized crime has acted in the past, particularly Mr. Shades, as you call him. He isn't the type we usually see in the line-up of goons that the police like to show off. I like Lucía's ideas about the Governor's political enemies. I would add his friends to the list too. Her theory about Clyde Ramsay seems like a long shot, but who knows."

"How about the Salvador Navarro Front?"

"I knew Gabriel Ruíz's father. We played Dominos together every Thursday night. He was a good lawyer and a decent man; a bit too fond of the ladies perhaps but an honest man. Of course, some apples do fall far from the tree, but I think Gabriel is very devoted to improving human rights here which must be both frustrating with our current government and not a little dangerous.

"As for the Salvador Navarro Front, I have no doubt that the *amparo* trying to stop the García land grab is justified. But you must be careful there too because the Front's people have allied themselves with some rather shady opposition politicians who I don't think would be much of an improvement over the Governor's gang."

"Were you working at the newspaper when Salvador disappeared?"

"*Aye*, now you want my story," smiled Ricardo. "Do you mind if I light up a cigar?"

"No problem but I'm going to open a window."

"My grandfather founded this newspaper in the mid-1920s when he came back from exile in New York."

"Exile! that sounds exciting."

"I don't think they thought it was exciting. Your mention of President Madero and Spiritism brought back my grandfather's story. My great-grandfather was an ardent supporter of Francisco Madero. In fact, I have a copy in my library of his book, '*The Spiritist Manual*' which he wrote under the pen name, 'Bhima.' When Madero and his brother were murdered, my great-grandfather, feeling sure he was next on the list, fled with his wife and children to New York. They managed to eke out an existence in Brooklyn, but my grandfather who was also called Ricardo got himself a scholarship to the then new Columbia School of Journalism. He graduated in 1920, but while he was studying, he worked on a newspaper dedicated to the ideals of the Mexican Revolution founded by other like-minded exiles.

"Anyway, when the Revolution was over, they came back to Ávila and with some capital borrowed from friends and family, my grandfather started El Diario. My father carried on the tradition both by going to Columbia and by editing the newspaper. When I got back from doing an M.A. at Columbia in 1980, I worked as a reporter until my dad retired. Then the Board appointed me as editor."

"So you were working as a reporter when Navarro disappeared."

"Yes, and it was I who oversaw the story. I had a source in the municipal government who called me when Salvador's mother came in to report his disappearance. The authorities wouldn't even see her. I wrote the story up and turned it in. Salvador Navarro was a well-known activist in the state of Tepetlán, and it was shocking that the authorities wouldn't pay any attention to his family. There were dozens of witnesses. The story that the authorities circulated was that he had tried to run off with the money the community had collected for their legal defense, and that his fellow villagers had caught and killed him."

"What happened to your story?"

Ricardo pointed to the old iron safe in the corner of his office. "It's there with all the other stories we never printed. There was a story, of course, in the paper which stated both the family's version of the disappearance and the government's cover-up story."

"Didn't people get indignant about the destruction of El Rosario?"

"You know about that too," said Nuñez. "Again, the government fabricated another story. The propaganda said that the people of El Rosario were selfishly holding up the development of a major civic project, the new airport, that would bring progress and prosperity to the city. The *campesinos* had been offered a good deal, but they were trying to squeeze the taxpayers for more money. Our citizens wanted the airport, so they chose to believe the government. Nothing much new in that."

Ricardo leaned back in his chair puffing on his cigar. "However, the part of your story which I find most intriguing is the disappearance of Jessica's parents because I don't remember reading anything about it in the press or even in Jessica's bios. It's sinister. Do you think their disappearance is related to Jessica's kidnapping?"

"It's hard to see how it could be directly related. Sami and Jessica know so little about their father's past; even what he was really transporting for the airline. Juan Carlos could have a connection to Ávila. It's weird that when they spent a weekend here as children, their dad was only interested in seeing the airport. What do they say? Isn't it that a criminal always returns to the scene of the crime? What I do know for sure is that Jessica was trying to contact her mother's spirit. That could be the key to why she agreed to get into a car with Javier Arias."

Pausing for a minute, the editor said, "What if we published a photo of Juan Carlos which didn't in any way identify him with Jessica, but says something like: 'Family seeks missing relative.' Let's do it as an ad sponsored by an anonymous family member, and I'll give one of the staff's phone numbers. Ads like that appear all the time in the press so that it won't look suspicious."

"It's a real shot in the dark, but I can't see what we can lose by it although if Beto finds out, he won't be happy. I'll get Sami to scan the passport photo he has of Juan Carlos, but meanwhile what do you think I should be doing?"

"It's a sensational story, Alma, and even if we end up being undermined by the Garcías, we'll still have a unique tale to tell. I say just keep doing what you're doing but be careful. The Governor may have some enemies, but he also has many dangerous friends. Power and money are deeply attractive. Don't disappear on me. I want you to call me at least twice a day."

"Do you have a tape recorder?" she asked, showing him the tape that Luz María had given her.

Ricardo buzzed his assistant who produced a machine. The first part of the tape revealed the séance just as Cécile had related it to Alma. When Leandro finished speaking, there were the sounds of chairs being moved, suddenly a man's voice spoke. "Jessica," it said, "could you give me your phone number in case Luz María is away, and I need to get in touch with you?" Then the recording abruptly ended.

"Mexico City," said Alma. "Norteño, my ass. That man's accent says educated in private schools and universities in Mexico City, no mistake," said Ricardo.

"Just one more question before I head out. Did you go to the British Academy here like almost everyone I've met?"

"No, but you're right, Ávila's elite would probably fit on the head of a pin. We all seem to connect instantly when we meet through shared family or friends. But to answer your question, my father was a Yankee-loving guy. He sent me to the American School in Mexico City. He disagreed with most of U.S. foreign policy, but he loved the States." Throwing his hands up in the air, Ricardo sighed. "Such is the schizophrenia we Mexicans have learned to live with."

Chapter 16

FRIDAY, JANUARY 8TH, MIDDAY

When Alma had asked Clyde for an appointment, he had sounded delighted. "Sure, come to the house around one, and we'll have cocktails." She wasn't sure about cocktails in the early afternoon, but she did want to get a better sense of the man.

The back garden of the Ramsey mansion rolled down to the eighth hole of the Chateau Ville golf course. The house was spectacularly contemporary: all glass, stone and fine Teak from Panama. As a maid in a pink uniform and starched apron led Alma towards the terrace at the back of the house, they passed through a two-story living room with floor to ceiling windows at one end and an enormous white stone fireplace at the other.

Clyde was checking the bottles in the bar when she stepped onto the covered patio. Where the terraced ended, an endless pool began which led the eye to the manicured golf course in the distance. "So, what can I get you, Alma? I've got some private label tequilas or mezcal if you prefer."

"How about a Diet Coke?"

"Always the *gringa*," her host said shaking his head.

When they were settled with their drinks on the rattan sofa, Clyde said grinning, "I hear Lucia has fingered me as one of the suspects in Jessica's kidnapping."

"Who told you that?"

"Beto, of course, he thought it was even funnier than I did." She noticed that close-up he was not as young as she had first thought, forty-five or so but in terrific shape. "But Lucia's usually sharp, so if she knew how goon-less the DEA had been, she would've discarded her theory immediately."

"How did you get involved with the DEA?"

"My parents are Americans, but I was born and brought up in Mexico City. My father originally was sent here by a big consumer goods company. After six years, they wanted to move him to South Korea. He said, 'No thanks, I'm happy here.' So, with a Mexican colleague, he started a small company. Servi-Corp provided trucks for local deliveries, temporary employees, health services; stuff foreign corporations didn't want to do themselves. My father did very well. He sold the company five years ago and retired to Santa Fe."

"And you, how did you fare as a kid in Mexico?"

"It was the seventies and eighties when I was growing up here. We lived in the fanciest part of the city in a big old house. I went to the American School where I was on the tennis and golf teams. The city was safe; the clubs let us dance until four in the morning and my friends who were all Mexican were fun: party guys and gals. I wanted to stay here for college, but my father insisted that I go to the States. So, I chose the University of Arizona where I thought I might be able to continue my Mexico City life---big letdown. The sports were there, but the party scene was dismal. I majored in psychology because that's where the girls were and minored in Spanish which turned out to be a lot more work than I imagined.

"When I graduated, I knew I wanted to come back to Mexico, but I didn't want to work for my dad. One day I was reading the Arizona Daily Star, and there was an article on the DEA. I applied and was accepted even though I was neither a lawyer nor had law enforcement experience. I got very lucky too in that they sent me to Mexico and not to Colombia. I stuck it out for eight years, but I was bored to death. In the mid-nineties, Mexican thugs were shipping a lot of marijuana and some cocaine from Colombia across the border but it was nothing like it is today with heroin, amphetamines and God knows what else. So, I spent my time, not chasing *narcos* as Lucia imagined but holding meetings on drug policy and playing a lot of golf. But I did research the money laundering angle of the drug trade which made me get an education in finance and banking."

"I'm curious what is it that makes you stay in Mexico besides your business, of course?"

"I have Mexican and American citizenship, but culturally I'm probably more Mexican than American. In a way, I'm neither. You can't imagine how I used to envy my Mexican friends when I was a kid. They were one thing. Even if they hated some things in their country, they belonged. I felt I didn't belong anywhere."

"Didn't you feel special because you had two languages and two cultures. If you didn't quite belong anywhere, you could fit in everywhere. I could figure people out so much faster than my American friends," said Alma.

"Maybe, my wife would like nothing better than to live in Houston where she spends half her time anyway. She doesn't understand when I say I want my kids to be one thing. It's great that they have two languages, but I want them to feel that they're Mexican. She doesn't get it; she looks confused and says, 'but they are Mexican'."

"So back to your story. How did you meet the Governor?"

"In a golf tournament, of course. Towards the end of the nineties, the North American Free Trade Agreement, you know NAFTA, was starting to be a big thing for Mexico. Humberto was launching his new political party, the PIYS, and he was looking for someone who could interest American and Canadian companies in coming to Ávila. I said, 'I'm your guy.' So, we went into business. When Beto came back five or six years ago, Humberto passed his half over to his son."

"What did you think when Jessica and Beto got engaged?"

Clyde got up and served himself a second tequila.

"I thought she was the hottest woman I had ever seen. I mean she is so stunningly beautiful. Sometimes I think how did two ordinary, okay, her parents were attractive people but nothing special, produce this extraordinary woman. As an outsider most of my life, I've had a lot of time to observe people. I guess too that I just didn't study psychology for the girls, people interest me.

A couple of months ago, Beto and Jessica had a cocktail party at their house which was probably Beto's idea. About twenty minutes after all the guests had arrived, Jessica walked into the room. She didn't even say anything; she just flicked her hair back from her face and waved to Beto. The room went dead quiet; people couldn't take their eyes off her. I have a theory about women. The interesting ones at some time in their mid-twenties, or maybe for some, it's mid-thirties, reach a point when it all comes together: their talents, their self-confidence, their ambition and it lights them up. If they're beautiful like Jessica, being near them is like being run over by a ten-ton truck."

"Perhaps I need a make-over because I haven't seen anyone dead at my feet yet," said Alma.

"*Aye* Alma," laughed Clyde, "maybe you haven't been looking closely enough."

"But how do you know what Jessica's parents looked like?"

"She showed me two tiny blurry photos which she keeps in a locket," he said enjoying the last drops of his tequila.

"Apart from being beautiful, what else struck you about Jessica?"

"You know what, Almita, I think you're interviewing me. I see you looking for quotes for a future article. I thought you were here with your detective hat on. The Governor and Beto are not going to like one little bit your prying into family secrets."

She smiled at Clyde and repeated her question. Shrugging his shoulders, he said, "Then don't misquote me. What struck me most about Jessica? She's shrewd. 'For Beto, marriage is having a glamor girl on his arm,' she told me once. 'He's in love with Jessica María, the TV star. I'm different. For me, marriage is a partnership. I need that sense of complicity that my parents had. My mother knew to the last detail whatever it was that my father was hiding. I want to close my front door and feel safe, and for that, I need to trust Beto absolutely'."

Clyde shifted in his chair and for some minutes looking out at the manicured greens of the golf club, said nothing. At last turning to Alma, he said, "Don't you ever get frightened? You're in the middle of some pretty nasty stuff. There are a lot of secrets floating around Ávila, and many people who don't want their dirty laundry hung out in public. I don't know why Beto hired you, but it could be to keep tabs on you. He isn't entirely his father's son, but he can play hardball too. Watch your back."

The mood of the interview had shifted. Was this warning coming from a disinterested but sympathetic Claude or was he the García's messenger? Alma felt it was time to wind down their talk.

"So, if you didn't organize the kidnapping, who did?"

"I think it was those bastards from the Salvador Navarro Front."

"But what could they possibly gain from kidnapping Jessica? They have you where they want you. You are going to have to renegotiate the land deal if you want the *amparo* lifted."

"Yes, but ten million dollars can go a long way in a war chest if you aim to question past land deals," he said. His face was now pink with anger.

"Do you think that's their strategy?"

"I think that *hijo de la chingada,* Gabriel Ruíz, has fired them up and put too many big ideas in their heads. I also think that elections are coming up next year, and they want money to finance opposition candidates."

"How are the negotiations over the ransom going?"

"Beto thinks that by late afternoon or evening they'll have settled on a number. The problem might be getting the funds transferred tonight or over the weekend. He wants Jessica home by Sunday at the latest."

"Now that I know you're such a keen observer of women, why did Cécile Reynaud give up such a promising consulting business when she married Humberto? I would have thought that with his contacts she could have doubled her client list. What was she advising on? Oh, yes, asset acquisition."

Alma saw a smirk cross Clyde's face. She could see he was debating if he should let one of his closely guarded secrets out of the bag. Lucky for her, the two tequilas had loosened his tongue. "That's what she told you, asset acquisition? She met Humberto because she was the representative in Mexico for a Panamanian bank. In other words, she was the one to go to if you wanted to open a shell company to avoid taxes. But when they married, the Governor didn't want a wife who was in such an iffy line of work. He was in the process of cleaning up his image and wanted to stay away from anything that smacked of money laundering.

"Did she tell you also how unfair the Société Générale had treated her?" She nodded her head. "I have a friend in their Latin American office in New York, and he told me that Cécile was caught taking kickbacks for the dicey loans she was recommending. The bank dropped her like a hot potato. I know you are going to keep what I just told you under your cute little hat, Almita. I wouldn't want it to get back to the Governor that I was telling tales out of school."

"Have you and the Governor had a falling out?"

"Look, my business is being wrecked by the Garcías. First, it was the *amparo* which has frozen up all my capital, and God only knows for how long that's going to last. Now what capital we have left, is being eaten up by this ransom business. They should have negotiated longer. I bet we could have gotten off with a million dollars, but no, the Governor insisted that we settle as soon as possible. If I were Beto, I would have settled quickly. Jessica is his wife. But the Governor wanting to settle so promptly? He's a real cold fish and was totally against Beto marrying Jessica. I just don't get it."

She gave Clyde a brief kiss on the cheek as she was leaving. Walking off the terrace towards the front of the house, she had a last view of him holding up the bottle of tequila trying to decide if a half a shot would do or if he could risk letting the golden liquid rise to the top of his glass. He talks a good story she thought tossing me just enough juicy tidbits to make me think he's my accomplice, a real buddy. But trust him? She smiled to herself as she unlocked her car. No way. He's as slippery as an eel.

Alma arrived at the house as her mother was serving lunch. Her father was away on a job, so it was just a subdued Kurt still thinking about his tennis shoes, and her mother bubbling over about her plans for the new Internet café who joined her at the table. Alma ate so quickly that her mother commented, "I could be cooking you corn mush for all the interest you take in your food."

"Sorry, Ma, but I have an urgent call to make." As Alma bounded up the stairs to her room, she heard her mother say to Kurt, "Hey, slow down! This isn't McDonald's."

Sitting on the edge of her bed, she punched Leandro Sousa's phone number into her cell phone. When he answered immediately, she was startled. "*Señor* Sousa my name is Alma Jaramillo. I'm an acquaintance of Luz María Fuentes and a friend of Jessica Maria's. Do you remember the séance you conducted for her a month or so ago?"

"Yes, of course, why are you calling me?" he said in a soft Portunol accent.

"Jessica has gone missing, and we're interviewing anyone who has had contact with her in the last month. Where are you right now?"

"I'm in the bus station in Puebla on my way to Mexico City."

"Could you make a detour to Ávila? We could talk tomorrow morning. Luz María is as concerned as I am."

"Are you with the police?"

"No, I'm an investigator working with the family," she said. She breathed a sigh of relief when he answered, "I guess I could change my plans. Jessica is dear to me, and I would like to help."

At four precisely, Gabriel knocked on the front door. Kurt ran to answer it. As they exchanged a complicated handshake, Alma kissed her mother good-bye. "I might have to go out later this evening too," she said sighing. Her mother shrugged her shoulders as if to say it's lucky you don't have to pay a babysitter at Los Angeles prices.

When Alma dropped into the front seat of Gabriel's car, he greeted her with a brief, "How's it going?"

"I'm pretty much on my own now. Beto seems to have lost interest in trying to locate Jessica's kidnappers. He, his father and the insurance company seem resigned to paying the ransom as quickly as possible. Clyde thinks she might be home by Sunday. The only people who are still cheering me on are Sami and Ricardo who by the way knew your father."

"My father looked forward to those Thursday night domino games if for no other reason than to escape the women in his life. Who else have you seen since yesterday?"

"This morning, Luz María, the Spiritist's 'little box.' She gave me the lowdown on Javier Arias, a.k.a. Mr. Shades which was fascinating. It seems she doesn't think he's very spiritually enlightened even if he talks a good story. She also gave us a recording of his voice. He's no *Norteño*, just a privileged guy from Mexico City." She was about to continue with Ricardo's idea about publishing a photo of Jessica's father when she stopped. Of course, she trusted Gabriel, but maybe some things were best kept to herself.

Instead, she continued, "I saw Clyde Ramsey just before lunch, and he's convinced that the Salvador Navarro Front is behind the kidnapping." She could see Gabriel's jaw tighten.

"He would, but why in heaven's name does he think the Front needs ten million dollars so desperately?"

"Politics and profit of course. His theory is that you guys are now so emboldened by your success with the latest *amparo* that you're going to challenge old land deals where the government might have been involved in monkey business. That's one theory, the other is that the Front is going to be participating in the upcoming elections, and you'll need cash to support opposition candidates." Alma looked at him out of the corner of her eye to see if he was keeping his temper in check. She didn't dare mention Ricardo's comment about the Front's supposed unfortunate choice of political friends.

Gabriel turned to her with a big grin on his face. "*Aye*, Almita, you're a tough one. You can squeeze information out of people like a juice extractor, nothing left but the pulp when you're finished."

"Yep," she laughed. "I do have a nasty way of getting people to tell me their secrets." Then she looked serious. "Too bad, I've failed so miserably to find Jessica."

"Hey, come on, it's like looking for a needle in a haystack. Tell me how many victims has the government managed to find? When they do, it's headlines all over the country."

"Okay, I'll stop being a crybaby. Tell me about who we're meeting this afternoon?"

"The Front is a very loose organization. We have a committee of ten men and women. I never know who will turn up for the meetings because they're all working several jobs, but somehow we get things done."

"Where are we meeting them?"

"At El Milagro one of the four villages which are involved in the *amparo*. As I told you last night, their land is poor, but ironically, they've benefited from the construction of the airport. The city has moved almost next door to them. In fact, over the last ten years, they've been little by little selling off their land."

Parking on the edge of the village which consisted of twenty-five or thirty adobe and cement block houses, they were immediately surrounded by a pack of howling street dogs. Gabriel left Alma to chat with the dogs while he went to look for *Don* Isidro who was the most constant attendee of their weekly get-togethers. Don Isidro's wife soon appeared to shoo the dogs away and to conduct Alma through the village.

Don Isidro's house was a warren of small rooms and patios. The first part of the structure had been built of adobe; later a second floor made of cement blocks had been added to the front of the house. At the back of the building, rebar wires covered with Coke bottles still protruded from the flat roof. A scent of soaking corn, slaked lime and toasting *tortillas* filled the air. When Alma was ushered into the front room, besides Gabriel and Don Isidro, she found four more villagers.

Don Isidro's wife slipped away but soon reappeared with two large bottles of Coca-Cola and a pail full of glasses. "This is Alma Jaramillo," said Gabriel "she's a reporter for El Diario de Ávila." As she clasped the hands which were held out to her, she remembered the village handshake her father had taught her. The whole hand was not gripped firmly, but rather just the fingers of the right hand were grasped with the lightest possible touch.

"Thank you for including me," said Alma. "Do you read our newspaper?" Chairs were pulled out as the eight of them sat down at a simple wooden table covered with a white hand-stitched cloth. A short man in a battered baseball cap answered, "We don't see too many newspapers here, too hard to get a hold of. We see the news on television." He held up his hands as if to say whatever that's worth.

No hundred-channel cable here, Alma thought. They'll have a few national channels which carry the top news stories written to accentuate the positive role of the government in power and a full selection of soap operas.

"I think Alma would like to know what happened here with your land, and how we plan to fix it," said Gabriel kicking off the meeting.

"Our land," said Don Isidro "since the Revolution, has been *an ejido* which means it was communally owned, but each of us tilled our own plot. Then about twenty years ago, the government told us that we did own the land and could sell it. The land is not worth much as farm land. It's too rocky and sandy. We earn a little money raising pigs and chickens, but most of us have jobs as gardeners or maids in the city. Since the building of the airport, the city has been moving closer to us, and some of us have begun to sell off our plots."

"When did things begin to change?" asked Alma.

"When Governor was elected," said an older woman wearing a *huipil* embroidered with a red and blue pattern. "Before the election," she continued, "the people from, what's the Governor's party?"

"The PIYS" said Don Isidro.

"That's right," said the woman. "Those people came around and offered us sets of pots and pans, blenders. I heard someone in another village got a washing machine. They said they were going to pave the road to the village and build a new elementary school much nearer to us if we voted for Humberto García."

"Then," said a younger man in a cowboy hat, "a bunch of engineers appeared one day to survey the land. 'What's going on?' we asked. 'Haven't you heard? This is going to be the new runway for the airport. The Governor is bringing a regional airport to Ávila'."

"A few months later," said Don Isidro's wife, "men in suits appeared and posted papers on the village walls. Next came two lawyers who presented us with the Government's offer for our land: one hundred pesos a square meter."

"We may not have had many years of school," said the man in the cowboy hat, "but we knew that one hundred pesos a square meter was not the commercial value of the land. We turned down the offer, but the lawyers said that they had a court order. We could keep our houses in the village, but the farm land was fenced off."

"There is a protocol under Mexican law which says that the land for expropriation has to be independently appraised," said Gabriel. "A town meeting also should have been held. None of that ever happened."

"Did you receive payment for the land?" asked Alma.

"Yes, some of us put down payments on taxis, bought old cars or new TVs. Then we watched and waited. A year or so ago, we heard that the land wasn't going to be used for the airport after all but had been resold to a company that was going to build factories."

"That's when I entered the picture," said Gabriel. "We are going to get a decent price for the land or force the government to return it."

Alma looked around the table at the faces staring up at Gabriel, but the reporter in her couldn't resist asking, "I understand that you're backing an opposition party that wants to take the governorship away from Humberto García's party."

A third man with a weather-beaten, deeply tanned face turned toward Alma. "*Licenciada*," he began formally.

"No, please call me Alma," she answered.

"*Licenciada*," he continued his face as unreadable as the adobe wall in front of her. "Why are you here? Are you going to write an article about the problem with our land? Or are you gathering information perhaps for the Governor? What's your interest in us?"

"Juan, she's a friend," said Gabriel. "Don't worry."

"Why shouldn't we worry? We never see newspaper or television reporters here. They aren't our friends. They use people like us to show up the government when it suits them, but later they walk away, bury the story. Leave us alone, *Licenciada*. Go back to the city where you belong!" As he stood up to go, his chair fell over; the sound echoed through the now silent room.

For the next hour, Alma sat quietly listening as Gabriel went over their next legal maneuvers with the men and women left around the table. "Mexico is changing," he said to the group as he walked to the door. "Maybe not as fast as we would like, but we have to be hopeful."

"Do you really believe that?" said Alma sliding into the front seat of the car. "That Mexico is changing?"

"On my good days, which mostly outnumber my bad days, how about you?"

"I don't think this is one of my good days. Can I reserve judgment?"

"I'm sorry about what happened back there with Juan. He's a school teacher who's been too long in the trenches, fighting the powers that be. Do you still think that the Salvador Navarro Front is involved in the kidnapping?"

"I don't believe our friends here in El Milagro are involved, but I haven't met all two hundred and fifty people in the organization. Who knows if there aren't a few more hotheads around like Juan."

"Alma, you are a terrible skeptic."

"Not really, I've learned that politics is like those Russian dolls, the *Matryoshkas*, you know you have to open the top one to discovered what's inside. As you open each doll, one by one, you realize that there is layer upon layer of hidden dolls. But it isn't just Mexico, can you name a country that doesn't have graft, where drugs aren't sold to kids, or minors, trafficked?"

Turning to look at Gabriel, she said, "Sorry to be so glum. Let's change the subject. I'm sick of politics. Remember that first afternoon when we had just met, and you were driving me back to look for Kurt? You told me how your father would take your mind off your troubles. Let's try it again. Tell me more about your childhood."

"Do you realize that that far-off day when we first met was only two days ago?"

"Yes, I think that the first thirty years of my life went by in ten seconds, and this week is going to last a year."

"Let's see. I told you that my mother is an anthropologist."

"Yes, you said that she lives most of the time in San Cristobal de las Casas."

"The three summers when I was five, six and seven were the best months of my life."

"Up to now, I hope."

"Well, of course," said Gabriel amused, "up until now. We spent a month each of those years in a tiny village on the shore of Lake Miramar in the center of the Lacandon Biosphere Reserve. Can you imagine what it was like for a city kid who took the bus to school every day, watched television every night, and shopped with his mother in a supermarket every Saturday to suddenly find himself living in a tropical rain forest? A rain forest filled with macaws, wild parrots, howler monkeys, tapirs, giant tortoises and more exciting than anything, maybe a jaguar or two. The trees were so tall that I could barely see the tops. We lived in a hut made of wooden posts which supported a thatched palm-leaf roof; there were no walls, and the floor was hard dirt. We slept in hammocks made from some local rope and ate, I suppose, *tortillas* and beans most of the time. I could run wild with the village children if we didn't go too far into the jungle."

"Did you learn any of the local language?"

"Yes, a few words but children learn to communicate without words. Sadly, it all came to an end with the *Zapatista* uprising. When my mother returned to her work there several years later, my father put his foot down. My summers became day camp in Ávila and nightly tortures from Esther. Now your turn, what were your summers like?".

"No jaguars that's for sure except in the zoo. What I remember most about being six was that it was the first time I saw the ocean. It must have been July or August; we had been living for about a year in Los Feliz. I missed my cousins terribly. There were very few children to play with in our building, and no gang of neighborhood kids who congregated on our stoop. We usually went back to the old neighbor on Sundays to have lunch with Alfonso, Julieta, and their kids. Then one Saturday my dad came home early from work and said, 'We're going shopping.' My mom and I jumped into the old pick-up, but when my dad pulled up to Sears, we were surprised. 'What are we getting here?' my mom asked. 'Tomorrow we go to the ocean,' my father answered. 'The ocean!' we shouted. 'That's way on the other side of Los Angeles.' We were doubtful because seaside L.A. was as strange to us as the jungle was to you.

"We were very timid because none of us had ever been in a department store before, but Alfonso had given my father a list of what to buy which we followed to the letter. First, we needed swimsuits. My mother chose a one-piece green suit which she showed me in the dressing room, too shy to come out into the store. My dad just grabbed a pair of trunks walking though men's wear. My bikini was exceptional. It was white with pink ruffles across the bottom and the top. It was the most beautiful piece of clothing I had ever seen. Next, we bought a red beach umbrella, and three chairs with no legs which my mother thought very impractical. We acquired three beach towels, a cooler and a thermos, suntan lotion, finally a bucket and shovel for me.

"I was so excited that night I couldn't get to sleep. In the morning, Alfonso and Julieta came by around eight. My mother had bought small steaks for grilling, made *tortillas, salsa* and great quantities of lemonade. We followed Alfonso for what seemed to me hours, frightened we would lose sight of him in the traffic. When I had almost run out of hope, we came over a hill and there it was, a huge expanse of blue as far as the eye could see. We gasped and breathed in that particular smell, the scent of the sea. It's totally unforgettable.

"We parked next to Alfonso on a long white stretch of sand and set up our umbrella and chairs near a dune a few feet from the water. My father took my hand and led me towards the water. I remember how warm the sand was and then how cold the sea felt on my feet. He reached down, cupped his hands, and scooped up the sea water. 'Stick your tongue in it, Almita' he said. I still can feel the first taste of the salt in my mouth. 'Yuck,' I said, 'it tastes sharp.' 'Yes, but that's what lets you float on top of the water as if you were in a hammock.'" Alma smiled with same delight she had felt that day.

"That's not fair; you win again. I had howler monkeys and jaguars in my story and you just had the boring ocean, but your story is so much better than mine."

"Why do you think I became a journalist?"

"Because you can tell a good story. Do you miss L.A., your life there?"

That day five years ago, when she had walked along the path that linked San Diego to Tijuana had been the worst in her life she told Gabriel. She remembered bumping Kurt's stroller over the cracks in the sidewalk, beads of sweat jumping off her eyebrows onto the burning pavement. The shopping cart with the suitcases which contained their few remaining possessions had bounced along slightly ahead of them. The old man pushing the cart had asked if they were leaving for good. A lump had risen in her throat because she knew it was true. Her old life was gone forever.

When they had reached the Mexican immigration booth, what had struck her first were the smells drifting through the fence: burning charcoal, grilled *chorizo*, onion, green chili, toasting *tortillas*, diesel fumes, day-old garbage. Then the sounds: car horns, loudspeakers blaring out *Rancheras*, the wail of street vendors. She could just make out beyond the fence blinking neon signs and people, people everywhere. The official had barely glanced at her Mexican birth certificate and her son's American passport. "¡*Felicidades*!" he had said. It was Mexican Mother's Day, and she hadn't even realized it. What she had grasped was that she was stepping into a void, a future she couldn't predict in a country she had never known.

When she had arrived in Ávila, she had hated everything about it. She spoke the language so she should have fit in, but she didn't. If she had been a tourist, she would have found it charming, exotic, but it was supposed to be home, and it wasn't. She had grown up in L.A. believing in the "American Dream." She had been told she could do or be anything she wanted. Then the truth was flung in her face. She wasn't wanted. Her talents, because she was born on the other side of a line drawn on a map, could be discarded like yesterday's trash. "But I was young, educated, resilient, and, I guess, lucky. I've built a new life, a good life here but, like Kurt with his shoes, I still from time to time mourn what I lost."

It was dark when Gabriel pulled up in front the Jaramillo home. He turned off the engine, and they sat for a moment not speaking. Then he turned to Alma, took her gently by the arm and pulled her close to him. He found her mouth easily in the dark. It was a long sweet kiss with a hint of passion to come. When Alma pulled back, she said, "Oh, that was nice." During the second kiss, she put her arm instinctively around his neck and began settling into the luxury of a longer more passionate kiss when a flash of light hit her in the eye. "What was that?" she said pulling away.

"Probably fireworks going off in our heads."

"No, it was like the flash of a camera."

"It's probably just headlights from a passing car," he replied reaching for her again.

Pulling away, Alma said, "The neighbors take particular delight in spying on couples fooling around in cars. Could we continue this tomorrow perhaps in a more private place?"

"How about dinner at my place tomorrow night?" Suddenly turning serious, he said, "Alma, please take care. There's a lot of bad stuff going down here in Ávila. I worry about you. Maybe you should get another reporter to work with you on the investigation or get a detective to accompany you. I've seen close up what the Garcías can do to people who challenge them. I've been lucky because I've got friends in high places but I've got several clients who will never work again because they took the Governor on."

She kissed him lightly on the cheek. "I'm listening to all the warnings. Don't think I'm not but I still believe I'm on the side lines. No one really cares about my investigation."

Chapter 17

SATURDAY, JANUARY 9TH, MORNING

When Alma awoke at 7:30 on Saturday morning, she first remembered the kiss, and a warm feeling radiated down the length of her body. "Umm," she murmured, "tonight should be fun." Too quickly, however, her thoughts were forced back to the reality of the day ahead. She had had two messages last night when she had turned on her cell phone. The first was from Stephen saying, "Sorry, drinks off tomorrow night." That was a relief. Slightly afterward, Beto had texted, "Gov wants us his house 8:30 A.M. important."

Showered and dressed by eight o'clock, she shouted to Kurt as she was closing the front door, "Of course, I'll be back by ten thirty. Get Grandma to wrap the present." Her mind was fuzzy as she drove towards the Garcías' hacienda. Tonight's dinner with Gabriel occupied her thoughts much more than her upcoming conversation with the Governor. She expected the Garcías to say that her services were appreciated but no longer needed. Nevertheless, she might be able to have an interview with Jessica if the family decided to go public about the kidnapping. The Federal Police would certainly be debriefing her.

When she pressed the buzzer on the interphone at the entrance to the Hacienda San Ignacio, a brusque voice answered instead of Álvaro's cultivated tones. A minute or two later, a burly man with a wire protruding from his ear opened the door. With a crooked forefinger, he indicated that she should follow him. As she crossed the threshold of the Governor's study, she saw Humberto García seated behind the massive desk. Beto was standing next to him, leaning over, listening to the Governor as he showed him something on an iPad.

She paused in the doorway studying the Governor. He was as handsome as the portrait that hung above him: fit, muscular, his face relatively unlined. It was only his silver-gray hair which gave away his age. He was dressed impeccably in a dark blue suit. His shirt, printed with the thinnest blue stripes, had a starched white collar. The tie, dark blue and no doubt Hermès, was decorated with minuscule crests. Was he now Nuevo Progreso's first Baronet? speculated Alma, amused at her little joke. Beto, on the other hand, was wearing an old sweatshirt which proudly proclaimed in faded letters, "University of Minnesota." His jeans, belted under his still protruding middle, were unfashionably baggy. His face was unshaven; his hair looked as if a comb was too blunt an instrument to tame it.

"Come in, *Señorita* Jaramillo," said the Governor beckoning her to take a seat in one of leather armchairs in front of his desk.

No polite kiss on the cheek, thought Alma. Beto simply nodded his head as if they were distant acquaintances who ran into one another occasionally on the golf course.

"We want to thank you, *Señorita* Jaramillo, for your service in trying to locate my daughter-in-law. The problem has now been resolved, and we will no longer be needing your help."

"That's wonderful news," said Alma, "but I think some of us, including Jessica herself, would be interested in finding those who committed this crime. I would very much like to continue the investigation."

"We no longer think, *Señorita* Jaramillo, that you are the person who can offer us the kind of inquiry we need. The police are professionals and are trained for his kind of work. We would like to give you a bonus, however, for your efforts but in exchange, you must forego publishing anything on this week's events."

The Governor, she thought now, seemed very anxious to be rid of her. Beto stood mute; his gaze fixed on the far wall as if trying to determine the carbon date of the Olmec head so beautifully displayed in its niche.

"*Señor Gobernador*," said Alma "when I agreed to take on this investigation, I never signed a contract. I understood that when the case closed and Jessica was safely home, I would be able to use the information I'd gathered. I have no problem sharing it with the police, but I can't agree not to publish the story."

"The reason, *Señorita* Jaramillo, that we cannot allow you to publish it, is that you would be totally prejudiced against my son, myself and our family. You have shown yourself to be disloyal, and if I may say so, it is overly generous of my son to offer you any compensation at all."

Alma sat in her chair for a minute stunned. "I don't understand why you would think that I am prejudiced or worse, disloyal. I have, in fact, uncovered a lot of information that the police neglected or overlooked. I'm totally confused." She turned to look at Beto who still refused to stop mentally evaluating the Olmec head.

The Governor tapped an app on his iPad and pushed the screen around to Alma's side of the desk. "I think perhaps that it is your emotions as well as your loyalties which are confused, *Señorita* Jaramillo," said the Governor while Alma gazed at a photograph of Gabriel and her caught kissing in the car. "That person with whom you appear to be intimately involved has created an enormous, and I might add, unnecessary, financial problem for my son and his partner, Claude Ramsey."

"I can assure you," said Alma angry now, "that my private life in no way influences my professional judgment."

"You are then the first woman in recorded history not to be under the spell of her emotions," said the Governor, his mouth forming a tight patronizing smirk.

A chauvinist too, thought Alma. She looked at the Governor and at Beto. "I don't want your money, but I will keep my per diem because I've more than earned it. I will never agree not to publish what I think is newsworthy as long as it doesn't harm innocent people. Now if you will excuse me, I have work to do."

As she left the room, she heard the Governor say in an almost inaudible voice, "If I were you, *Señorita*, I would be prudent. Yours has proven to be a risky profession."

When the door of the Hacienda closed behind Alma, she knew her cheeks were burning. She couldn't remember when she had last been so angry. The nerve of the man, the arrogance, no wonder Lucía was peculiar and Beto, not much better. How could Catherine still love that *pendejo*! The block she had to walk to recuperate her car did nothing to calm her indignation. I'll show them, just wait, she promised herself.

As she slid the key in the door of the car, she suddenly felt a sharp object pressed into the small of her back. Next she heard the man's voice.

"This is a gun, Alma. Remove the key, turn left and walk up ahead to the black car with the tinted windows." He gave her shoulder a slight shove to get her moving. Alma's heart began to beat so rapidly, she thought it might explode. Her stomach lurched.

"Now open the back door and slide in," the man said.

She did as she was told and as she sat down, a hood was thrown over her head and her wrists were bound with an elastic cord. "My friend in the back seat has a gun too, Alma. So, don't think about annoying him. We only want to talk to you."

The engine of the car sprang into life, and the car pulled out onto the ring road.

They're going to rape me or worse, thought Alma, her whole body shaking with terror.

"This is the thing," said the man in the front seat. "Our people are very unhappy with you, Alma. You have been sticking your nose into certain matters which are private. Me and my friend are your alarm bells. We're taking the trouble to warn you to start being a good girl, to mind your own business. You can write all the stories you want about what happens outside of Ávila, but what's published in our city is controlled by people wiser than you and me, and that goes for your editor too. He needs to choose his friends more carefully."

The voice paused for a moment. Why does he sound so familiar? thought Alma. And the car, the leather seats and seamless shifting gears, have I been here before?

But the terror of what was soon to come pushed all other thoughts from her mind.

The man at the wheel cleared his throat and spoke again.

"If you are thinking of running to the police, I wouldn't bother. We control them. You also should think about Kurt, Alma. We wouldn't want that car taking the children to the birthday party to have an accident, would we? How terrible to lose so many children when just by cooperating, you could avoid an accident. Your parents also, Alma, Jesús and Sofía, you wouldn't want them to be found hanging from one of Ávila's bridges. Your friend, Gabriel, we've been keeping an eye on him, too. If he continues to stand in the way of progress, he could easily disappear like his idol, Salvador Navarro. Now, Alma, do we understand one another? I need you to say, 'yes,' loud and clear." The man beside her poked her with another sharp object.

"Yes," said Alma. "I understand you completely."

"Good," said the man. "I'm going to stop in a few minutes, and because we are such considerate guys, we are leaving you off very near your car. My friend is going to remove the bands from around your wrists, and you will step out of the car and not remove the hood until we've pulled away. The hood is a small gift, a memento of our talk. We are watching you, Alma. Just remember every minute of the day, we are watching you."

As she stood trying to insert the key into the lock of the car, she began to retch. A few people had stared at her as she removed the hood from her head, but they had quickly hurried away. She glanced at her watch. It was only nine forty-five. How could her whole life have changed in forty-five minutes? She knew she had to act, but her brain refused to function. If she started to drive, perhaps something would come into her head. Up ahead she saw the familiar green Starbucks logo, she pulled into the parking lot and slowly walked into the cafe. She ordered a coffee, placed it on a table, walked to the restroom and locked the door behind her. She punched in Ricardo's number. What would she do if he didn't answer? When he picked up, she tried to remember what he had told her to say years ago if she got into trouble. Yes, she had to say, "Mayday."

"Mayday, Richie," she said barely able to formulate the words.

"Where are you?"

"Starbucks on the ring road."

"I'll be there in ten minutes. I'll use my son's car. It's a gray VW Golf. Stay in the building until you see the car in front."

When she dropped into the front seat of the car, Ricardo looked at her with such concern that the spell of the morning's events was finally broken, and she began to sob.

"I'm so stupid, Richie, why did I think this couldn't happen to me? Everyone kept warning me."

"Do you think you were followed?"

"I don't know. My mind went blank."

"I'm taking you to my house where we can talk privately. I want you to call home and tell your family not to leave the house; not to open the door to anyone, even a neighbor."

When her father picked up the phone, she repeated Ricardo's message word for word.

"Alma, what's going on?" asked Jesús.

"I'll be home as soon as I can, Pa. Don't worry but please do as I say."

"What about Kurt's party?"

Oh, God, the party, thought Alma. "Tell Kurt that he won't miss the party." What a liar she'd become.

The Nuñez' house was buzzing with activity, but Ricardo showed her quickly to his study and shut the door. "So, what happened?"

Alma related her conversation with the Governor and Beto and then, the terrifying ride in the car. "They sent a warning to you too, Richie," she said finally.

"Well, it wouldn't be the first time, but I never had a ride in a car with goons. Can you describe them?"

"I never saw either of them but the driver, the one who led me to the car and did all the talking, had an odd way of speaking. He sounded familiar. It was as if he had memorized a script from a film. It seemed like an educated man trying to speak like a hood. The other man in the back seat never spoke at all, but he had on some expensive aftershave. It was such a strong fragrance that it was distracting."

"Well, maybe, we have a first here," said Ricardo, "sophisticated thugs. And the car? Do you remember anything about the car?"

"It reminded me of Beto's Mercedes because it had that leathery smell, and it rode so smoothly. It was black with tinted windows, but that's all I can tell you. What am I going to do, Richie?"

Her hands had begun to shake again.

"Alma, I can't make that decision for you. I can help you when you decide what's best for you and your family, but the decision can only be yours."

Alma had never had any desire to smoke, but she strangely wished she had a cigarette to concentrate on, to still her hands. She began to realize that she had never taken a decision as important as this. She had been brought to the U.S. as a baby, nothing to say in that choice. She went to a school where her parents had enrolled her. Even UCLA had fallen into her lap. Kurt was wonderful, but he had just happened. She had let nature take its course. The decision to leave L.A. was forced on her by politics and economics. Her jobs, well, she had sought them, but they had not involved any momentous choices. The men that she had been involved with had slipped into her life and then out of it just as easily. Had she been tied too tightly to her mother's apron strings? Probably. Maybe she was too hard on herself, but no, she thought, I don't remember ever anguishing over a decision.

"Aunt Renata told me that for her Beto was a weak man because he hadn't built his life on any real values. I know right from wrong, but I don't think of myself as a brave person. You know someone that leads a crusade or runs into a burning building to save people."

"I think Aunt Renata meant strength of character. Look at the Governor, he's strong but to what end?"

"Yes, he's a bully. His talent is for intimidation. I wonder if something terrible happened to his children if he could survive it? How do people become brave, Richie?"

"I guess for some it's when the abuse they're suffering finally becomes intolerable or they turn into heroes because their family, their friends or their beliefs are threatened. Look, Alma, you have all the qualities of a good journalist. You can write, you have the values we're talking about, people open up to you and you're curious. If you decide to let someone else finish the story, you'll still get most of the credit and believe me, I have a couple of competent guys who would do a fine job wrapping it up."

Alma stood up and walked to the window. I'm not the first person to have this problem, she mused. Many other people right this minute must be wondering what comes first their job or their personal life. Although probably the stakes in their decisions aren't quite as high as mine are.

She turned to her boss, "How will you protect us?"

"What I'm going to talk about Alma is physical protection. First, you must get Kurt out of the country for a few weeks. Can you send him to his father in L.A.? Second, your parents. My wife's family has a big ranch in the state of Veracruz. There're people around day and night because of the animals, and, because Veracruz also has plenty of problems, there's security. Third, do you know Carlos Nuñez Sandoval, the mayor? He's my first cousin and like a brother to me. He'll be running for Governor against the García machine next year. His right-hand man is Pedro Ramirez, our police chief. There's a small apartment in the mayor's official residence where we've hidden people before. You'll be safe there."

"Why did you stress the words 'physical' protection, Richie?"

"Because it isn't only a problem of keeping you out of the hands of the bad guys. There's a psychological toll of going into hiding. Your movements will be restricted. You'll have to live with body-guards around you, day and night. Your family will be far away, and probably you won't be able to communicate with them. You'll be scared. It takes some people a long time to recover. Look, I'm painting the worst possible picture. Most people recover just fine. They end up with the satisfaction of finally being able to stand up to those who want to harm them."

Alma continued to stand by the window watching a familiar street scene: a fruit seller peeling mangos and a gas truck blasting its annoying siren. A world so safe and well-known suddenly gone strange and menacing. What had the Governor said? Oh, yes, that she was under the spell of her emotions. Well, despite what he thought, decisions like this one always had to be based in part on feelings. How could it be any other way? But if she walked away now what would her future as a journalist be? She hadn't chosen this profession to report on weddings and baptisms. Her mind cleared. If I'm going to be taken seriously and be the reporter I want to be, there's only one choice.

"What's going around in your head, Alma?" asked Ricardo.

She walked over to Ricardo. Taking a deep breath, she said, "Too many things. I'm frightened, angry, and I feel stupid for walking into a trap, but I can't let this story go. I can't walk away. So, let's get started. We have to get Kurt an airplane ticket. I need to call Kenny and to get home before my family gets frantic."

"Alma, are you sure that you've thought this through."

"I started this investigation, and I need to finish it. I have to believe that you're right; that we'll all come out of it in one piece physically and mentally. It's a risk I must take, or I'll regret it my whole life. Of course, if it turns out badly, I'll----but I don't want to go there. Can I call Kenny from this phone?"

Ricardo smiled, "First a big hug," which he gave her with such force that she thought he might have cracked a rib. "No, don't touch that phone. It has been bugged for the last three years. I use it mostly to throw off the Governor's people about the stories we're working on. Here," he said handing her a new iPhone, "this will be yours for the duration. It's registered to my gardener's son. Do you have Kurt's passport number on you?"

"Here, it's on my phone," she said while dialing Kenny's number on the new iPhone.

Kenny answered immediately. "Kenny, it's me, Alma. Sorry to call so early on a Saturday morning."

"No problem, the girls have been jumping on our bed for the last hour. What's up? Is Kurt okay?"

"Yes, he's fine, but I need to ask you a big favor. Can he come up to L.A. for a week or two?"

"Sure, when?"

"This afternoon?"

"This afternoon. Are your mom and dad sick? What's going on?"

"No, everybody's fine. I have a problem related to work, my work on the newspaper."

"You're in trouble, aren't you? Hey, just a minute, Helen. Let me finish talking to her."

"Yes, I've had some threats, and my editor thinks that I should get my family out of the way for a little while," she said, trying to keep her tone as natural as possible.

"Maybe you should get yourself out of the way for a while too."

"No, it's something I started and I have to finish, but I'll be fine. Richie is going to surround me with bodyguards. Our lives aren't normally like this, really and truly, and it will be over soon." Alma paused for a minute before her next question. "Kenny, you will send Kurt back when it's all over?"

"Alma, what kind of a guy do you think I am? I know what you've done for Kurt. I also know what I'd feel like if Helen left me and took the girls. It would break my heart. Of course, I'll send him back the minute you say so. Helen says she thinks we can get him temporarily into a school here."

"Thanks, Kenny and thank Helen too. I'll send you a WhatsApp when we have the reservation booked."

When she opened the front door of her family home, Alma didn't even notice Dulce nipping at her ankles. She was prepared for the worst: tears for sure, outright rejection of the plan, hostage taking, she being the hostage.

"Mom," said Kurt running up to her, "we're late for the party. I called Max, and they said they'd wait for me but we have to get going right now."

She led her son into the kitchen where her parents were enjoying a second cup of morning coffee.

"Let's all sit down for a minute," she said, "I have something to say."

"But mom---,"

"Kurt, sit down, now." Both her parents looked at her quizzically.

"What's the matter, Alma? Kurt has been impossible all morning. You'd better get him to that party," her mother said.

"Kurt has to go upstairs and pack his small suitcase. He's going to be visiting his father for a week or two. You two are going on a much-deserved vacation to Veracruz. Upstairs, Kurt," she said pointing to the door.

"But why do I have to go today? Can't I go tomorrow? Dad won't mind."

"There'll be other parties, Kurt. I promise I'll take you ice skating with Max and the whole gang as soon as you're back."

"That's what you always say and then you don't do it."

"Upstairs, Kurt, and don't forget your computer."

"Alma, what in God's name is going on?" said Jesús. "I didn't know what to think when you called earlier."

"The story I have been working on has become dangerous," she said flatly.

"I told you, Jesús," said Sofía her voice shrill, a tone higher than normal. "You said I was imagining things, but I know my daughter. You must stop this right now, Alma. How could you have put yourself and us in danger? Talk about crazy!"

Alma looked directly at Jesús.

"Dad, this is about Humberto García and how he has been abusing this city and this state for years. Also, a serious crime has been committed, and I intend to find out why and who's behind it. Look, Ricardo has been through this before; he's giving me and you all the protection we need. No harm is going to come to anyone, but I need your help and support. Kenny has agreed to take Kurt until it's safe again here. Ricardo's wife is going to pick you up in front of Sears at the mall and take you to Veracruz. She'll be staying there too. I'm sure it will be comfortable and, maybe, interesting."

"How can you talk about 'comfort' or 'interesting' when you are putting our lives and your life in danger. I don't understand you anymore, Alma," said Sofía crossing her arms over her chest as if to say I'm not moving from here.

The room was silent for a minute except for the furious stamping of feet and banging of doors from Kurt's room. Her father turned to her mother.

"Sofía, I have never ordered you to do anything in the thirty-four years we've known each other, but if you don't come with me to Veracruz peacefully, I will drag you there. I'm scared too. I'm terrified, in fact, but Alma's right. Someone must stop these people and if Alma's the one, so be it. It's time."

"But, Papi, you more than anyone know what that man is capable of," pleaded her mother who was now crying.

"Yes, I know," said her father. "Alma, the time has come for me too. I want you to tell my story to Ricardo, to Gabriel. They should know what happened to El Rosario. What more do we need to know or to do?"

"As soon as Kurt and I leave, call a taxi. Don't take anything with you. Just walk out of the house as if you were going shopping."

"Who's going to take care of Dulce, Miss Smarty Pants and what about the house and my store?" said her mother angrier than ever.

"Lock everything up. Dulce ought to love the farm. The police will be watching the house. Listen carefully. Ricardo's wife is called Elvia. I have a new cell phone but unless it's an emergency, don't call me. Here's the number. Ricardo has arranged a safe house for me," she said as she went around to where her parents were sitting. She put an arm around them and whispered, "I promise nothing is going to happen to us."

Drawing in a deep breath as she walked out of the kitchen, Alma repeated over and over to herself: *Por favor, Virgencita,* take care of us, don't abandon us now.

When Kurt stepped out of the house and saw the two large black SUVs with their uniformed drivers and bodyguards, the party seemed to vanish from his mind. The wailing of the van's siren and the sight of the bodyguards hanging out of the windows of the two cars fascinated her son but did nothing to calm Alma's nerves. She knew that the vehicles were armored, but still she kept waiting for cars to pull up alongside and automatic weapons to start firing.

When they were about an hour into their journey and her mind more at ease, Alma put her arm around her son's shoulder and pulled him close.

"Is it tough for you these two different lives you lead, one in L.A. with your dad and one here with me?"

The boy thought for a moment, "No, I've gotten used to it. The only thing I don't like is when Grandma Lauren makes me speak Spanish to her friends."

"Does she have friends who speak Spanish?"

"No, they have no idea what I'm saying, so what's the point? They just say stuff like 'Isn't he smart' which is dumb too because how do they think I could live here if I couldn't talk to anyone?"

"I think your Grandmother Lauren is proud of you which is nice."

"But it's embarrassing, Mom. It makes me feel different, and I hate that."

Alma told him about Clyde who said he wanted his children just to be Mexican so that they felt they belonged somewhere. What did Kurt feel about that?

"I like being two kids, the American Kurt and the Mexican Kurt, but I wish I had a different name here. It's okay, it's fun, Mom. You worry too much."

As Kurt nodded his head and stretched out his legs, Alma looked at the shoes he was wearing. "Why did you put on those awful old shoes to go to L.A.? They're too small for you. What are your dad and Helen going to think?" A few seconds later the penny dropped. "I see," said Alma, "one way or other you're going to get those fancy tennis shoes back, aren't you?"

Kurt bowed his head, but she could see he was pleased.

"I think, Mom, maybe it isn't such a good idea to tell Dad and Helen about the guys who stole my shoes."

"I think you're right," said Alma. "We should keep that to ourselves. They might worry."

Chapter 18

SATURDAY, JANUARY 9TH, AFTERNOON

After Kurt had checked in for his flight, Alma looked at her watch. They still had an hour before he had to be at the gate. Lunch, she thought. She had totally forgotten that they haven't eaten since breakfast. As she turned to ask Kurt what he wanted to eat, a voice called out, "Alma?" A few feet away she spotted Steven Bennet rushing towards her carrying a briefcase and waving in the air what looked like his cell phone. A second later, he was on the ground, felled by one of the bodyguards, and she and Kurt were pushed behind their other protector.

"What the hell!" Steven shouted as a sizable crowd started to gather.

"Raul, no, he's a friend. Oh, so sorry, Steven. Please help him up, Raul." Alma stepped over to Steven whose phone and briefcase had slid out of his hands, and whose suit now didn't look so freshly pressed. She helped gather up his belongings as the bodyguards shooed the curious spectators away. An airport policeman walked over, but one of the bodyguards took out a card which seemed to satisfy the man's concerns. He nodded his head and walked away.

"Alma, what's going on? Who are these men? I guess this is your son, Kurt, right?" said Steven not without a little indignation.

"Yes, this is Kurt." The boy promptly stuck out his right hand to be shaken and politely said when it was, "I am pleased to meet you, sir."

"These two men are Raúl and Raulito, and, well, they're my bodyguards." The fact that the two men had the same name only added to the confusion, and Raulito was hardly "little Raul" either. He was more barrel-chested and muscular than his colleague.

"Have you had lunch, Steven? I think there's a food court over there," she said pointing to the far end of the airport.

When everyone had filled their trays with the fast food of their choice, Kurt went to sit with the Rauls. "They want me to show them my new video game," he said with a wink.

"Now, Alma, for the fifth time. What's going on?" said Steven.

"I was fired this morning by the Garcías. Well, it was Humberto *padre* who did the talking. Beto just looked like he wanted someone to throw him a life preserver. When I left that tongue lashing, I was briefly kidnapped by two men who made threats against my family and me. My editor, Ricardo Nuñez, and I decided that it would be best if Kurt and my parents were to take a vacation until the whole Jessica saga blows over. His cousin, the mayor, assigned me several protectors and a temporary residence."

"Curiously or maybe not, I got fired last night too."

"What, but why?"

"This is the most complicated assignment I've ever had and believe me I've been involved in some wild kidnappings. Just before I sent you that text last night, Humberto showed up at Beto's house. It must have been around 10:30; we were waiting for our friend, Mr. Metallic Voice, to confirm our final offer of ten million dollars. We also needed to know where to transfer the money. We were sitting in the living room drinking a beer and eating a sandwich, both of which Humberto refused as if he'd been offered arsenic. God, that man is an arrogant prick! Then Humberto's phone rang; he looked at the caller I.D. and headed into Beto's study across the hall. Even the closed wooden door didn't prevent us from hearing the shouting. After about ten minutes, he reappeared. He looked furious. 'It's over,' he said. 'They've accepted the ten million dollars. The money has to be wired tomorrow morning.'

"Beto and I looked at one another and then Beto asked why the kidnappers had called Humberto and not him. I said that if I didn't sign off on the deal, Lloyds wouldn't pay up. The Governor didn't answer our questions; he just picked up his jacket and started walking towards the front door. He turned and said that he wouldn't be asking Lloyds to honor the insurance policy. 'I preferred to pay the whole amount myself.' He thanked me and said he sent my colleagues his regards. 'I'll see you at 8:15 tomorrow morning,' were his parting words to Beto."

"But why did he refuse the insurance money?"

"Oh, that's easy," said Steven. "The kidnappers didn't want the money traced. After the victim is returned safely, we always try and recover the ransom. We are in the insurance business, but we also protect our shareholders. We call in Interpol and anyone else who can help us get the money back. Maybe Humberto will change his mind later, but my impression is that he has kissed the ten million dollars good-bye. I think he knows or suspects who's behind the kidnapping and that they have something very incriminating on him."

"Do you have any more idea after the days you spent talking to Mr. Metallic Voice who he might be?" said Alma taking a final sip of her coffee. "You had a lot of time with Beto too, do you still suspect him?"

"Look, Alma, as I said before, most kidnappings are carried out by criminals who have been tipped off by a disgruntled, greedy, current or ex-employee of the victim. But believe me, I've seen everything. Husbands who have their wives kidnapped and vice-versa. Business partners too, that's not uncommon. Classmates. You get a little cynical after a while. I don't see Beto extorting money from his father because despite everything there's a lot of affection there, but his wife's demands might have been more persuasive. Clyde Ramsay, he's a cynical bastard like me, and the Governor doesn't scare him. Then there are the Governor's political enemies or even his so-called friends. The Salvador Navarro Front can't be ignored either. Jessica's friends, family or acquaintances? Those Spiritist, for example, they are a strange bunch. Her friend, Gloria that lead was never checked out. I, myself, wouldn't rule out anyone." Steven threw his hands up in the air. "I think this one has us stumped."

"But don't forget that it's the Governor's thugs who threatened me."

"Maybe, but you don't know if those guys came from the Governor or some other interested party. Sorry, Alma, the waters here in Ávila are too muddy for me to see to the bottom of this mess. What are you going to do next?"

"I hope to be on the spot when Jessica is released tomorrow. Also, I'm like a dog with a bone. This story will stay buzzing around in my head until I know what it's all about."

Steven accompanied Kurt through security, together with the airline employee who was seeing her son to his flight. They turned and waved before disappearing through the Passengers Only doorway. Kurt looked like a miniature businessman pulling his small suitcase with one hand and clutching his computer with the other.

In the car on the return trip to Ávila, Alma looked at her watch. It was just after 3 P.M., time to call Gabriel. "Hey, you've got a new number," he said when he picked up.

"Richie lent me one of his phones. Things have gotten complicated. I'm so sorry but our dinner for tonight is off."

"What's up? Where are you?"

"I'm on the highway returning to Ávila. Kurt is on a plane heading out of Mexico. My parents have decided to take a vacation to parts unknown, and I'm no longer living at home. You warned me and I didn't listen. I feel lucky to be alive right now. Can I call you back when we can really talk? But Gabriel, be careful. There was a message for you too. I'll call you later, *un abrazo*."

When she arrived at the mayor's official residence, the two Rauls showed her to her apartment and posted themselves at what looked like a reinforced steel door. The apartment was small but comfortable. It included an alcove kitchen, a sitting room with a sofa, two chairs and a desk, a bedroom with a single bed and finally a bathroom big enough for one slim person. No exterior windows; thank God, she would be safe here. She unpacked her toothbrush, toothpaste, two pairs of panties and a simple night grown. Her skirt, blouse, and sweater would have to do for the next couple of days.

Just as she was about to stretch out on the sofa, Raulito knocked on the door. "The mayor would like to see you in his office if it's convenient."

The mayor's official residence ,which was used exclusively for his office and big official events, had once belonged to a rich Porfiriano family. Built towards the end of the 19th century, the elaborately curved staircase and large reception rooms must have been perfect for lavish evenings of dancing and showing off Paris gowns.

The mayor, Carlos Nuñez, ushered her into his office as soon as she knocked. He looked a little like his cousin Ricardo; but taller and stockier. His checks were covered by a closely cropped gray beard. His voice was deep and gruff in contrast to his warm brown eyes which showed concern.

"I'm so sorry, *Señorita* Jaramillo, that you and your family have had to abandon your home temporarily. We have tried to keep

Ávila a safe city, but our country is living through a very difficult time."

"I can't thank you enough, *Licenciado*, for taking me in but please call me Alma."

"Only if you call me Carlos or Charlie as Richie does."

"Delighted. Would you thank Captain Ramirez for me also? The two Rauls are very efficient." She pictured Steven spread eagle on the airport floor with his hands pinned behind his back.

The mayor, relaxing into a worn leather chair behind his desk, explained that the police investigation into Jessica's kidnapping had been mainly handled by the Federal Police, but he'd been in constant contact with them. There was, however, one piece of the puzzle which he hadn't passed on to them which Alma might find interesting after her experience this morning with the Governor. Last Tuesday, midday he'd received a call from Humberto García on his private land line which was tapped because, as she could imagine, he'd received more than few threats over the years. If the Governor had thought it out, he would have realized that he was being recorded, but he'd been one angry, out-of-control guy. Inserting a tape into a recorder on his desk, Carlos said with obvious delight, "Listen to this."

"Hello," she heard the mayor say as he answered the call. The Governor's voice came screaming down the line. "*Hijo de puta*, did you and your faggot friends think you were going to ruin me by kidnapping my daughter-in-law? Do you think that I'm the only one behind my party? As far as I'm concerned, you can keep that girl forever. I'm not paying a penny to rescue her because this isn't about her. It's about me and politics. ¡*Vete a la chingada*!"

Alma sat back in her chair. "Has he ever called you before with messages like that?"

"No, never. We pretty much avoid one another and communicate through our staffs, if necessary. But that's not the end of it. Listen to the message I got yesterday afternoon about 5 o'clock." He fast forwarded the tape.

"Hello," again the Mayor's voice. Then "Carlos, Humberto here. How are you? Listen I wanted to apologize for that call last Tuesday. You can imagine the stress we were under when the kidnappers contacted us. I jumped to some very hasty conclusions. No hard feelings I hope. You'll be glad to hear that Jessica's coming home on Sunday. I have a favor to ask you because we don't want any more screw-ups. Could you tell Captain Ramirez to put a hold on his part of the investigation? I've asked the same of the Feds. When Jessica is safe and sound, we'll be in touch again."

Carlos turned off the recorder. "I agreed, of course. But what do you make of these calls?"

"The timing of the second message makes sense because both the negotiator from Lloyds and I were fired last night or this morning. Thank you, Carlos. All I can say is that I'm going to add this information to all the confusing data in my head and try to process it."

Suddenly exhausted Alma returned to her hideaway and lay down on the sofa for a ten-minute nap. Just as she was dozing off, her old cell phone rang. She picked it up quickly and looked at the caller I.D. she immediately answered when she saw it was Luz María.

"Alma, where have you been? It's Luz María. We've been trying to reach you all morning. Leandro is staying with me, and he wants to talk to you about Javier Arias."

"Sorry, Luz María, I've had quite a day. Could you two meet me at the Sanborns near the Mayor's residence?"

At this time of day there would be lots of people in the restaurant, and with the two Rauls, it should be safe. She wouldn't be giving away where she was staying either.

"Okay, we'll be there in twenty minutes."

Alma picked a booth. The two Rauls seated themselves a few tables away. Luz María and Leandro slid in next to her a few minutes later. Leandro was a man in his fifties, much better looking than his photograph. He smiled broadly at Alma and shook her hand gently taking precaution not to squeeze too tightly. He knows his own strength, she thought.

"Thank you so much, Leandro for taking time out of your trip to see us. I don't know if Luz María told you, but we are particularly interested in locating Javier Arias. Did you make friends with him? Do you know where he lives in Mexico City?"

"I wouldn't consider him a friend; I think of him as does Luz María as a new soul or perhaps a lost soul. He worried me because he was a young man, but he seemed weighed down by so many troubles. He called me the last day I was in Mexico City, maybe three weeks ago, and suggested we have coffee because he wanted to discuss something with me. I arranged to meet him in Polanco.

"We talked about the séance in Ávila, and I asked him if he had a family. He said he had an older brother who was always in trouble: drugs, women, money. His brother had gone to good schools and started university but had begun selling drugs and running with a rough crowd. I asked him about his parents. He said that his mother had been sick off and on for some time and that his father had another woman. The boys saw him rarely.

"Then he asked me what Spiritism taught about the end justifying the means. I said that it depended on how bad the means were. It certainly wouldn't help him for his next reincarnation; doing good work was what earned us a better life. Frankly, his eyes glazed over while I was speaking. I thought that he'd made up his mind; nothing I could say would change it. We parted company, and I haven't heard from him since."

"So, Javier has a brother and a mother," said Alma. "Did he mention anyone else?"

"No, only the absent father."

"Have you had any call back from your aunts, Luz María?"

"No, they promised to call tomorrow morning after church."

When Alma returned to the apartment, it was already 6:30. "Just ten minutes," she said as she stretched out on the sofa.

"Hey in there, open up. I'm here with dinner." Ricardo's voice unmistakably.

"What time is it anyway?" asked a sleepy Alma.

"Dinner time, it's after eight."

"I conked out for over an hour."

"I should think so. It hasn't been an exactly restful day," said Ricardo unpacking a big pizza and a six-pack of her favorite beer. He asked how the trip to the airport had gone; she related her encounter with Steven and their conversation. She added her meetings with Carlos, Luz María, and Leandro.

Between bites of pizza and sips of beer, they discussed the way the Governor's role in the negotiation had gone full cycle from Tuesday to Friday. "You know what I really don't get, Richie, is this. If the Governor is being forced to take the whole burden of the ransom on himself because the kidnappers are holding something over him, why go to all the trouble of a kidnapping? Why not just blackmail him outright from the beginning?"

"Because, Alma, I think crimes are like the rest of life. We think we have the perfect plan and then there's a screw-up. The kidnappers had a straightforward idea: kidnap Jessica María, ask for twenty million dollars, bargain probably until the family offered fifteen million dollars. But something went wrong. They had to speed up the negotiation maybe even accept a lesser payoff. I think they panicked. In the end, they forced the Governor's hand with some information which was very damaging."

"But why did the original plan go off the rails?"

"I think it was you, Alma. You stumbled onto something that sent the fear of God into them, and they had to implement a very thrown together Plan B. What's your most important discovery?"

"Javier Arias, Mr. Shades, without a doubt."

"Okay, what do we know about Arias, and who could be associated with him?"

"You heard his voice. He's a guy from Mexico City, with a privileged background; not rich maybe but private schools and, possibly, a good university."

"What else do we know about Javier?"

"He was helped by two accomplices, maybe a woman, certainly a man. Now I think that they're his brother and his mother. He's good at insinuating himself into people's lives. He's smart, charming. I would also say that through his brother he has a connection to organized crime."

"Alright," said Ricardo, "let's start to work out a few scenarios. You know who, why and how? Can we start to put the pieces of the puzzle together?"

"Before we do that," said Alma, "I have another idea. Up 'til now, we've thought of Jessica as a pawn in this kidnapping. You know that it's a straightforward financial transaction: money in exchange for her life. I've been thinking today, what if it's about revenge?"

"What do you mean?"

"Look, Jessica has her admirers, mostly men, but her staff and Luz María seem to love and admire her. She has, however, a few people who dislike or maybe even hate her, namely, Lucía, Catherine, her Aunt Renata and the Governor. She also has a few individuals who could resent their financial dependence on her, like Sami and Gloria."

"The question is how desperate or cruel do you have to be to carry out a crime as despicable as kidnapping?" said Ricardo. "Frankly, I see money as being a much more likely motive than revenge. Also, call me a *macho,* but I see this crime as being planned and carried out by men."

"Maybe, you're right about the money angle, but as far as it being a man, I disagree. Some of the women I just mentioned seem to me to be callous enough."

"It's getting late. I have three young reporters who I can assign to check out the most likely suspects. They can start tomorrow first thing."

"Okay," said Alma taking out her notebook. "I think the suspects break down into three groups: Desperate Business People, the Governor's Political Enemies, and the Wild Cards. In the first group are Beto, Claude, Gloria Sandoval and Jessica, herself. They all might have been desperate enough for money to try a stunt like this. Steven has plenty of evidence that kidnapping can be a family affair. None of them are particularly principled, and some are professional actors. Some like Clyde have access to the underworld. You'll remember that it was Clyde who suggested getting kidnapping insurance.

"Among the Governor's political enemies are the various political parties he's been associated with and, of course, the Salvador Navarro Front. Could Javier Arias be an urban guerilla? He wouldn't be the first modern day Robin Hood out to save the world, robbing the rich to give to the poor.

"In the third group, the Wild Cards, we have the Spiritists. Maybe I'm wrong, and Javier Arias is a genuine believer. Perhaps he thought with a cash box full of dollars, he could spread the word of the Fidencian Christian Church to the far corners of the world. Next we have Sami. He's sensitive and secretive, and we no idea what his financial situation is. But it can't be that good. There's Cécile Reynaud, also. Clyde trashed her successful C.V., and Lucía has evidence of the Governor's skirt chasing. We also can't forget Aunt Renata who even offered herself up as a suspect. That seems too obvious, however. She's such a goody-goody.

"Lucía, Beto's sister, hates Jessica. She's smart if unstable. But how she could be connected to Arias is beyond me. Martha, the cook, certainly knows Jessica well and could want a life independent of the Garcías. How she'd love to go to Paris! Then there's Catherine. She barely copes in her limited, protected world. Her life seems constrained by her religion, but there's an older woman involved in the kidnapping, and she is her ex-husband's stooge."

"Just hearing all the options has exhausted me," said Ricardo. "Let's pick three prime suspects so I can get home to bed."

"I'd say your guys should check out Beto, Clyde, and Gloria. I'll get in touch with Luz María again to see if she has anything new on Javier. I'll also see what I can find out about Catherine, Cécile, and Lucía."

As Ricardo picked up the beer cans and the pizza box and stuffed them into a black garbage bag, he said, "Hey, what an idiot I am! I almost forgot to tell you. We had a call about the ad we put in the paper with Juan Carlos Lara's photograph. You know Jessica's father. It was a woman, sounded older. She says her name is Ana Cardoso de Pérez, and she thinks the photo is of her brother. I asked her to come into the office tomorrow morning, and if she seems legit, we'll be over here to talk to you, say at around 10:30."

When Ricardo left, Alma pulled out her phone and called Gabriel. "Hey," she said softly.

"God, Alma, I've been sick with worry. Can you talk now? What's going on?"

When the whole story of the morning's events had been related and commented on, he said, "Alma you're going to hate me. I think I lost you your job. The guys who took that picture were, I'm sure, tailing me. I've felt for the last couple days that I was being followed."

"Look, Gabriel, the Garcías were going to get rid of me anyway. Beto had hinted more than once that the Governor didn't want me on the investigation. He's got too much to hide. Jessica is supposedly being released tomorrow. I'd love to be there when it happens, if it's not some isolated spot in the mountains. I'll call you if I find out anything."

There was a brief pause on the line. "Alma, I've been thinking about you all day, and I was so looking forward to this evening."

Hanging up Alma had to smile to herself. Maybe, just maybe, she speculated Gabriel's broken heart was starting to mend.

The unaccustomed bed and the events of the day made Alma's dreams that night a series of frightening traps from which there was no escape, only prolonged and frustrating struggles. First, she was enmeshed in a giant web spun by an iridescent green spider as big as a man. The snare which stretched across the entrance to the Governor's study was made from long strands of bubble gum which stuck to her hands and hair. The spider web gave way to a spooky house composed of empty rooms in which she was held captive. She could hear footsteps echoing from the other rooms but no front door, window or person offered her a way out. When she awoke at three A.M., she was covered in sweat. Groaning, she rolled over hoping that the three hours until daybreak would pass quickly.

Chapter 19

SUNDAY, JANUARY 10TH, MORNING
AND EARLY AFTERNOON

A knock on the front door woke Alma from a deep morning sleep. Since the bedroom was windowless, she had no idea of the time. "Who is it?" she called out.

"Raulito, I've got some breakfast for you." She turned on the overhead light and looked at her cell phone, ten o'clock; she hadn't slept that badly after all. She found a terrycloth robe in the bathroom and opened the front door. A paper bag awaited her with yogurt, sweet rolls, a small carton of milk and two apples. She thanked Raulito and asked if she could reimburse him. "Compliments of the mayor," he said and went back to reading the sports page in El Diario.

Alma showered while the water boiled for coffee. She had just finished her apple and yogurt when she heard a second knock on the door. "Alma," Ricardo's voice called out, "I'm here with Ana Cardoso."

The woman who entered ahead of Ricardo looked to be in her early sixties. Tall, slim, classic features, light olive skin, she was dressed in black slacks, a floral print blouse and a black cable-knit cardigan. Her thick shoulder length gray hair seemed to curl under naturally in an attractive pageboy. She wore red lipstick, and her eyes were highlighted with black eyeliner. Alma could immediately see that she was uneasy. Her eyes darted around the room and then settled on Alma as if to say, please make what I'm doing not be the worst mistake of my life.

"Can I get you both some coffee?"

"No thanks," her guests answered in unison.

"The *Señora* Cardoso has a very interesting story to tell us, Alma. She has been very brave to come forward. It tells us a great deal about the mysterious disappearances we've been looking into over the last week. Do you mind, *Señora*, if I record your brother's story?"

"No, if I have come this far, I would like what I'm going to tell you to be on the record." Her voice was full-throated, confident. Alma felt that the woman needed to relate her account without interruption. If there were doubts, they could go back later and verify the information.

"It brought back so many memories when I saw my brother's picture in your paper on Friday," began Ana. "I hadn't seen him for more than twenty years, and then it was only for a few hours. He left Ávila more than thirty years ago. I should tell you, however, the whole story from the beginning. My parents were Dutch. At least they had Dutch passports. They were also Jews,

Sephardic Jews, originally from Spain but their community had been in Amsterdam for four hundred and fifty years.

"I never knew my grandparents. They and most of their families died in the concentration camps. My parents who didn't know each other before the war survived in different ways. My mother, Raquel, came from a well-to-do Amsterdam family. Her father was a banker. She was fluent in French, Ladino, and Dutch. My grandfather was able to save her because he had business dealings with Trappist orders in Belgium, and in 1940, when she was fourteen the nuns agreed to accept her as a novice in the Scourmont Abbey. She stayed with them until 1945. My father, Abram, came from a poor family. He was sixteen in 1940, staying with a brother in Rotterdam when the war broke out and the terrible bombing of the city began. He always said he survived because he had the instincts of a water rat.

"My parents met in a displaced persons camp at the end of 1945. Most of the people there were on their way to Israel. My father, however, had an uncle in Mexico who had immigrated in the 1920s. He sponsored my parents' trip to this country. For a couple of years, my parents lived in Mexico City. My father worked with his uncle as, I guess you could call it, a 'motorized peddler.' His uncle had a small van in which they packed pots, pans, cloth and, most of all, Bibles. They sold their goods in the small towns around the southern and central part of Mexico. That's how my father discovered Ávila. They stayed here for only one night, but he decided he wanted to live here. Why? He never explained it. I think it was because it was small, peaceful and out of the way.

"There wasn't a synagogue here, of course, so my brother never had a Bar Mitzvah, but we celebrated the holidays and lit candles and said prayers every Friday evening. My father opened a small jewelry shop which my mother managed, and he, a die-hard tinkerer, repaired gas boilers, lawn movers, whatever was mechanical. I think, despite being a world away from Holland, they were content. My mother never got over her fear of author-ity. An unexpected knock on the door could send her into a total panic. I do believe that the pure terror she sometimes experienced made David and me very fearful too. Her panic attacks annoyed my father. 'It's nothing, Raquel. Go lie down for a minute. It's only a neighbor at the door,' he would say.

"We lived in an apartment over the store which by the way, still exists. My brother, David, was born in 1950 and I, in 1952. At six, we started at the neighborhood public school, made friends and became Mexicans. I tell my children that we were like all those new drinks you find in the supermarkets these days. You know those vodkas flavored with mandarin orange or raspberry. We were Mexican, but, like many immigrants, we were a bit exotic.

"Our favorite bedtime story was my father's account of Rotterdam during the war. David loved to hear about the air-planes, German or Allied, which flew over the city constantly. He and my father began to build model airplanes from small kits when David was very little. I don't think my brother ever doubted he would become a pilot. When he was eighteen, he joined the Mexican Air Force and was trained to fly cargo planes. He wanted to fly fighter jets but for some reason didn't quite make the grade. In 1981, he was assigned to the Mexican Army air base here in Ávila. You might remember that before the civil airport was built, we had a small military airport.

"Then something terrible happened. My parents were killed in an automobile accident on the way home from a wedding in Mexico City. Here they had survived the War, and they were killed coming home from my cousin Esther's wedding. David and I were beside ourselves. They were the only family we had really ever know. I took over the jewelry store, but it was too lonely living in that apartment surrounded by ghosts. We had a client who brought in his watch every few months to be serviced. Jaime was an accountant ten years older than me, but within a year we were married and living in one of the new suburbs on the edge of Ávila. I sold the store and gave half the profits to David.

"We had David over to dinner at least once a week. I wanted him to get out of the Air Force and go into civil aviation which was booming. Towards the end of 1983, maybe it was November, I can't remember because I was pregnant with my first child and in kind of a daze. Anyway, my husband had gone off to work, and I was enjoying a second cup of coffee when there was a tapping on the back door. It was David. He lurched into the kitchen and pulled down the blinds. His uniform was filthy, and he was pale as a ghost.

"He said he was in very serious trouble and had to get far away from Ávila. He needed new clothes and money. I didn't ask him any questions, but I couldn't imagine what had happened. I gave him one of my husband's old suits, and the nest egg we kept in the house for emergencies. He told me that he had to go away and not to tell anyone he had been here. It was now, he said, very dangerous to know him. He said to burn his uniform which I did immediately. A few days later several officials knocked on our door looking for him. We said we had no idea where he was. I told my husband that I had given his old suit to a beggar and replaced our emergency fund the next day from my savings.

"Thank God, the baby came. It was my first daughter. She saved my life. Imagine losing your parents and your brother in a few short years. I thought of him often, picturing him in Paraguay or Ecuador, some country where people didn't ask too many questions. I always hoped that someday, somehow, I would hear from him. We had three more children over the next ten years. My husband wasn't Jewish, but he was a good man and happy to participate in the dinners I organized for the Jewish holidays, and, like my mother, I still light candles and say prayers every Friday night."

Ana suddenly stopped speaking. She looked around the room. Then smiling shyly, she said, "I need a cigarette. Can you wait while I go outside for a minute?"

"What do you think?" Alma said when the door was closed. "I'm totally intrigued," answered Ricardo.

"Julia, my youngest, was only a few months old," continued Ana when she returned, "and everyone else was out that summer Saturday when the doorbell rang. Thank God, we were still in the same house. I couldn't believe my eyes. There was David. Ten years older but still as handsome as ever. We hugged each other so tightly I lost my breath. He asked if I was alone. 'Come,' he said, 'let's take a ride. It's safer.'

"With the baby in the back seat, we drove on little-used roads to the old military airfield which was now abandoned. I could tell David was nervous. Every few minutes he would check the rear-view mirror. 'This was probably a bad idea, too dangerous,' he said more than once. We parked at the end of the weedy runway. David put his head down on the steering wheel. 'Fate is so cruel, Ana. All I ever wanted was an ordinary life. But I ended up living like our father did during the war, hidden, staying in the shadows. I must have asked myself a million times over the years, why me? Why didn't the gunman choose the pilot in the first bunk?' I asked him what had happened. Why did he have to hide? Why did he run away? "

Ana stopped telling her story for a moment and reached into her handbag. She drew out a dirty plastic folder containing several sheets of the paper covered in tiny script. "I'm going to read you my brother's account of what happened to him because I think you should hear it in his own words."

"'On the night of November 11th, I was on duty at the Ávila Air Force Base. I had been given leave for three days but the wife of another pilot was having a baby, and he had asked me to switch days with him. It was all the same to me, so I did. We were an out of the way airbase, basically a refueling stop. We had half a dozen cargo planes which were used to drop supplies when the coastal areas were flooded or there was an earthquake, but I played a lot of poker with the other airmen. We had a small barracks where the pilots, cook and maintenance people slept. The commander of the base was a washed-up officer, an old drunk who kept his job because someone in power remembered him fondly from cadet school.

"We had lights out at eleven o'clock as usual, and I was fast asleep when I felt someone shake my shoulder. I opened my eyes, and there was a large man dressed in civilian clothes pointing a gun at my head. He put a finger to his lips and beckoned me to follow him. He had my uniform which had been folded at the foot of my bed under his other arm together with a pair of my shoes. When we got to the recreation room outside of where we bunked, I started to speak, but he pointed the gun at me and ordered me to dress. When I had finished dressing, he threw me an aviator jacket which was hanging on a peg on the wall.

"Still speaking in a whisper, he ordered me to walk towards the planes. I think it was only when the cold night air hit my face that I realized that this was not a nightmare, but it was so outside any experience I had ever had that I seemed spellbound. When we neared one of the Lockheed C-130 that we flew, he tossed me a key and ordered me into the pilot's seat. I suppose as he walked around the plane, I could have tried to escape, but I had become paralyzed with fear. Ten minutes hadn't gone by when a car pulled up. Three men got out: the driver who appeared to be in his early twenties and two goons. The cabin and cargo doors of the plane were open, so I could see everything that went on. The two burly men opened the trunk of the car and lifted out what appeared to be a body or maybe an unconscious man. They threw him onto the floor of the plane. The driver hovered in front of the car, but his face was perfectly reflected in the headlights. A look of revulsion crossed his face when he saw the body.

"Just then the gunman turned around and said to me, 'None of your business' and closed the cabin door. He shouted to the driver to park the car and wait for our return. Suddenly the runway lights came on, and he ordered me to get going. 'But where to?' I asked. 'The Gulf' was his answer, but I was to fly north of the city of Veracruz so as not to appear on the airport radar. I had flown many times to Veracruz but never at night and never without constant communication with the air controllers in the region. We did reach the coast without a problem and after about twenty minutes, 'the boss,' as I now thought of the man sitting next to me, ordered me to fly lower. When I indicated that I was as low as it was safe to go, he knocked on the cabin door. I heard the cargo door open, the sound of a scuffle and a loud bang as the door was shut again. The boss turned me and said, 'Okay let's get home.'

"It was then that I realized that this man would never let me walk away from the airfield alive. I decided that the only way to survive was to get them as disorientated as possible. The ride back was as rough as I could make it. 'Can't you fly better than this,' he asked me. 'Weather has changed,' I answered. When we approached Ávila, I radioed to the control tower that they should turn on the runway lights although I had no idea who was there, and I didn't recognize the voice that answered me. The landing was the most violent that I could manage. The boss next to me cracked his head on the plane's ceiling. I thought that we might blow a tire. I sped as fast as I dared to near where the rest of the fleet was parked. I slammed on the brakes and while the gunmen were recovering, jumped out of the plane and ran, darting under the wings of the other planes. Luckily, the runway lights had been turned off almost as soon as we landed. The men followed me, of course, shouting, swearing and shooting, but I got away. I knew the airfield like the back of my hand. I hid in the bushes around the field for a few hours; then, I hitchhiked to my sister's house. I swear that the young man driving the car for the thugs was the politician, Humberto Efrain García de León, Ávila's present Minister of Agriculture, and I have never doubted that the man pushed out of the plane was Salvador Navarro, the community organizer from El Rosario.'

"I was speechless when he finished reading his account. When I recovered, I said 'But, David, those kinds of things don't happen in our country.'

"'Well, they did,' he said putting the sheets back in the plastic folder and handing me the packet. 'Keep this safe for me, Ana, and if something happens to me, I want you to deliver it to the newspapers. But be careful. Humberto García will do anything to hide his role in Salvador's murder.' We chatted while he drove me home. 'What have you done with your life for the last ten years?' I asked him.

"'I never left the country. I'm married and have two kids. Here let me show you a photograph. This is Renata. Isn't she beautiful? And that's Sami. He's a good-looking boy and very smart. After all these years, I think I'm safe, but I'm not going to tell you any more about my life so as not to endanger yours.'

"When we reached the house, David kissed me and the baby good-bye. I had this terrible feeling I would never see him again. As he instructed me, I buried the papers in a forgotten corner of the back yard. My life went on; the children took up much of my time. They were such happy children. Susana, the oldest and Julia, the youngest had a real talent for dancing, like my brother, David. All the girls always wanted to dance with David.

"Maybe ten years after David had come by the house, I saw a picture in Vogue of a stunning young model named Renata. I just knew it was David's daughter. A few years later she started to appear on television and changed her name to Jessica María. When she announced that she was engaged to the Governor's son, you can imagine the anger and sorrow I felt. How could she marry the son of the man who had ruined her father's life? Since I never found a mention of her parents in the articles, I was sure they were gone. I was sick about the wedding but felt helpless to stop it. Two of my children were still at home, and my husband had his business. I knew I had my mother's terror of authority, but I couldn't see anyway of exposing the Governor that wouldn't place my family in danger.

"My husband died two years ago. My children are now all over the place. My two boys live in San Diego. Susana married a Spaniard and lives in Barcelona. Can you imagine after five hundred years, someone from our family returning to Spain? Julia is in Argentina learning the tango. About a year ago, I dug up the document my brother had given me and had a copy made, but I still didn't know what to do with his story.

"This Thursday a fancy car from the federal police with a uniformed driver pulled up to my door. Two young men got out. They showed me their credentials and said that they were part of a special task force investigating corruption in our state government. They asked if I was David Cardoso's sister. They said that they knew he had deserted the Air Force in November 1983 but since he was such a decorated airman, they wondered why he had run away. They said that there had been reports of an unauthorized flight the evening of November 11, and they wondered if he had been involved. If he were still alive, they would like to hear what had happened to him."

"So, you gave them the document," said Alma.

"I gave them the copy of the document and told them it was the only one I had. It seemed at the time like an easy way to bring David's story to the attention of the authorities without putting me in the spotlight. But the next day I saw your ad in the newspaper with David's picture, and I remembered that he had asked me to go to the newspapers, not to the authorities. So, I called Mr. Nuñez."

Alma picked up her bag, took out the photograph of the séance and showed it to Ana. "Do you recognize anyone in this photograph?"

"The Governor's wife of course. Oh, no, the man with the sunglasses, he was one of the men who came to my door, the special agent from the Federal Police. Is he involved with the

Governor? With David's enemy? What have I done? "she said fear now raising the level of her voice to almost a scream.

"No, I don't believe he's involved with the Governor, but I don't think he's a member of the Feds either," said Ricardo. "Ana, you've done a very brave thing for your brother, but I would feel much better if you went on a visit to one of your children, the further away, the better."

Ana took a tissue from her purse and began to wipe her tears. "After all these years, I thought I was finally doing something to clear my brother's name and instead I have messed it up."

"No, you haven't," said Alma. "His story is going to get out and soon. But we must get you to a safe place. Do you have your credit cards with you? We need you to get to the airport as soon as possible and book a flight to Argentina or Spain."

"But my two dogs and my cats who will look after them?"

"We'll take care of everything. We'll find a neighbor to feed them."

"Maybe Spain is best," said Ana. "I've been trying to persuade my oldest grandson who is ten that he should have a Bar Mitzvah."

"Let us know a phone number of where to reach you when you arrive at your destination," said Ricardo. "We don't want to know where you are; just how to get in touch with you."

Alma threw herself down on the sofa after Ricardo had returned from organizing Ana's trip to the airport.

"Richie, this is crazy. Do you realize the bomb we have in our hands? We now have proof that our Governor was involved in the death of Salvador Navarro and most probably the deaths of Jessica and Sami's parents. How is Jessica ever going to be reconciled to having married the son of her parents' killer?

"You once said that the elites in this city could be fitted on the head of a pin, but Jessica wasn't even part of Beto's world, although our politicians do seem to like glamor girls. You know what it is, it's like some puppet master is controlling our fates. The Spiritists, of course, wouldn't be at all surprised. I wonder if Javier Arias knew the Governor's dirty secrets, and if that's how he lured Jessica into his trap? If I were writing a novel, I would be embarrassed to include something as farfetched as Jessica marrying Beto or for that matter Javier Arias discovering Ana Cardoso's secret. What do writers call that?"

"Deus Ex Machine," said Ricardo smiling. "The probability of Jessica and Beto meeting is rather low, but since her only vacation, as a child was to Ávila, she would've had an interest in revisiting the city. The children knew deep down that Juan Carlos was somehow connected to this place. If we do manage to reveal the Governor's role in the deaths of Salvador, Juan Carlos, and Rosalba, then Beto and Jessica are going to have a tough time, but I worry more about how to pin the Governor's crimes on him. He's so slippery and has been so clever in covering his tracks that he could escape again.

"Your other point about Javier Arias discovering Ana Cardoso's secret is easier to explain. Look, we know that the person or persons behind the kidnapping know Ávila well. There've been rumors for years about the disappearance of Salvador Navarro, and I've heard it mentioned many times that dissidents in those years were disposed of in the Gulf. Didn't they even bury Osama bin Laden at sea? Maybe for different reasons but bodies lost at sea are rarely recovered.

"Would getting the information on David Cardoso be that hard if you had access to Air Force records? I don't think so. How many deserters from Ávila were there in November 1983? I bet just one and who was his next of kin, Ana Cardoso. This is a small city; people can be found easily. The Arias family were fishing for information, and the visit to see Ana paid off. Yes, they got lucky, just as poor David was so terribly unlucky. It makes me totally convinced that Clyde is our man. Who else on our list has friends in high places that could give him access to Air Force records?"

"Maybe," said Alma. "I know that this might sound flimsy, but Clyde is a professional. I can't see him using Arias and his amateur night family. Not that they haven't been efficient. Still, I see Clyde going right to a trustworthy connection in organized crime and asking the professionals to handle it."

"Sorry, I'm the kind of newspaperman that goes with hunches. I'm putting my three staffers on Clyde, right now. What are your plans for today?"

"I'm just about to call Sami to see if he knows where Jessica is being released, and if it's anywhere I can get to, I want to be there. I'll call you later."

"Okay, but you don't leave here without the Rauls."

"You think I haven't learned my lesson? Thanks for everything, Richie."

When Sami picked up, and after chatting for a minute, Alma asked if he had any new information about Jessica's release. "Beto just called me about an hour ago and said she was going to be dropped off in front of the Santa Teresa village church at 6 P.M."

"What? In the middle of the fair? The fireworks start at six. That's insane! Why do they want such a public place?"

"Beto had no say in the matter, but I imagine the kidnappers want to avoid a shootout. Even if the police are standing down, they must want a place where the presence of so many bystanders makes that impossible."

"Are you going to be there?"

"Yes, I'll leave for Ávila in about a half an hour."

"I'll be hiding in the background."

As she was looking over the slim pickings for lunch, namely an apple and some sweet rolls, her old cell phone rang. It was Luz María again.

"Alma, my cousin from Monclova called a few minutes ago. I feel so awful. No one in the family knows Javier Arias. My aunt even made fun of me when I described him. 'He couldn't be a Coutiño. You said he had little hands. I bet he has tiny feet too.' What have I done? Jessica's kidnapping is my fault."

"I don't think anyone would say that, Luz María. If they hadn't gotten to her through you, they'd have found another way," said Alma placing the phone between her shoulder and her right ear so she could start to peel her apple.

"Yes, but I should have known that he wasn't a Coutiño, even a Coutiño who had lived in Mexico City for most of his life. What Coutiño ever spoke fluent French?"

"What's that, what did you say?" said Alma dropping her apple and putting the phone close to her ear. "Javier Arias speaks French?"

"Oh yes," said Luz María. "One day we were coming out of a restaurant downtown, and there was a couple arguing over a map. Javier went over to them and started to speak in what seemed to me to be perfect French. The couple was pleased. You know how nice it is when you find yourself in a foreign country and someone speaks your language. I asked Javier later where he had learned French. He shrugged his shoulders and said. 'Oh, I studied it at school.' Truthfully I was so concerned with other things, I didn't think anything more about it."

"Thank you so much, Luz María. That's the best piece of information I've had all week."

Alma was so excited that she dialed Sami's number wrong three times before she finally got hold of him. "I can't tell you yet, but I think I know who's behind the kidnapping. Was there a private website set up for Beto and Jessica's wedding?"

"Yes, it's huge."

"Are there pictures of the guests?"

"Yep, all sixteen hundred. There were two hundred tables."

"Can you give me your username and password for the site?"

"Sure, let me look them up."

Alma immediately accessed the site and to her surprise, the username and password worked. It was all there: the invitation, the guest list, the bridesmaids, the best man, the families, photos of the church wedding and the reception. Please Oh please, she thought make the photos be labeled, and to her relief they were. If Louisa Michel and family were invited, they were not going to be among the most honored guests. So, Alma started at table one hundred fifty and worked her up way up towards table two hundred. She was not surprised that the Governor's political friends had so many tables and Jessica María's friends seemingly, so few.

At table one hundred eighty-six Alma began to despair. Perhaps Cécile's family didn't go because they didn't know anyone. Or perhaps they didn't make the cut. Then at table one hundred ninety-three, there they were: 'Mr. Shades' whose real name she now knew was Philippe Rebollero Michel; his brother, Guy Rebollero Michel, his mother Louisa Michel de Rebollero; his father, General Miguel Rebollero Sánchez. Everyone in the family was smiling for the camera except Mr. Shades.

Alma sighed a huge sigh of relief, she had found them. It was Cécile all along. Lady Bountiful, dressed smartly in Dior or Channel, was when you came down to it a common criminal. The lady banker who took kickbacks, the Panamanian bank representative who promised a tax-free safe haven for your ill-gotten nest egg had up the stakes. How could I have missed it, Alma thought. Now that it had been thrown in her face, it seemed so obvious. But of course, like finding gold nuggets in a stream, you had to pan all the pebbles before the prize appeared.

She called Ricardo, "You have to come back right now. I don't know it all, but I know a lot."

"The problem," said Ricardo after congratulating Alma, "is that all we have is circumstantial evidence. We can prove from Luismi's evidence that three people abducted Jessica. We can prove that Philippe Rebollero used a false name to ingratiate himself into Jessica's Spiritist group. We can prove that Cécile knew about the Spiritist meetings. We can prove that our intrepid trio visited Ana Cardoso and collected incriminating evidence against the Governor. I suppose we can prove that Philippe picked up Jessica at her home the day of the kidnapping using the alias, Javier Arias.

"But we go back to our brick wall, a governor who doesn't want anyone sniffing around in his business and for good reason. He won't prosecute, and I'll bet you anything that Beto won't either. Jessica has a mind of her own, but she will be under enormous pressure to keep her mouth shut. The only person I can think of who would like to get his money back is Clyde, but, if he blows the whistle on the Governor, he'd better have a Plan B in Houston."

"Why do you think Cécile got involved in such a risky scheme, Richie? Why did her cousins go along with it? Kidnapping a TV star and blackmailing a governor who plays hardball, what was she thinking?"

"You know you mentioned revenge last night and I poo-pooed it, but now I think you were right. Cécile saw her golden future going down the drain. Just like Catherine said, our Governor gets a different woman for every new phase of his life. I bet anything there's a prenup which allows Cécile to keep her expensive wardrobe, her jewelry and paintings but no alimony, no right to property and no financial settlement. She just never figured the fairy tale would end; that Humberto would decide to trade her in for a new model. 'Hell, has no fury like a woman scorned.' I'm not saying that the money is secondary because it isn't, but her first impulse was to stick the knife in deep, to wound. The cousins seem like lost souls. Their excuse for stealing other people's money is their sick mother, pathetic. Their guilty father who abandoned his children years ago was played for privileged information, what a bunch!"

"Let's dig a little deeper, Richie. Let me call Álvaro Jimenez, to see if Cécile is still in Ávila because if I were she, as soon as the money was deposited, I would have flown the coop. Also, maybe I can get an address for the Rebolleros. Do you think Captain Ramirez would be willing to check out an address if we could find one?"

She tried to sound as casual as possible. "Álvaro, it's Alma Jaramillo. I met you a few days ago at the Governor's hacienda."

"Sure. How are you?" said the cheerful secretary. "I imagine you've been trying to reach Cécile. She left for Paris last night, but I can give you an email if it's urgent." Alma nodded her head to indicate to Ricardo that she had been right about Cécile.

"Actually, I wanted the address of Louisa Michel, her cousin."

"Whatever for?"

"We've decided to do a story on the First Lady of the state of Tepetlán, and I just wanted a little background. You know about the year she spent in Mexico as a teenager. That sort of stuff."

"She took her address book with her. For the short stay, she said she was planning; she certainly took a lot of stuff with her. I'm at home, but I could look for it tomorrow."

"Do you have any idea where they live in the city just in case I have to make a trip in today?"

"I think they were living in a rented apartment in Polanco. Louisa was receiving chemotherapy at the Military Hospital."

"Does Cécile have a chauffeur? Could you give me his name and number?"

"Look, Alma, I don't think the Governor would like me giving the press personal information about his staff."

"I think you're right, but I'll never say where it came from. Please, Álvaro."

"Okay, but don't tell anyone that I gave you his number. He's Eduardo. I think the last name is Bello."

"It's almost four o'clock Richie. I need to leave for Santa Teresa at around five. Should we see if Captain Ramirez would be willing to try and get some information out of Eduardo?"

"Nothing to lose as far as I can see," said Ricardo rubbing his hands together.

Chapter 20

SUNDAY, JANUARY 10TH, EVENING

A lma had barely enough time to finish her apple and to text Gabriel, "5:45 Plaza S.T. see u there." While she was brushing her teeth, the police chief returned her call.

"Alma, Pedro, here."

"Hi what's up?"

"I think my mind was somewhere else when you called about the Cécile Reynaud's chauffeur, a guy named Eduardo Bello."

"Yes, did you contact him already?"

"Sure, we had his info on file from the background check we ran on him when he was hired by the Governor."

"What did he tell you?"

"He gave us an address in Mexico City where we, of course, can't operate. I called a friend in their Metropolitan Police, and he's sending a squad car to check the place out. I told him 'no confrontations and no arrests,' just ask a few questions. I'll call you when we get a report. One question, as we're standing down on

Jessica's release and you're tight with the family, could you fill me in on the details later this evening?"

"Of course, Pedro, I'll call you when I know anything, but I think this is one kidnapping that will be buried very deep."

Alma could do little to spruce up her appearance. She longed for her old Calvin Klein jeans and her fleece jacket because she knew it would be cold later. She also longed to hear how Kurt's trip to L.A. had gone and what her parents thought about the ranch in Veracruz. Tomorrow she would try to call them when she hoped the Jessica drama would at least be contained, if not over.

She arrived at the far side of the Plaza Santa Teresa with the two Rauls in tow about five-thirty. They'd had to park three blocks away. It looked like the fireworks were drawing an even bigger crowd this year. In the middle of the square, two dozen small stands had been installed selling everything from cotton candy to popcorn to corn on the cob to Cokes and lemonade to *tacos*, sopes, and *tamales* to peanuts covered in salt and lime to ices made with fresh fruit juices to pieces of pineapple dusted with chili to small bags of *chapulines*, fried Mexican grasshoppers. The smells alone were worth a visit. How much the four Jaramillos had enjoyed last year's fair picking out a favorite snack, finding a free bench and getting ready to 'ooh' and 'aah' over the fireworks which seemed every year to get bigger and more elaborate. Last year the high point of the display had been a tower which when ignited had blazed with a sketch of the church while spelling out in sputtering letters '*Santa Teresa Siempre*'. Kurt had been beside himself with joy.

As she looked for a strategic spot to watch the action, her phone rang. "Hey Alma," said the police chief, "I've got some news. The neighbors say that our three friends apparently moved out last night. At least they were seen loading a van at about midnight and pulling away at about one in the morning. The woman in the apartment across the hall said that she thought they were gone but this morning she heard their door close and people going down the stairs at about 7 A.M. She's at the back of the building so she couldn't see if anyone came out the front door. Unfortunately, the people in the apartments that face the street were asleep."

"Did the neighbors get a license plate number for the van? If so, I'd check the border crossings at Laredo and Brownsville. I have a feeling that sooner or later there will be an investigation into the kidnapping."

Alma positioned herself on an iron bench which was half hidden by the hanging branches of a Ficus tree. When Gabriel slid in next to her a few minutes later, he gave her a quick kiss and said, "Ávila's teenagers are going to hate you. You've stolen their favorite spot."

"No funny business," she reminded him, "the Rauls are watching your every move. Remember what happened to Steven."

"So, what have you been up to this afternoon?" Gabriel asked taking her hand in his. "But you're cold, be right back." Before she could fill him in on her big discovery, he was running back to his car for a spare hoody he kept in the trunk. When she next cast a glance across the square, she saw Beto perched on the curb in front of the church looking up and down the street. He was dressed in what must be his best suit. His tie was neatly tied, his hair freshly cut and combed, his face shaved.

She spotted Sami standing on the bottom step of the church with what looked like a blanket under his arm. Not a muscle moved on his face. But who's next to him? It can't be, but it was, Governor Humberto García de León! Strange she didn't see any bodyguards near him. He was dressed casually in a tan windbreaker and khakis. Protecting his ten-million-dollar investment, she muttered.

The late afternoon light was fading fast. It can't be long now, Alma said to herself. The traffic on the street was intermittent. Most people who were there to see the show had already found a place to sit or stand. There was an air of anticipation in the crowd. The younger children too excited to stand still were running circles around the legs of their parents.

The first rocket shot into the sky at six twenty as a few stars became visible. "Just in time," said Gabriel as he slipped the hoody over her shoulders. The crowd cheered as the bright pink, blue and white sparks spread across the sky like spray from a waterfall. The resounding boom hit the plaza a few seconds later. The next rocket twisted towards the sky throwing out a trail of red, green and blue glittering fire until it exploded in a shower of sparks high in the heavens. The faces of the crowd were lit up with a rainbow of color. Squeals of delight could be heard across the plaza.

Alma glanced at her phone to check the time. "No Jessica yet," Gabriel whispered. He too was watching as Beto paced up and down in front the church. The crowd behind the stocky figure was oblivious to the drama that had occupied his every waking hour during the last week. As a large burst of four different cascading shapes of light and color splattered across the sky, a small very battered green taxi came sputtering to a halt in front of the church. Beto stood mesmerized for a second, but as the door started to open, he rushed over and stuck his long arms into the back of the car. In a second Jessica was out of the cab and in his arms. The taxi, slinking away in the dark, was forgotten. As each succeeding twisting, darting, whizzing flash of light in the sky became more spectacular; the crowd lost interest in the strangely silent, embracing couple on the curb. Jessica and Beto clung to each other as if to let go for a moment would mean a lifetime of separation.

Alma didn't bother to wipe away the tears that rolled down her cheeks. Gabriel slid his arm around her and pulled her close. For a brief minute, the noise and light from the fireworks stopped. They're preparing for the big finale, she thought. It was in these few seconds of the crowd holding its collective breath that she saw the Governor walk up to the embracing couple. She knew he wanted them out of the public eye. She smiled as Jessica and Beto paid not the slightest attention to him.

She and the Governor heard the whine of an approaching motorcycle at the same time. As the rider stopped in front of the embracing couple, rockets flew skyward from the four corners of the plaza: four, eight, twelve, sixteen blasts of light in every color imaginable illuminated the night. The noise was deafening, but Alma had risen to her feet transfixed by the helmed man in black leather balancing one foot on the curb.

"No," she shouted as he drew the automatic pistol out of his jacket.

She started to run towards Beto and Jessica screaming, but it was the Governor who reacted first. The muffled shot that rang out as Beto's father fell on the assassin surprised the people standing closest to the couple. They looked around to see if some joker was tossing firecrackers into the crowd.

The screams only started as the Governor slumped to the ground. From out of nowhere two bodyguards leaped on the black leather figure before he could get to his feet and take aim again. As Alma neared the chaotic scene at the curb, she could see Beto, his suit covered in blood, cradling his father in his arms. Sami had wrapped Jessica in a blanket. The harsh flash from an iPhone camera for a moment lit up the miserable scene. Sirens sounded in the distance.

POSTSCRIPT

SIX MONTHS LATER IN MAZUNTE, OAXACA

The sun was a large red ball slowly sinking into the ocean's horizon as Alma, admiring the view, took a small sip of her white wine. The waiter had cleared their dinner plates away, but she was happy to see that they had left a half of a bottle of wine with which to while away the rest of the evening. The sound of the waves rhythmically pounding the shore and the sweet smell of the sea had lulled them into a dreamy mood.

"Whose idea was this?" said Gabriel.

"You mean the restaurant or the trip?" she said.

"Either one or both," he said smiling. "Why do I even ask? I'm sure both were yours! What do you---?"

"Gabo, wait! Isn't that Sami walking in the door with that good-looking older man?"

"Sami, Sami," she called jumping out of her chair, waving.

Sami turned to his companion, pressed his arm and gestured towards the bar. As he approached the table, Alma threw her arms around him. "I can't believe this coincidence," she said. "You remember Gabriel Ruiz, I'm sure."

As the men shook hands, Alma called the waiter over. "I hope you'll let us buy you a drink?"

"Sure, a rum and Coke would be great."

"What are you doing here? I thought this was our secret spot."

"Blowing off steam the same as you two. I've been coming here for years," said Sami.

"I'm sorry I haven't been in touch more. It has been a crazy six months. I have a million questions," she said, "but you're probably in a hurry. What news do you have of Jessica María? How's she doing?

"Let's see; she's been in Miami for five months now. I stayed with her a few weeks ago for a long weekend, and I think she's giving the move her best shot. Her apartment on the fourteenth floor of a new building right downtown has a spectacular ocean view. She's decorated it herself, and it looks great. But wait a minute. Is that an iPad, Alma? Is there Internet here? Let's try and Skype her. Here's her Skype address."

"Hey, Jessica," said Alma when a thinner but if possible, more beautiful face appeared on the screen.

"Oh, my God, Alma and Sami. Is that Gabriel too? Hello. Where are you guys?"

"In Mazunte, having a reunion. You're the only person missing."

"Yes, well, Mexico is a little difficult for me right now," said Jessica.

"Isn't it strange that here I started out in the U.S.," said Alma "but am now back in Mexico while you have left Mexico and are starting a new life in the U.S. It's as if something circular is going on in our lives. Your Spiritism friends would probably have something to say about it."

"Yes, I'm sure Luz María would have a theory. What's more neither of us had much choice in the matter," said Jessica. "You had to repatriate because your life in L.A. became too difficult and I left Mexico after the kidnapping and my problems with Beto. I felt, I guess the best word for it is 'betrayed,' but, more than anything, I didn't feel safe."

"So how are things going in Miami?" asked Alma.

"Do you remember what my new Aunt Ana told us about her mother after she lived through the War? My grandmother was always afraid. I'm like that. I will only answer the door to people I've known forever. I can't sleep unless I've checked the alarm system five times. I'm afraid of crowds and enclosed spaces. Loud noises practically make me jump out of my skin; I have soothing music playing day and night in the apartment. The therapist says it will take time. I'm glad the Rebolleros are in jail, but I'd feel better if Cécile was locked up too."

"Just a minute. Is that Valentina we can hear in the background? How is she?"

"She's singing a song to Erica in English. She loves her new kindergarten. She misses her daddy, but she perked up when Erica arrived. Thank you again, Sami, for getting Erica a visa."

"Glad I could be of help even though you've dumped me as your agent."

"Exaggerating as usual. I've got an American agent now, Alma, as well as Sami. They've gotten me an audition for a new Netflix series. The show is a comedy about the dizzy First Lady of a small Latin American country. You're allowed to laugh; I think it's funny myself. I need to get back to work, so I call my agent about five times a day. By the way, I have a new stage name, Jessica Lara. I've also put the '*El viaje inmortal*' project on the shelf."

"But what about Beto? Are you guys in touch?" asked Gabriel, noting that the expression on Jessica's face became less animated, more serious.

"When we first moved to Miami, he came almost every other weekend. We talk on the phone a couple of times a week; I still have a lot of ties to Ávila. But it's complicated. You know I was in the hospital for five days right after I was freed. I was too freaked out even to go to the Governor's funeral. The day I got out of the clinic your story, Alma, about Humberto García's involvement in the destruction of El Rosario and the disappearance of Salvador Navarro made headlines all over the country. Sami and I were elated on the one hand and horrified on the other. David's story, well I mean, my father's story finally explained his odd behavior and for the first time, we understood who was probably behind my parent's disappearance.

"I was thrown for a loop when Beto rejected outright the evidence that the Governor had been involved in either crime. He brushed off your father's evidence, Alma, and my father's account too, as uncorroborated testimony from two unreliable sources who probably had a grudge against Humberto García. 'The fact that my dad died to save us, Jessica, is enough proof for me that he was a decent man,' is what he said. The fact that the Governor had paid the ransom to keep Cécile from revealing his secrets didn't cut any ice with him either."

"Beto tried to kill the story," said Alma. "He sent lawyers, and then he sent threats. Ricardo just said, 'Not this time, Sonny.'"

"After that first blow-up," said Jessica now looking dejected. "I stayed for three more weeks in Ávila trying to change Beto's mind, but he just kept repeating the same thing. 'You know how much I love you. My dad and I worked tirelessly to get you home as soon as possible. I even hired Alma to find you. My father refused to take the insurance money so you could be released quickly.' Of course, I felt guilty too. How could I have fallen for Javier Arias's story? How could I have gotten into that car and not left word where I was going? I was so fascinated with the idea of contacting my mother that all common sense went out of my head."

Suddenly Sami put in his two cents. "Hey, stop beating yourself up. Falling for a fake story doesn't mean you deserved what you went through. When you got home, you were a mess, emotionally and physically. You were so fearful about your safety you couldn't get out of bed. Beto couldn't understand either how much we needed justice for our parents."

For a moment, the Skype connection went blurry, but Jessica's voice finally returned. "Remember, Sami, how I lost it when Beto said that our dad was probably involved in drug smuggling. When I told him that the airline had been investigated and was clean, he dismissed the report with a wave of his hand. I feel that the sense of trust and partnership we had is gone. I had to get away from Ávila and from Mexico."

"Maybe when the shock of his father's death wears off," said Alma "he'll be more willing to listen. He must miss you and Valentina."

"I've heard that he's thinking of running for Governor," said Gabriel. "His father's colleagues want a García in the statehouse to stop any effort to clean up the government."

"I had to laugh last week when Catherine called to ask me to persuade Beto not to run for governor," said Jessica. "'It ruined his father's life. Why does my son want to repeat that tragic mistake?' She moaned to me. She calls me often. We seem to have realized that neither one of us is as bad as we used to think. I got to go, guys, it's Valentina's bedtime, and then I'm going with friends to check out a few clubs. Nothing like a little *cha-cha-cha* to cheer you up. *Besos*."

Sami took a long swallow of his rum and Coke and then smiled. "Just one little piece of family news then I want to hear about your accomplishments, Alma. Our Aunt Ana who looks so much like our dad it's uncanny has suggested that we have a memorial service for our parents. Jessica and I have bought a plot in a cemetery and had a stone carved with their names on it. They're not there of course, but in our minds, they've been put to rest. Our new-found cousins will come to the service as well as Aunt Renata. So, small though it is, we have at last a family. Before she left for Miami, Jessica gave Renata the deed to my parents' house and told Gloria she had a year to straighten out the spa business.

Jessica said she had a lot of time to think while she was cooped up in that little room."

"I'm so glad Sami that you and Jessica found Ana," said Alma. "Now much of what I'm going to tell you about the investigation into Jessica's kidnapping comes from Clyde and my new buddy, Captain Ramirez. Lucky for him, Clyde got hold of the Governor's bank accounts before Beto became so protective of his father's image. Clyde has been on the backs of the Attorney General and Interpol almost daily trying to recoup the ransom money. What's known is that three million went to a private bank in Las Vegas. That part was the Rebolleros' payoff. The other seven million was transferred to Panama to an account in Cécile's name.

"As you know the day after the Governor's murder while she was still in the hospital, Jessica identified the Rebolleros. She suspected from the first that they were in cahoots with Cécile. Our Attorney General began working with the FBI and warrants were issued for their arrest. When Philippe, a.k.a. Javier Arias, started to use his new American credit cards, the U.S. authorities nabbed them easily. I understand that they're going to be extradited back to Mexico and that they have agreed to testify against Cécile.

"Prosecuting Cécile is going to be more difficult. She's claiming that Humberto gave her the ten million in exchange for a quiet divorce, and she has a paper to prove it. The Governor must have signed the document when she showed him David's statement about the night of Salvador Navarro's murder. Ironically, Humberto's young mistress confirmed Cécile's story. Ana Carolina, a twenty-three-year-old 'model,' assured the Feds that the Governor had promised to make her the future first lady of Mexico, no less. But Cécile is far from off the hook. She must explain why she transferred three million dollars to the Rebolleros.

"In an interview, Cécile had with the French police, she claimed she had no idea about Jessica's kidnapping or the attempted murder of her stepson and his wife. Extradition is never easy, but the Attorney General has great hopes that the Rebollero's testimony will convince the French to send her back."

"Do you think it was Cécile who ordered Beto and Jessica killed?" asked Sami.

"I haven't a doubt in the world. Her three cousins were following orders. Cécile was always the mastermind. She had to kill Jessica to protect their identities. Killing Beto wasn't gratuitous; she was punishing Humberto. But as we saw the Governor was not entirely the man we thought he was, he loved his children."

"The rest of the actors in the plot were methamphs' addicts and are behind bars we hope for a long time. I still find it hard to believe," continued Alma, "that Cécile could have dreamed up such a desperate plan and that the cousins went along with it. The only person who wasn't surprised was Steven. He just said, 'What did I tell you!'"

"You know what I find creepy," said Gabriel "is how that verse from Pablo Neruda's poem that Luismi sent to Jessica turned out to be the Governor's epitaph. You remember the lines:

In this part of the story, I am the one who
Dies, the only one, and I will die of love because I love you,
Because I love you, Love, in fire and blood."

"Yes," said Sami taking out his phone, "let me read you what Lucía wrote to me a few months ago. 'Like everyone else I find it hard to reconcile my father's sacrificing his life for Beto's when he didn't have any qualms about having people killed who thwarted his political ambitions. But then he was always full of contradictions. He loved us but never spent time with us. His public persona was that of an affable man: articulate, ambitious, hardworking, loyal to his friends. In our home life, we saw his ego, his lack of empathy, his insensitivity. He was incapable of understanding that his neglect, wreaked havoc in our lives. Why then do Beto and I have such different images of our father? I see a man who, although he loved us, nearly destroyed us while Beto sees a man who, despite his flaws, was a shining example of paternal love. We were raised in the same home, go figure!'"

"Amen," said Gabriel. "On a more positive note, have you been following Alma's triumphs, Sami? She not only wrote what will be an award-winning series of articles for El Diario de Ávila about the Garcías but she also published two articles in Proceso. Two big dailies in Mexico City have asked her to write articles on government corruption. She's also had stories in the L.A. Times and in the Spanish newspaper, El País."

"I was definitely going to ask for her autograph," said Sami smiling.

"But you didn't mention the not so good news," said Alma. "Even with Ricardo personally calling the U.S. Ambassador, I couldn't get a visa to the U.S. to interview the Rebolleros. We'll see what happens in five more years."

"Hey, it's getting late," said Gabriel. "Let me find the waiter and pay the bill."

When Gabriel was out of earshot, Sami turned to Alma. "So, what's going on with you two?"

"It's good. Besides having a great time together, we can talk about everything. He's patient too. I've needed time to work out some other issues in my life. The decision to pursue the story of Jessica's kidnapping after I'd been threatened made me think about what I had been doing with my life. Here I was thirty years old and still living with my parents. I saw I needed to take on the responsibility of paying rent, buying groceries and figuring out childcare. In other words, I needed to grow up.

"It wasn't easy. My mom was still upset about the danger I had put the family through by pursuing the Garcías. She was even more unhappy when I announced that I'd rented a little house about a mile away. Kurt just thought it was stupid. You know for kids if you're comfortable why would you change anything. I forgot to pay the phone bill last month, and half the time my dad puts bread and milk in the fridge, but I feel good about my new life. We see Jesús and Sofía often, but finally, at thirty, I'm independent. Well, as independent as you can be with a son and a dog. I've also decided that Ávila is going to be home at least for the near future."

Alma kissed Sami goodbye and joined Gabriel at the door of the restaurant. "You ready to call it a night?" he asked hugging her.

"You know Gabo my life would be perfect if we could just move Ávila twenty minutes inland from Mazunte," she said as they walked out into the warm night air.

THE END

ACKNOWLEDGEMENTS

I am very grateful to my family for their support, encouragement and help. Thank you Sarah Lorenzen, David Hartwell, Tricia Breen, Brian Breen and Sue Real.

I am also eternally indebted to my friends: Erica Marin, Susie Jaye, Flora Botton and Nancy Rocha for their very useful suggestions, corrections and most of all for their kind interest.

Thanks also to Veronica Bulnes for the delightful maps at the beginning of the book.